Island Secrets
A Queens of Kiawah Story

NINA FOXX

ALSO BY NINA FOXX

And You'd Better Not Tell
Momma: Gone
Catfish
Marrying up
Just Short of Crazy
No Girl Needs A Husband 7 Days a Week
Going Buck Wild
Get Some Love
Dippin' My Spoon
Do Right Woman
Stuff That's Kinda True: Ghosts of Scorpions Past
Do The Write Thing: 7 Steps to Publishing Success
(w Kwame Alexander)

ANTHOLOGIES

A Letter for My Mother (editor)
Wanderlust: Erotic Travel Tales (Contrib)
Can't Help the Way that I feel (Contrib)
Reaching Beyond The Saguaros (Contrib)
Ley Lines (Contrib)

AS CYNNAMON FOSTER

Eastern Spice
Southern Comfort
Northern Passion

NINA FOXX

Island Secrets

A Queens of Kiawah Story

NINA FOXX

CLEVER VIXEN MEDIA, LLC

Seattle • New York

NINA FOXX

Clever Vixen Media LLC books may be purchased in bulk or special discounts for sales promotion, corporate gifts, fund-raising, or educational purposes. Special editions can also be created to specifications. For details, contact Clever Vixen Media, LLC.

Visit our website at CleverVixenMedia.com.

10 9 8 7 6 5 4 3 2 1

Library of Congress Cataloging-in-Publication Data is available on file.

Cover Design by Kristin Bryant
Cover Photo Credit: iStock

ISBN: 978-0-615-90216-6

Printed in The United States of America

NINA FOXX

For Marcea.

Who welcomed me into her world and introduced me to the beautiful setting that made my imagination run wild.

NINA FOXX

1
Door Dings and New Things

Denise savored the warm breeze left behind by the summer storm that had skirted the barrier islands, imagining it to be a caress from Charles across her cheek. Even after all this time, this place was magical to her. Thankful for the lull in the blistering heat that normally sat on the shoulders of the South Carolina Low Country, she drove her convertible with her top down. Days like this made her glad that she'd run from the stress in Chicago and moved to hide away in this hipbone of the country, even if these days were tinged with sadness.

Old trees stretched over the narrow road, meeting in the middle and creating a green, mangled tunnel. In an earlier time, she would have spent evenings in her studio, re-creating the tunnel on canvas, hoping to unlock some of its secrets. Charles used to laugh when she talked about the things her paintings revealed. He didn't believe, like she did, that sometimes her eye saw things that were hidden beneath the surface, things that other people missed. On each trip to Kiawah Island, Denise had imagined that she had been traveling through the century of secrets the canopy of trees must have shared. Today was no different. This time, like other times before, she fancied herself being transported to a simpler place, maybe not hundreds of years ago back when Kiawah Island had been a plantation, but certainly one where she was not a widow, back when her

husband had been beside her and they'd ventured out to Buster's
Place, hidden deep in the swamp, together.

Ten years ago, when they'd first come this way, there'd been
almost nothing here. There were very few people and homes on
Kiawah Island when they'd first built their place here, and even
less on Bohicket Road and surrounding areas, but the PGA tour
had discovered their little golf course and put the tiny island on
the map. After the famous golfers and television cameras had
left, people kept coming. Then, Buster's Place had just been a
spot that she and her friends would go, mainly by boat, when
they decided to fall off their diets and enjoy some fish, fried
South Carolina style. Her stomach growled as she remembered
the taste of Buster's famous fried oysters. Last season, some
golfer had discovered the place, and it had been featured on that
grease-worshipping TV show, *Diner's, Dives and Drive-ins.* Since
then, you could barely get a skiff anywhere near the shore or a
car in the parking lot on any day except Monday, the day when
the tourists were turning over and headed back to wherever
they'd come from. Monday was when the large antebellum-style
homes that the owners rented to seasonal people were filled with
cleaning teams, preparing for the next batch of visitors to check
in and when most of the few public eateries stood empty.

Not that there were many. The islands were dotted with only
a few local places other than the Beach Club, a haven that many
of the regulars retreated to during high season when the rental
homes were full. A member's only establishment, it was where
they went when they wanted to get away from all of the people
that had brought the bustle of the city with them.

Denise slowed as she reached the clearing that served as a
parking lot, rounding the bend in the road. The way the gravel

gave way to reeds and water was unexpected no matter how
often she came, leaving her with the feeling that the road had
coughed her up and spit her out into the light-filled space at its
end. Buster's sat on the water's edge and was nothing more than
a shack on stilts, raised high enough to avoid the occasional rise
of the water above flood-level. Every time she came here, Denise
found herself amazed that the place was still standing, somehow
avoiding being damaged by the various storms that came through
the Low Country every year or being bulldozed by the forward
march of gentrification, masquerading as progress. Trees reached
down to meet the reeds that grew up out of the shallow water
around the place creating a living cave with the restaurant
ensconced in the middle.

Today, there was but one boat in the small clearing, and
Denise didn't recognize it. Her eyes moistened as she took in the
sight. In her mind, the boat in the middle of the clearing would
always be one that her husband had piloted. She'd become
accustomed to a crowd, and the lack of one surprised her almost
as much as it relieved her. Still, she frowned. The boat looked
almost too big to be in this small space, a few more inches and it
might be beached. Any other day, the cove would be full of a
myriad of vessels, but few would be larger than a small rowboat
or powerboat. Compared to those, this boat was a jarring sight
cutting a hole through the middle of the picture-perfect
backdrop of the swamp and its lone building. Denise's brows
knitted. This boat was a symbol of what was happening to
Kiawah and neighboring Seabrook Island. Normally small, quiet,
and steeped in history, modern intrusions kept making their way
into the island life, trying unsuccessfully to blend in with what
felt as if it had been undisturbed for centuries.

Denise bit her lip as she fought back the surliness that brewed inside her. Whenever she noticed the juxtaposition of old and new, she had feelings of unease. The contrast reminded her of Charles. He had always been opposed to the renovations and newness that kept creeping into what had been their retreat, protesting every time they returned from the city at whatever had changed while they'd been in Chicago. The quaintness of Kiawah Island, now fading, had been something that attracted them to the area in the first place. Denise had grown to love this place, but he'd had an even deeper appreciation for it and had come down to the island whenever he could, a few times without her.

It was hard not to be angry, but how could she be angry at the man for dying? Even as she thought it, a wave of stress swept over Denise but she resisted the pull, refusing to let herself be drawn back into the funk she'd felt for months after Charles was gone. She'd never seen his body, and no matter how much they'd assured her that the artifacts she'd gotten were his, she wasn't quite convinced. The few things left after his disappearance were her new reality and these had been hard to accept. Together they'd had everything and suddenly he was dead, supposedly falling overboard after a heart attack at the helm of his boat that he'd loved so much, but that was just a theory, and not one she believed. Of course, the police wanted to tie a neat bow on things, so that was what was on the record, for now. But it didn't feel right. Charles had been one to dot every I and cross every T. Normally, as far as she'd known, he'd never gone out boating alone and he was a very strong swimmer, so the whole story didn't seem plausible.

He'd been gone almost a year, and that made Denise even more angry. Her coming to the Island alone had never been in their plan. It had been Charles who reminded her of the local folklore - the idea that the island was both protected and haunted by the spirits of the slaves who had worked the land and toiled in the rice fields hundreds of years ago. "That makes this place special," he'd said. The island was supposed to have been the place where they'd grow old together. Instead, it was now the place Denise ran to hide from the task in front of her as she mourned Charles's absence from her life while continuing to fight with the insurance company. There were still no biological remains, only a wallet and some clothing, and without that, there was no physical proof that Charles was actually dead. No proof, no insurance money, and no closure.

She slowed and pulled her car into a narrow space between an SUV and a pickup truck so large it overshadowed everything around it. Denise pursed her lips. "I don't know why people think these things make sense," she mumbled to herself, unimpressed with the monstrosity of the car.

Denise killed her engine and grabbed her bag from the passenger seat. Just as she was about to open her door, a loud thud and then a jolt shook her car. She looked up in alarm in time to see a pair of male legs jump down from the cab of the truck.

The door trapped her inside her car. Heat rose from her body. Did he not see that he'd hit her car? "Hey!" she shouted. Obviously, this guy was not a regular, probably one of those who had seen the restaurant on television. Why couldn't city folks leave their city manners back where they belonged? This was not how things were done here.

After too long, he slammed his door and hit the button on his remote. The car alarm screamed in response, its beep-beep cutting through the stillness of the cove. Finally, he noticed Denise. "Oh, hi there. Did I give you a door ding?"

He felt familiar, but she was too annoyed to care. Denise couldn't see his face past the large sunglasses that covered it. "Door ding? More like a dent." She waited for him to step aside and hopped from her car. "You really need to be more attentive." Her words were sharp as she made no attempt to hold back her annoyance.

"I'm sorry, Ma'am. I couldn't see your car. It's so low."

"My car is not low. Yours is ridiculously high." She rubbed the door with her thumb, her back turned towards the man. "You want to give me your insurance information?

"Is it that serious?" There was a hint of a smile in his voice. Denise could not believe his arrogance. "Maybe not to you, but to me, yes. You clearly have no idea how hard it is to match this paint. It's special edition." She bristled as he spoke. The candy color red had a metric glow to it, and now, a whisper of a scratch. The color had been Charles's idea, even though Denise would have preferred something just a little more subtle.

The stranger seemed at a loss for words. After a pause, he finally answered. "Okay, I can give you my insurance information." He reached for his wallet. "But I'll make sure it gets fixed for you even if I have to take it all the way into Charleston."

"You probably will have to do that. There is no body shop or car dealer anywhere on the island." She folded her arms across her chest like a shield. Just like she'd thought. A tourist. A local would know that. He looked vaguely familiar, but most of his face was shielded by the brim of a hat. "I'll just take a picture of your card and driver's license." Denise glanced at her watch, looking down to shield her eyes from the sun. If he didn't hurry, the humidity would have sweat running from places where Denise didn't want it to run from.

After what seemed like too long, the man held out his driver's license and insurance card, and Denise used her phone to take pictures of each without really looking at them. "Thank you," she said, her mouth drawn into a thin line. If she didn't hate newcomers before, she edged closer to that now. She dropped her phone into her handbag without even looking at the information.

He held out his business card. "Call me first?"

Denise snatched it from his hand, a grunt emanating from her throat. People were always trying to get away with something. Denise glanced at it, then shoved it down into the outer pocket of her shorts. She's look at it closer later when she was out of the bright sun. She trudged away from him, leaving him standing there watching her make her way across the gravel parking lot and up the three wooden steps that led to the veranda of the restaurant.

NINA FOXX

2

The Boat in The Cove

Her eyes didn't have time to adjust to the light before she recognized Yolanda's loud cackle. Denise removed her sunglasses, a broad smile spreading across her face and relaxing the wrinkles that had appeared in her forehead earlier. She spotted Yolanda immediately, in the usual back corner of the restaurant. She was holding court, surrounded by four of their friends. Since here were regulars, they traded friendly insults with the people working there, only separated by the stainless steel counter tops that separated the kitchens from the front of the house which was filled with long, picnic tables that ran the length of the building.

"Here she is," Yolanda's yell filled up the wooden building.

Jillian's slim shoulders moved up and down in time with the silent laugh that remained trapped inside her body. She pressed two fingers to her lips in an apparent effort to keep the sounds inside.

"You know that Diva Denise always has to make an entrance." Samantha added.

"Right." Yolanda's booming voice gave way to laughter and they exchanged hugs all around.

"Why do I have to be the Diva? Every last one of you has

some Diva in you." Denise's smile grew as she took in the style that made their group the perfect friends. Samantha stood beside Yolanda, as quiet as Yolanda was outspoken, but Denise couldn't miss the ever present smirk on her face.

Yolanda laughed. "But you have more than the rest of us. You know, you bring it with you all the way from CHI-cag-O."

"I don't know why you act like you aren't from the city." She waved her friends' ribbing away. She was used to it. This teasing had become part of their ritual. The ones who arrived first enjoyed free rein to tease the others who came later.

"We used to be from the city. You're the only one of us who goes back as much as you do," Yolanda said.

"I don't go back. I live there. Or I used to, anyway." Denise hugged Yolanda first. "I vacation here. Some of us have to work. Oh, right." Denise continued. "You don't live in the city anymore, right? Is that why you remodeled that big old house down here?" She winked, a smirk hiding in the corner of her mouth. She couldn't resist teasing Yolanda about the never-ending remodeling project she was undertaking on her house on the Island.

"Do I hear some hate?" Yolanda turned to one of the other women. "I think I'm hearing hate. She knows we spend the majority of the year on Kiawah now." Yolanda and her husband ran a small tech company together and Yolanda spent most of her time serving on corporate boards.

"I'm right here. Don't talk about me. Talk to me." Denise totally respected that her friends had chosen to move most of their lives down to the island, but she needed big city-level excitement that nearby Charleston had yet to be able to provide. Sure, there had been lots of development on Kiawah in recent years, but it was still a pretty sleepy place, at least when compared to Chicago. Plus, unlike Yolanda and her husband, she and Charles had yet to fall into the "more money than God" category of wealth, although Charles had been working a major project before he died that he'd sworn was going to put them into a whole other tax bracket, if there were such a thing. She needed to go back to Chicago to make a living, at least until her money started making one for her. A big part of her really wanted to be on the island full time, but she has yet to divest herself fully of city life the way Yolanda had.

"We'll talk about you whether you're here or not," Yolanda said and the group erupted in laughter.

"You spend the majority of your time down here because you're old. You both know that people come to Kiawah to retire, right?" Denise answered.

"We're far from old," Yolanda said, picking at her shirt, "We just enjoy flexibility in our lifestyles. And we trust in ourselves. You'll get there one day."

"One day." Denise knew all about Yolanda's flexibility. Her husband had invented too many things to count, and his company was one of the few that still paid for patents. Between that and Yolanda's office supply company being bought out by some big company again - the two of them might not ever have to look for another traditional job in this lifetime. Working from home had become their jobs.

"Some of us still have things we do." Denise waved them off.

"Don't get it twisted, friend, "Yolanda said. "We have jobs. We think about things."

Denise's eyebrows shot up. "Golf isn't a job."

"No, it's not. But the thinking I do about my money and how

to make more of it while I'm playing golf, is."

Everyone laughed, and Yolanda hugged Denise.

Denise welcomed their teasing with the warmth it brought to her soul. She needed it. Her friends had been her rock during her grieving. They kept her on her toes and without them, she had no idea how she would have made it these past few months.

"I'd like to know why you only go all in on me. Samantha here is technically a summer person, still, right? I mean she still lives it the city; they only come down here because her husband owns a golf condo."

Samantha stepped forward. "No ma'am. Do not bring me into this."

Yolanda smirked. We are not discussing them. Besides. They golf year-round and their golf time itself adds up to damn near half a year."

Denise was only dejected for a minute. She leaned in. "You see that monstrosity out there?" She motioned over her shoulder, back towards the parking lot and the waterfront.

Before they could answer, a loud clang sounded in the restaurant and they all turned just in time to see the proprietor, Dabner, wiping his hands on his stained apron. "Don't look at me like I'm crazy. Y'all are regulars." He scowled at the room.

"What's his issue?" Denise asked.

Yolanda shrugged as they turned away. "His panties have been all in a bunch since we got here. You know how he can be."

Denise did know. He was notorious for his attitude. Dabner had been a central part of the TV show when the restaurant was featured, but now regretted it. "He likes things to be the way they've always been."

"Yes, the two of you are peas in a pod." Yolanda winked.

"You always have something smart to say, Yolanda," Denise sighed. "It's that boat in the cove, isn't it?"

"Oh. That." Yolanda looked away sheepishly. "Now that you mention it, it is kind of large."

"Is that what you call it? That thing is at least a 45-footer. It's got to be drafting the bottom. Good thing it's not low tide or it would be stuck in the seaweed." She bit her lip as soon as the words left her mouth. She'd promised herself that she would only think forward, and the idea of boating jarred her backwards into the past. Denise knew she'd probably never experience that again, at least not in the same way.

Yolanda raised her eyebrows but refrained from comment on her friend's pain.

There was a lump in Denise's throat. She had loved boating with her husband. It was their thing, and she'd been quite content to be his First Mate. It struck her now that this was one of the things she missed most about him. After the memorial, she'd gotten rid of a lot of things, but the boat had to go first. Yolanda had convinced her it was the best thing to help her move on, and as far as she could see, it had been. Not to mention that the money from the sale had helped her to bridge the gap in her finances. Charles had taken care of everything, so when he died, she was easily overwhelmed by requests for payments from creditors. And of course, there was that little matter of life insurance not paying. No body, no payment, at least not until he was officially declared dead. The drastic change was so much in her face, Denise wasn't sure which she'd been mourning, the husband or the lifestyle.

It dawned on Denise that all eyes were on her, and not in what felt like a good way. Alarm bells went off in her head. Her eyes narrowed. "What don't I know? Why are you all looking at me like that?" She searched their faces for answers. Something was going on, and she was obviously the only one who had no idea what.

Dabner yelled again. "Rich folks come up in here and disturb the nature," he bellowed.

Yolanda snickered. "Y'all see how he treats 'the nature' as if it's his own proper noun."

"That thing is too big for my cove. Who knows what them anchors will drag up?" Dabner shook his head and wiped his hand on a cloth he pulled from his apron pocket.

A smile spread across Denise's face. "He acts like the anchor is going to dredge up a hidden body or something."

Yolanda almost choked on her drink. "Oh, here you go again. Your imagination is just a little too overactive."

"Yeah, one tiny thing will have you making up a whole story. There are no bodies in my cove." The owner glared at them.

Denise shrugged.

"That we know of," Yolanda cut in. "No bodies at the moment, but I'm sure there are plenty of souls of Black folk. Who knows what happened down here when this was a plantation?"

"Or since?" Denise added.

The owner poo poo'ed her comment, waving his hand as if he could make the thought and the words disappear. "The only hidden bodies are in your head. Besides, anything that happened two hundred years ago would just be dust now." He wiped his hands on his apron and busied himself behind the counter.

Yolanda sipped on the straw in her pink, frosty drink. "It's just a boat, woman. You should feel how it glides through the water." She clapped her hand over her mouth as soon as she'd uttered the words.

Denise's mouth dropped open. "Glides through the water? Wait, you guys have been on that boat?"

Grins broke out all around. "Yup, we came on that monstrosity. You won't be hating when you're riding to the Beach Club in it." Yolanda raised her eyebrows and then lowered them.

"I can't believe you. That thing is way too big and conspicuous to be in this little cove. Whose is it?" Denise glared at her friends. Why were they acting so crazy? "Did one of you buy a boat and not tell me?" Not that that would surprise her, Denise thought. Buying a water toy was not out of reach for any of these women.

"Not me. I don't know a thing about boats, you know that." Yolanda's eyes were wide as she tried to look a little too innocent.

Denise glanced from friend to friend, and each of them averted their eyes as soon as they met Denise's. They were up to something. She could feel it. She pursed her lips. "Alright. Someone had better tell me something."

"We thought it would be fun to ride the boat over here—"

"Instead of driving for twenty minutes? Of course, that makes tons of sense. That would only burn a little bit of fossil fuel."

"Since when do we care about that?" Yolanda laughed. "Any other time you would be right there with us."

But this was not any other time. She had not been able to get on anyone's boat since she'd sold Charles'. "How many engines are on that thing? Two?" Denise asked. Truth be told, she was just a tiny bit intrigued. She'd had such great fun on their boat. She fought back the wetness that was trying to well in her eyes.

Yolanda touched her elbow. "Are you gonna be okay, friend?"

Denise wiped at the corner of her eyes with her index finger. "I'm fine. How many engines?"

No one answered.

"Why are you looking at me like that?" Denise hated it when her friends acted so silly. "You guys are always coming up with some crazy stuff!" She hated it even more when she was on the outside of their shenanigans.

"Because you know more about the engines on my boat than they do." A voice boomed over her left shoulder. Denise whipped around to face the man who had just come through the door. She had to look up to see his face, his eyes still covered by his sunglasses. He was already standing way too close to her for someone she didn't know. She could practically feel the vibrations of his breath on her ears. Instinctively, she took a step back.

Yolanda's face was plastered with a nervous grin. "Denise, I'd like you to meet Trent Wilkerson. He's down from—"

"New York. I know." A chill ran down Denise's spine and memories of college came rushing back. She'd been too angry in the parking lot, not to mention blinded by the sun, to recognize him. She knew he was familiar! She and Trent had crossed paths before, and she didn't recall it all being good.

Her eyes brushed over his body. He was much thinner and fitter than she remembered him being. Age looked good on him. Something had kept her following his career over the years and she'd even felt slightly happy for him when he'd finished out his basketball career with the Knicks. She'd lost track then, or just got too involved with her life with Charles to keep following him.

"Denise." Trent removed his glasses and looked down at her. "You look just like I remember."

"Before or after you dented my car?" Against her will, Denise blushed.

"What don't I know?" Yolanda looked back and forth between them, confused now. "Trent, you didn't say you knew Denise."

"You never told me your friend's name, so how could I?" His eyes remained locked on Denise, raking her body. "We go way back."

And they did. Denise took a deep breath as the memories of Trent and her, both good and bad, returned. She swallowed hard. He was her one who got away or the one who broke her heart, maybe both. She wasn't sure then and she certainly wasn't sure now. All she remembered was the feeling of being humiliated, and then he was gone, whisked off to what Denise had imagined to be the fabulosity of an NBA career.

"A blast from the past." Denise's mouth went dry and she could think of nothing else to say. Her feelings got all jumbled up inside her as the last twenty years rushed back at her.

"Is that all I was?" Trent's voiced softened and the air around them grew still as everyone held their breath. Denise didn't answer him. There was no need to reply to something that he already knew the answer to.

Finally, it was Yolanda who cleared her throat. "Well, unless you want to let us all in on whatever it was that you two shared, we need to order, or you know that Dabner will lose his cool."

Dabner already stood behind them, his hands on his hips,

glaring straight at Yolanda. She held up her hand. "C'mon, people." She directed everyone towards the counter.

Denise glanced over her shoulder, meeting Dabner's angry gaze. "Yeah, he hates it when you take up tables before you order—" Her words were cut short as Trent grabbed her elbow. The palace wasn't fancy, and there was a process to it. You stood in line to order, then found a table while you waited for your food to be prepared.

She jerked away. "Don't!" He had no right to touch her.

Shock showed on Trent's face. "You can't still be angry for something that happened twenty years ago. I'm a different person."

She drew in her breath. Trent might be different, but it still stung the same. The memories came flooding back like it was yesterday. Denise remembered that she had allowed herself to become the gal pal, all the while hoping that Trent would fall for her, but he'd dated her friend instead. Then, when they'd finally gotten together, it had ended in a fiasco with health department visits and multiple friends all tied up in some kind of bad love quadrangle with Trent at the center. Just when she'd begun to feel as if she might be special to him, she'd discovered that she'd been nothing more than a notch on his bedpost. She should have known. She'd trashed the painting he'd inspired because it had too many shadows she hadn't liked.

Denise opened her mouth to speak, but just as quickly closed it. Why were they still staring at her? She took a deep breath, knowing that if she appeared too flustered, they would all be nosier than ever. "No," she said too quickly. "I'm not angry. That would be silly." She was only remembering one side of the story. Because of what had happened with Trent, she'd found Charles.

He'd picked her up, dusted her off, and the rest was history. She turned to Trent. "I am, however, a little perturbed about the dent *you caused.* If you came on the boat, why did your oversized excuse for a vehicle nearly total my car?"

"You were always good with a story." Trent smiled. "My assistant brought it over for me. He's going to take it to the mechanic. Is that acceptable?"

"You folks need to order," Dabner's voice boomed over the loud buzzing in the room before Denise could answer. "People are waiting on those tables, and you need to hurry up and get that Big Ass boat out of my cove. It's disturbing the wildlife."

Yolanda laughed. "Dabner, you know you don't care nothing about no wildlife."

"Maybe not. But I'm gonna be the one wildin' out soon if y'all don't respect my process." He almost laughed, despite himself. "You see what I did there? We got a line out the door and it's over 90 degrees outside. Get your fish and then get to getting out."

Get out. That was what she'd told Trent all those years ago. He'd been good, but he'd been just as bad at the end of their relationship, both times. *Both times.* Denise was annoyed at herself now. First, for allowing herself to fall for him twice back then, and second, she was annoyed because even after being married to Charles for so long, it still mattered to her. It shouldn't, and she knew that. Charles had been good for her. He'd been older and wiser and he'd known just what she'd needed to move on from that bad relationship with Trent. Only based on how she felt as she remembered it all, it seemed that she hadn't really moved on.

"So, I'm guessing there's no love connection here, then?"

Yolanda's eyes were wide.

"Is that what you were hoping for?" Denise measured her words. "You thought that the poor lonely widow needed some company and that I would be impressed by the big boat and massive car?" She laughed. "We're too old for these kinds of games. And all of you should know me better than that. This shop is closed. I'm good as things are." Denise wasn't sure she believed it herself, but it was going to take more than somebody like Trent to get her back in the game. Her husband's matters weren't even settled yet. Who wanted to get all tangled up again? She certainly didn't, right? A chill ran through her, even though it was scorching outside. Maybe the third time would be the charm.

3
Put your finger on it

Trent could practically see dark clouds of their past swirling around Denise as she stormed out of the restaurant. His stomach churned. He regretted being the source of any of the pain she might have been feeling. He'd done a lot of growing since their college days.

"You okay?" Yolanda asked. Her breath came fast and heavy. "I had no idea she would react this way. I'm so sorry." She paused. "I know she'll come around. I mean, I guess she will. But isn't it funny that the two of you knew each other after all?"

Funny, indeed, Trent thought. How was he going to get himself out of this pickle? He had no idea how he would explain that yes, he'd come to Kiawah to follow up on a crazy lead, and now he was being "fixed up" with his mark. And to make matters worse, he hadn't counted on feeling the way he had when he saw Denise. Sure, his breath had caught in his throat when he'd realized that not only had he already known the wife of the man he'd been investigating, but he used to date her. "You think she will?" Trent really didn't expect an answer but that didn't stop Yolanda. If only they had given him all of this information up front, he could have excused himself from the case. It was probably too late for that now.

"I'm sure of it. She's actually not angry at you, although, it looks like you didn't end well." She raised her eyebrows, her face full of expectation. "You can fill me in later because I can't remember any of those things she mentioned. And you certainly left out the pro basketball part."

Trent smirked. As if he would fill this woman in on anything. The past was best left in the past. "Denise hasn't changed." He thought back to college, when he and Denise had first known each other. He still remembered exactly where he'd met her, on the campus of Loyola. She'd come to a basketball game with a group of girls and she was so beautiful, she just stood apart from them, like a supermodel. He'd been unable to take his eyes off of her. Trent smiled as he remembered. Denise had walked past him and he'd been stopped in his tracks. "That woman always could tell you every little detail about everything, so I have no doubt that the details were as fresh in her mind as if they'd happened two weeks ago." She'd always had a helluva memory. A true Painter's eye." Fact is, he hadn't been ready for someone like Denise. He'd been too immature and clueless to appreciate a woman like her, no matter how young she'd been.

Yolanda laughed; her slap on Trent's back moved him forward unexpectantly. "I know, right? But I do think her anger is more about her admitting that it's time to move on than being about you. Don't you?" She'd taken the liberty of filling Trent in on all the pertinent details of Denise's recent life, but of course, he hadn't really needed the information. He knew most of the details.

Trent shrugged. "I hope so." His eyebrows raised. "I sure hope so."

"Well, don't worry, because I know so." Yolanda looked at her friends, their eyes focused on her and Trent. "She's had a hard year. Trust me, I know."

Trent licked his lips. He bet she did know, especially if they were as close as she made them out to be. His phone buzzed in his pocket and he put his hand on it to still the vibration. "I don't want to crash your party," he said. "I'm going to go."

"You don't have to, you know. It's no trouble. You could stay and eat with us."

Trent gestured in the direction of the door. "That's a very tempting offer. I could do that, or I could go and make sure the boat is ready." He needed a few minutes.

Yolanda squealed, demanding everyone's attention. Dabner shot her a warning glance from behind the counter. "We still get our return ride?"

"Of course you do. A promise is a promise. I have to move the boat to the marina anyway. I need to make a few calls though." Trent held his phone in the air. "Business never stops. I need to call my partner." He forced a smile.

Yolanda could barely contain herself. "I'm still glad I could convince you to come over and join us."

Trent chuckled. "Yes, of course. I'll be outside when you're ready."

She clapped her hands together like a school girl. "Great! We'll meet you outside in a bit."

Sweat immediately appeared on Trent's forehead as he left the restaurant. He glanced over his shoulder and walked away from the building and towards the water's edge. The gravel was loud under his feet as he rounded the corner of the building. A small skiff bobbed in the shallows. It was almost still, moving slightly with the ebb and flow of the water, without the help of a breeze. There should have been a person waiting in it to taxi him out to his boat, but instead the skiff and the shore were empty.

Trent's contact was on autodial. He bit his lip as he waited for the phone to ring. How in the world was he going to spin this? His partner would never believe that he'd come all the way to the Carolina's to meet the wife of the man he was supposed to investigate, and he kinda already knew her. He really wouldn't believe that had not made the connection earlier. What a rookie mistake. He could barely believe his luck, if that is what it was.

Rivers answered on the first ring. "Tell me something."

Trent cleared his throat. "Er, nothing to tell really. I actually was able to meet her pretty easily."

"I didn't think it was that big a place, and you went to school together so I thought you might know each other."

Trent didn't comment, instead cleared his throat. How was he supposed to know that of all people, she would be one that he knew?

"That's good to hear," Rivers laughed. "You're faster than I thought. What did you do, walk up and knock on the door?"

"No, nothing like that. You're not going to believe this—"

"And you aren't going to believe what I have to say," Rivers cut him off. Trent should have known that his partner would be true to his personality. He never really listened to anyone, not even when he needed to. He wasn't a bad partner, just an oblivious one. "We have a new clue."

"A what? After all this time? It's been a year."

"I know, right. We have a finger."

"A finger?" Trent pulled his phone slightly away from his ear and looked at it, then put it back to his ear again. Was Rivers drinking on the job? "Can you hear me?"

Rivers continued. "You're good. I said, we have a finger. Picture this, two girls playing on the beach, picking up shells—"

"What beach?"

"Don't interrupt. Doesn't matter. Are you going to let me tell my story or what?"

"Go ahead." Trent bit his lip as he forced himself not to interrupt Rivers and glanced over his shoulder. Yolanda and her gaggle of friends would be out soon, and Trent knew from experience that Rivers was the kind of man who would tell you everything in due time, all you had to do was be patient enough to listen.

"As I was saying. Two girls came across what turned out to be a finger over on one of the neighboring islands. We think it belonged to Charles."

Trent's mind raced. "Do we think or do we know? It would have had to have been out there awhile."

"It was," Rivers continued. "It was very badly decomposed but something in the water seemed to have partially petrified it. We are analyzing it now. I'll send you a picture."

"There couldn't be any fingerprints on it left at this point. It's been almost a year."

"Only a partial. But the bones have distinctive fractures that could help us out. We are trying to get medical records now to see if there could be match."

"Does the family know? Any remains at all will help the widow with her insurance claims. Not to mention give her some type of closure." Trent could only imagine what that nightmare was like for Denise.

"Are you listening to me? We have to make sure it's him first. I doubt it will help her. It would take more than a finger to prove his death. People cut digits off all the time. Oh, and this one looks like it was cut."

"As opposed to what?"

"Chewed, my man. Whoever this belonged to, it's a clean cut with no teeth marks. He was not shark bait. And if he was, this finger was amputated first.

4

Foul play on the Fairway

There had been no body. Charles's boat had come in, he just hadn't been on it. Perhaps that was why Denise had been so annoyed at Yolanda and her so-called plan. There had been no closure, so how could she possibly think of opening a new chapter? She wasn't ready to get back on anyone's boat, literally or figuratively, so Denise had passed on the boat ride back to the other end of the island.

It hadn't made sense really. Charles had been the most conscientious and careful human she knew, so there was nothing but disbelief when she'd learned that Charles had taken his boat out alone and had been in an accident. She tried to reconcile that theory in her mind, but something didn't feel right. Seeing that boat in the cove had made Denise feel these things all over again.

Eventually, they'd come to the heart attack theory. That, at least, had been plausible, even though her husband had prided himself on being the picture of health. Still, there was no way in hell she was getting on a boat with Trent or anyone else, and she absolutely had no intention of letting her meddling friends think that their tired plan had worked. They weren't kids anymore, so why did they insist on playing kid games?

Trent had been bad for her in college, and sure, she might be a little lonely, but for the most part, Denise was fine with the way things were, even if things with her husband's estate were still up in the air. It was a lot to deal with by herself so she certainly didn't want to complicate things with even a hint of romance.

She'd considered trying to explain all that to Yolanda, but thought better of it. Her friend was the type that just wouldn't stop when she got an idea. Denise shook her head and held back the tears that were struggling to escape. She'd left her friends to take their joy ride on Trent's boat while she drove back to her house alone. Normally, that drive relaxed her but this time memories kept intruding on her peace.

It was hard not to think of times past. Everything about her life now reminded her of her life with Charles. She smiled. The sooner she stopped thinking in the past tense, the better. Still, it was hard with so much left unanswered. She closed her front door gently, leaving the hiss of the cicadas outside.

They'd built the house to let nature in. The vestibule had three glass walls, and other than closing the door, you could still feel like you were outside. Denise paused and sighed heavily, listening to the silence in her house. Everything about the place, from the location set away from the water to the paint on the walls, reminded her of what had ended so abruptly just a few months before.

Tears stung Denise's face. All of her friends thought that Charles had had a heart attack and she'd let them believe that, despite her suspicions. Although that is what the authorities had come to, she had so many doubts. Denise wanted to believe what they told her. The heart attack story would certainly wrap things up and put a ribbon on them, but a voice at the back of her mind kept whispering that there was more to the story, and the longer she stayed on Kiawah, the louder the voice got. She hadn't shared her thoughts with anyone and hadn't planned to until she knew for sure what had really happened to Charles.

The police finally presented what they'd said were Charles's effects to her and that should have brought some type of closure, but it hadn't. His water-logged wallet. Some keys. For all she knew Charles was down in Cuba chilling with Tupac.

She wiped a tear away from her cheek and took a deep breath in an effort to keep herself together. She had to think of something else or she would lose it and she didn't want to do that.

"Be present now." She mumbled her yoga mantra under her breath and made her way to the kitchen, glancing at the framed picture on the front table. Charles, with his golf buddies, smiling. Charles, standing next to her, grinning like the cat that had stolen the mouse. Charles, with his secrets.

"You let me worry about that," he used to say. She'd done that, and where had that left her? Denise's eyes narrowed as she whispered to an empty house, "What are you hiding, Mr. Martine?"

The phone rang, drawing her back to the present. Denise's first instinct was to let it go to voicemail. She didn't really feel like talking, and certainly not when she didn't recognize the number. Besides, most of her friends would know to text her first.

She picked it up on the fifth ring. "Hello?"

There was no reply. Instead, she heard a clicking sound, and then silence.

"Hello," she said again, and then the phone went dead. Annoyance swept over her. More and more, telemarketers and robocalls were taking over cell phones. The Do Not Call registry was a hoax. She placed the phone face down on her hall table, not planning to look at it again for the entire evening, if she could avoid it.

Denise located a bottle of her favorite Merlot and poured herself a glass, then retreated to her living room to watch the golfers pass her house. They lived on the 14th fairway. The back of the house was mostly glass, set in a way that she could watch golfers maneuver their way through what seemed like an easy hole, only to be surprised by the not-so-infrequent alligator hiding behind the pampas grass or soaking up the sun.

The sun was going down, so there would just be a few people finishing up. Denise settled into her chair, appreciating that most of the people on the green would not be able to see her from her vantage point, nor would her neighbors. The houses were strategically placed so that no one really could see another, even though they weren't that far apart.

Before she had time to take a sip of her wine, Rascal, her four-pound Yorkie, jumped into her lap. A gift from her husband, Rascal went with her almost everywhere and was now a veteran on the trip from Chicago to Kiawah Island. Although she knew he was never far away, Denise was still startled and had to grip her glass to avoid a red wine stain on the area rug beneath her feet.

The dog sat back on his haunches and started to bark at her. She glanced at the clock over the mantle and frowned. They had a few hours until seven, his normal feeding time. "It's not time to eat yet," she said. "Do you need to go out?" *How could such a small creature make so much noise?*

She sat her glass on the small round table beside her and scooped up the small dog, dropping him in front of the patio door. She moved the security plank, and slid the door open. The curtains fluttered in the breeze.

"Wanna go out?" Denise asked. Instead of going outside, Rascal sat down and continued his barking, his back towards the door.

She sighed. "What is it? You're going to have to be more clear if you need something from me." She closed the door and then checked the dog's water dish. "You know I hate it when you do this." For half a second, Denise was annoyed at Charles, but then felt immediately guilty for feeling that way. True, Rascal had been an unsolicited birthday gift from him and was now added to the list of things he'd left her to sort out on her own, but he did bring her a sense of companionship that had been a source of comfort recently.

All Denise wanted was to relax and enjoy her evening, but that was lost on the dog. Annoyed, she grabbed Rascal and took him to the laundry room. His small crate was in the corner. "It's obviously time for you to go to your room." The dog wiggled in her hands, so she gripped him tighter and placed him inside the crate, shutting the door behind him.

Rascal made a few circles, then sat back and trained his overly expressive eyes on Denise. "Oh no you don't. Don't look at me like that." She turned to head back to her wine, but Rascal started his yapping again.

"Dang it, Dog," she said, closing the washroom door behind her as she left. *Was it that hard just to find some peace?* Denise hoped to dampen the sound of the dog and pick up where she'd left off. A sense of relief came over her; the dog was muted well enough that Denise could barely hear him.

Satisfied, she settled back into her chair. She sipped her wine, enjoying the bouquet as it took over her nose and taste buds. She let her eyes close and swallowed, feeling herself sink into her chair cushions. She finally felt like she might relax for the day. Two golfers walked past the window, oblivious to her presence. Just as the edge she had been feeling eased, a loud thump sounded above her head.

Denise's heart raced and she froze, looking up at the ceiling. The sound had come from the guest bedroom. Was someone in the house? Her stomach tied itself into a knot. She placed her glass back on the table slowly, trying to be quiet. If she wasn't alone, she didn't want them to hear her.

Her first instinct was to run, but where would she go? Her phone was on the table just inside the door, where she normally left it. Denise walked across the wood floor as silently as possible, holding her breath while she prayed that the wooden floorboards would not creak. She grabbed the phone from the entryway table, snatched the door open and ran through it, planning to call the guards from the street.

The few seconds that it took Denise to make it down her driveway felt like an eternity. Her own heartbeat thundered in her ears and her hands shook as she tried to call Island Security. The whole time, her feet did not stop moving. With her head down, she frantically pressed the emergency button on her phone. Just as she got to the asphalt of the street and rounded the bush at the end of her driveway, her egress was stopped. She ran right into Trent, bumping him so hard that she bounced slightly backwards. He grabbed both of her arms, steadying her.

"Whoa," he said. "Slow down. Where's the fire?"

Unable to comprehend for a minute, her voice caught in her throat.

"Niecy—"

Her old nickname snapped her back into the present, and things slowed down. "Denise." She no longer liked to go by the nickname she'd been called when she was in school. It felt somehow—not serious.

"Sorry. What's wrong? You look like you saw a ghost."

Denise swallowed her annoyance at Trent. "I think someone is in my house. I heard a noise."

Trent's face took on a more serious look. "Where? Are you sure?"

"No, I'm not. But I wasn't going to stick around to find out. I was calling security." Her body betrayed her and her eyes filled with water. "This is just too much to deal with right now."

Trent glanced towards the house. "Okay, you wait out here. I'll go and check it out for you."

Denise opened her mouth to protest, not wanting to accept help from Trent. How had he managed to waltz back into her life again after decades? Her face flushed hot. Damsel in Distress was not her style.

Trent didn't wait for her to answer. Instead, he headed towards the house.

She followed close on his heels. "I left Rascal. My dog." Denise could barely get the words out in between breaths. She didn't even consider staying behind as he'd suggested. Trent stopped right outside the door so suddenly that Denise ran into him again, this time, her nose bumping his back.

"I'll go first." He peered through the gaping doorway. "I'll let you know if it's safe.

Denise rolled her eyes. "If you think I'm staying out here, you're crazy," she said, grabbing his hand. Warmth emanated from Trent's body. "What if there are more of them out here?"

"Where?" His eyes scanned the interior of the first floor.

Denise motioned towards the upstairs, where the noise had come from. The mid-century modern house had both a front and a back staircase, and the front stairwell was just steps from the door. Trent started up the steps, walking on his toes. Denise could hear the thunder of her breathing inside her head as it mixed with the muffled sound of Rascal's barking from the washroom.

Trent hugged the wall as he led her into the master bedroom, to the right of the top of the steps. They paused outside the door and Denise stood by it, behind Trent as he pushed his way into the room. He went through the master and then into the ensuite, turning on the lights as he went. Denise heard the shower door open and close, and then Trent returned, this time throwing the folding closet doors open. "Does this look okay?" he whispered.

Denise's eyes swept the room and she nodded. As far as she could tell, nothing looked out of place at all. She opened her mouth to speak and Trent shushed her, placing his finger to his lips and shaking his head. The floor outside creaked, and he motioned to the hallway. Again, Denise's breath caught in her throat. Her eyes widened. There *was* someone in the house. Alarm bells rang in her head.

Trent moved to the hall, and once again, Denise followed close behind. What was going to happen if they found someone? she wondered. Neither one of them had a weapon, or at least she didn't believe that Trent had one. Why would he?

The door to the back bedroom was slightly ajar. Denise swallowed hard, her head pounding. Trent peeked through, and

then pushed it open forcefully, exploding into the room. She
looked around frantically.

"The bed." Her throat was suddenly very dry. "Someone's
been sitting on it." Denise pointed to the far side of the queen
bed that dominated the odd-shaped room. The blue bedspread
was clearly disheveled in one area.

"You have any guests?"

Denise shook her head. "No one should be here but me."

Trent nodded and continued into the room. He pushed
the small bathroom door open with his foot, peering inside. He
looked back at Denise and shook his head. "If there was
someone here, they're gone now."

Denise rubbed her temples, the tension once again
melting away from her body. She spun around and sat on the
bed, suddenly overwhelmed. The peace she'd come to know the
island for was so far, illusive.

"You sure you heard someone here?" Trent's nose flared
as he spoke.

The raised eyebrow that went along with his tone was
one that Denise remembered, even though they had been friends
years ago. He was doubting her. "I'm not crazy," she said, her
face darkening. "Someone was here." She put her head in her
hands, remembering the sound of someone walking overheard as
clear as day. That had been no imagination. "Look, I appreciate
you trying to help, but you really didn't need to ride up in here
on your white horse. Island Security could have handled this."
She jutted out her chin. She didn't need to be rescued. She could
take care of whatever this was herself, the same way she had
been taking care of herself since her husband disappeared.

Trent nodded, but there was a look of skepticism on his face.

"Let's get some air in here. Can I open a window?" He strode towards a window and wound the old-fashioned window-crank open before she could answer.

Denise welcomed the burst of fresh air, but as soon as Trent got the window open, the door to the back stairwell floated open, too. She gasped.

"What?" Trent stopped in his tracks.

She pointed towards the door that now stood ajar. "I'm sure that door was locked."

5

Island Insecurity

By the time Island Security rolled up in their Rolls Royce, both Trent and Denise were sitting outside the house on the front steps. Denise dabbed at her forehead with a napkin trying to hold back the sweat that was appearing there. Trent sat close to her, not caring if the contact between their bare arms made him sweat. They both listened to the hum of the crickets together, barely talking above a whisper.

The security guard parked at the end of the driveway, slamming the car door with a thud. His radio squawked as he walked towards them, telegraphing his approach. Denise froze as Trent rose to his feet.

"Did you call us, Mrs. Martine?" The guard was slightly overweight and sweat stains appeared on his light brown uniform.

Denise rolled her eyes. Why in the world would he ask that when he already knew she had? "Yeah. I did. I think there was someone in my house," Denise said. She stood and spoke quickly. "An intruder."

"Whoa," he said, "slow down. Can you tell me what happened?" He reached behind him and took out a pad, flipping it open. "Start from the beginning."

Denise could feel her frustration building. "What's to tell? I came in, sat down, and then I heard someone walking overhead."

"How do you know they were footsteps?" the guard asked. "These old houses make noises all the time."

Trent cleared his throat. "Do you want to go in and take a look?"

"We'll get to that, Mr. Martine."

Denise flinched.

"I'm not—"

"It's okay, Trent," Denise cut him off. "The house isn't that old. We did a complete remodel a short while ago. And I know what footsteps sound like."

"Okay," the guard sad. "I'm sure you do. But sometimes our senses play tricks on us."

Trent put his hand on Denise's shoulder as she rubbed her forehead. "Look. I think you can investigate better from inside the house, don't you?"

"I promise you, I know what I'm doing, Ma'am. I'm just following procedure." He folded his notebook shut. "How long have you been on the island?"

"Why is that even relevant?" Denise seethed with anger.

Trent stepped between the security guard and Denise. "Okay, look, there doesn't appear to be any signs of forced entry."

"Did you see anything?"

"No," Trent replied. "I checked the house out from top to bottom. If you don't want to take a look, maybe we should call the real police department or something."

"We are the real police around here. We have exclusive

jurisdiction on the island." He paused, squinting. "You're not the homeowner, are you?"

Trent shook his head.

"I'm the homeowner," Denise chimed in. "So are you going in now?"

He took his time answering. "I think I'm ready. I know you're frustrated, but I have to ask these questions to assess the situation and understand how much stress you're under."

"The door is open. Stress has nothing to do with hearing footsteps in a house that is supposed to have no one in it but myself." Denise turned the knob and then stepped aside so that the guard could make his way in. She and Trent followed.

"Where were you when you heard the footsteps?" he asked.

Denise pointed in the direction of her chair. He took the few steps to the chair and surveyed the room, his eyes coming to rest on her one glass that was still sitting on the floor next to the chair where she'd left it.

"You were sitting here?" he asked.

Denise nodded.

"And where were you, Sir?"

"I wasn't here yet," Trent replied.

"And the footsteps were, where again?"

"Over head. They were upstairs," Denise said.

The man looked up towards the ceiling. "And how much did you have to drink?"

"C'mon," Denise's voice was just shy of shouting. "Two sips. I had two sips. I'd only been home a few minutes. Don't you want to take fingerprints or something?"

By this time, Trent was becoming impatient, too. "Why

don't you just tell him what happened and then they can go from there?" He had a worried look on his face and spoke slowly, hoping to calm Denise.

"There was someone in my house," she repeated. "I heard them."

"But you didn't see them?"

Denise sighed. "I didn't have to see anyone. I <u>felt</u> them. My dog did, too. He kept barking and that confirmed it for me. There was someone here, in this house, that wasn't supposed to be. Are you going to do anything about it?"

"I understand how frustrated you must be, but we need to look at the evidence," the man said. "<u>Feelings</u> aren't exactly evidence."

Denise sighed, holding her hands up and then dropping them to her side. "Can we call the real cops?"

"There's no need for that," the security guard answered. "I can help you. We can figure this out."

"Like do you even have a gun?" Denise asked. "Do you have a license to be a real cop or are you a rent-a-cop because someone was in my house. I live alone. This is a problem for me and I want to know what you're going to do about it."

"Okay." He made a slow-down motion with his has. "I didn't do this. I came here to help you." Something that looked like frustration appeared on his face. "So if you want to tell me the facts, we can then check the visitor logs and see what we can see."

"Last time I checked intruders don't sign visitor logs." Trent pursed his lips. He was developing an even deeper respect for Denise and the amazing amount of restraint she was showing.

"Let's start from the beginning," Trent said. "We believe that someone was in here. Can you at least check your logs to see who came on and off the island like you said? Don't you sign most people in?"

"Most people." The security guard nodded, "Yes. But no one signed into this house in weeks."

"People lie though, right?" Denise asked.

He nodded. "They do. But not often."

"What about workers?" Trent asked. "They can come and go?"

The guard looked from Denise to Trent, studying their faces. "Workers get day passes. Even so they're vetted carefully." His phone buzzed. "Excuse me." He unlocked his phone and read the screen, finally locking up and slipping it back into its holster. "Sorry about that. Look, Mrs. Martine, I'm sorry for whatever you think happened here. It's clear you have been under some stress. When that happens, our mind will often play tricks on us—"

"Tricks? I'm not sure I like what you're suggesting."

The guard held up his hand to stop her. He reached into his pocket and took out what looked like a stack of paper and flipped through it. "This is the visitor log. I see no new visitors today. We had no workers on the golf course, no landscapers, nothing. Everyone is off on Mondays to make way for housekeeping. So, if someone was in your house, they snuck onto the island and we're going to figure that out."

"Great," Denise said. She folded her arms across her chest.

"I'll check the logs again, Ma'am." He walked towards the door and paused just outside them. "I'll see if there is something we missed but I don't think so. You know there's a lot of strange things that happen here in these islands. People around here like to believe in ghosts stories and all sorts of things, but there always and explanation. If anything is amiss, we will figure it out. Sometimes, our mind just plays tricks on us. You two have a good day. I'm going to leave my card—"

"Don't bother. I know where to find you." Her words dripped with disdain. The guard tried to hand her his card, but she made no moves to accept it. He sighed, instead giving it to Trent as he left.

Denise stood across the room and let Trent close the door behind the guard as he left. "You don't look like you believe he'll do anything."

"I don't. Why would he? He didn't believe a word I said."

Trent didn't answer. There was no need to make her anymore uncomfortable. He'd done enough already, hadn't he? "I can stay awhile if you want."

Denise sighed, then walked over to her couch and sat down, letting herself sink into it. "Might as well," she said, picking up her wine glass. "You should join me. I have a feeling it's going to be a long night."

6

Let me in

Yolanda stood in Darren's door and he barely looked up. "Darren, I'm talking to you." She tapped the stack of bills she had in one hand against the other. He didn't even flinch as the loud thwack sound erupted into the previously silent room. "Are you listening?"

Darren continued pecking on the keyboard. "Huh?" His face was locked on the screen in front of him.

"I asked you a question. I thought you said you paid these?" She shook the envelopes in her husband's direction. "Why is Citibank calling me?" Yolanda hated bill collectors more than anything on earth. Every time one called, it reminded her of the terrible fights her parents used to have over money when she was a child. She used to hide in her room but knew this wasn't the same. Hiding her head in the sand never got her anywhere before and it certainly wouldn't solve anything now.

He shrugged, waving her away. "I dunno babe. I just paid them. Did you talk to them?"

"You know I don't answer numbers I don't recognize," Yolanda said.

"You said it was Citibank. That means you recognized it."

"That's not the point, Darren. You know how I feel

about this." She rubbed the index finger of her free hand against her temple, in a circular motion. There was a headache coming. No matter how much money she had, she could never stop worrying. "Are you sure you paid them?"

"Babe, I did. Stop worrying. It's fine."

She wanted to believe him. Yolanda took a deep breath and felt her shoulders relaxing as she allowed some of the tension to creep away. "Sometimes you let these things slip through your fingers."

"I promise. Payment just crossed in the mail." Darren's eyebrows twitched a little, but he didn't look up again. "Either that, or it was a robocall spoof. You know how many numbers are being spoofed nowadays."

"But they knew my name, Darren. Who does that?"

He walked around his desk and took his wife into his arms, planting a kiss in the middle of her forehead. "Honey, you have to trust me. Didn't I promise to always take care of you?"

Yolanda still had some doubts, but she wanted to believe her husband. She put her nose into the space where his collarbone met his neck and inhaled, enjoying his scent. For some reason, that always made her feel safe. "You'd better."

He pushed her back to arm's length. "I have to get back to work, you sexy woman. You're distracting me."

"What are you working on anyway?" Yolanda sat on the edge of her husband's desk. He never told or bothered to explain things to her, but she never stopped asking.

"You wouldn't understand it, but I'm close to a breakthrough." Darren sat back at his desk. "I'll explain everything to you when it all falls into place."

Yolanda didn't want Darren to see that her feelings were

hurt. "I understand a whole lot more than you give me credit for. I'm not stupid." He never shared anything with her and treated her like she was a child. "How am I supposed to support you if I never know what you're working on?"

"I never said you were stupid. I just want to keep you from the stress of it all." Darren flashed his Colgate smile. "Baby, you help me just by being you. Keep doing that. Plus, I know you have a party to plan." He didn't wait for her to answer or to leave, instead he immediately went back to pecking away to his computer screen.

Yolanda pouted. "Okay. Fine." Darren was so engrossed in whatever he was doing that he probably didn't even realize that her "fine" meant she really wasn't. After being married so long, Yolanda knew when she was being dismissed and she hated it, so why couldn't Darren tell that she was annoyed? Her nostrils flared and she turned and left the room. She wished he would let her in.

7

Sankofa

Although Denise's house was not that far away from Yolanda's, they seemed worlds apart. Yolanda's house sat on the edge of a pond that would have been stagnant if not for the fountain that had been installed in the middle. Today, the water that blew up into the air evaporated before it came back down. The heat was so oppressive that it made Denise feel as if she were seeing a mirage around every corner.

After passing through the security guard stand that was supposed to keep undesirables off the island, Denise's home was one of the first you came to when you crossed over the small landfill-created bridge that signaled the entrance to Kiawah Island. Denise scoffed at the thought of that; clearly, the guards and the fortress-like gate had been ineffective the night before.

After the guard left, Trent had not spoken of the intruder again, leaving Denise to feel as if he'd turned his nose in the air, refusing to believe that there had actually been anyone in her house, or at least it felt that way. He'd damn near agreed with the guard, practically dismissing her as a lonely, hysterical widow. He'd seen the open window and door, just as well as she had, yet he'd looked at her as if she'd imagined the whole incident. Denise could still see the look on his face. He'd raised his right eyebrow in the air the same as he used to all those years ago, with not one ounce less of sex appeal, even though they were both so many years older. She'd felt judged. Even so, she couldn't help but feel grateful that he'd shown up when he did. Skeptical or not, Denise had felt safer after he'd gone through the house. That wasn't all she'd felt. She hated to admit it, but she'd actually enjoyed his company. It has been years since they had spent any time together, but she'd found herself slipping back into old familiar patterns like it had been yesterday, not twenty years. It had felt good, like an old pair of well-worn jeans, despite the drama.

Yolanda's house was further into the ten-mile island, behind another, more-grand gate. This one marked the entrance to what had been the plantation proper and now separated the mere houses from the mini-mansions. Like many of the homes in the area, Yolanda's house had been built in the style of old plantation houses, with a double, Tara-esque, raised stairway that led to the front door. It was supposed to frame the entrance, but to Denise, it looked like a mouth. In actuality, the steps were an eye-catching way to ensure that the home was raised out of the reach of the swamp and pond behind it, as well as the alligators that liked to submerge themselves there. The island's alligators were pretty passive, but every now and then there would be a scary story of a tourist and a near miss or worse.

The guard recognized her and waved her through the gate. Denise gave half a wave back, now doubting that this second gate was any more effective against intruders than the one by her house. After yesterday, she realized that the gates were supposed to make the owners feel exclusive, if not safe, but they could do nothing if someone really wanted to get in. They'd failed her, hadn't they?

Denise yawned. After her encounter, she hadn't been able to sleep at all, and now she was suffering because of it. Trent had stayed almost all night, but there was no way she was going to set tongues to wagging by having him stay with her as he'd suggested. Just before dawn, she'd ushered him out, and now blushed as she thought about it. Wasn't she a grown woman? Did she really care what people said or thought?

The driveway at Yolanda's house was full already and the garage door was open, revealing a garage filled with stuff that one acquired living an island life, including matching sets of golf clubs, shoes and tennis rackets. Denise exited her car, pausing a minute outside the garage. Her breath caught in her throat and she paused a minute. She would no longer need a matched set of anything.

Yolanda's garage looked like a reflection of itself; things were neatly arranged so that both sides were exactly the same and all of the recreation items formed a frame or border around the cars that sat in the middle.

These were the only small differences between the sides of the garage, yet it was easy for Denise to tell which side belonged to whom. Yolanda's Tesla sat on the left, without so much as a speck of dust on it, juxtaposed against the hybrid Ford on the opposite side. You could only tell they matched because of the vanity plates. Darren's car was Yoda1 and Yolanda's, Yoda2. The cars seemed to be at opposite ends of a spectrum, just like Yolanda and her husband, Darren. Yolanda, like her car, the Tesla, did everything she tried quickly and with gusto, while, Darren, her husband of many years, was slower, meticulous and yet very dependable, like his Ford, at least on most days. They were the perfect foil for each other.

As the air-conditioner cooled off her car, a bead of sweat popped onto Denise's forehead. The Low Country's heat would get her if she dallied too long. She flicked a fly away from her face and bypassed the elevator that went from the garage to the main floor of Yolanda's house. Denise preferred the simplicity and the speed of the stairs.

No one locked their doors this far into the island and Yolanda was no exception. Denise pushed the door in and announced herself, barely struggling to be heard over her friend's high-tech doorbell chime. Her announcement caught in her throat as she was thrown off guard by the tune of "Dripping With Finesse." Laughter emanated from the kitchen just as Yolanda rushed out to meet Denise.

"Cher! So glad you came." Cher was Yolanda's favorite endearment—for everyone, even though she was neither French nor from New Orleans where the greeting was common. "Are you okay?" Yolanda wrapped herself around Denise, immediately kissing the air to either side of her friend's cheeks. News travelled fast. Denise was sure there was more than a little speculation about why Trent had been over at her place last night.

Why did it feel as if Yolanda's questions were so full of judgment? Denise slipped out of her shoes and nodded. "I'm fine."

"You need a drink?"

"You know I do." Drinking would help take her mind off of things. "Cardi B on the doorbell?" It was Denise's turn to give judgmental looks. "Rap is young people's music. We ain't young."

"Speak for yourself. That's the music I grew up with. You did, too. You just need to get the stick out of your butt and admit it. You're as much a 90's baby as I am."

"We didn't grow up with Cardi B."

"You need to move forward with the times, girl. Only old people can't appreciate new music. It's proven. You're old when your brain fixates on an era."

"You've been listening to Darren too much." Denise rolled her eyes. "I can't with you today. I'm too tired."

Yolanda waved her hand in the air. "I forgot. You like Jazz, right? It calls you? Whatever, girl. You're too much for me when you're in your Hotep mood. Anyway, it's Darren's doing. New toy. You know how he is."

"Very classy." Denise pursed her lips. She did know how Darren was. He'd been very close to Charles for a long time. They'd been almost inseparable during the times they spent on the island.

"Hey, he's a frustrated hacker. He's hooked something up that will allow him to download music from iTunes. He can change the doorbell every day if he likes. It makes him happy, so I don't judge. He has no complaints about my shoe habit. No man is perfect and he's entitled to his toys like everybody else. I can't help it if his toys are high tech."

"You've got a point. I'm just tired." Her mouth curved into a slight smile. Ever since they'd met, years before, Darren had been a tinkerer, and the home he shared with his wife reflected it. Disneyland had nothing on the McAlister home. It was the most connected one that Denise had ever experienced. It was almost a pleasure to visit at the start of each season to see what Darren had cooked up. Denise needed all the fun she could get. Darren had been the perfect partner in crime for Charles. Charles had the ideas and Darren built then. Or at least he'd tried to. It didn't always work out, but as Charles would say, you only needed one hit.

"We're drinking champagne today." Yolanda didn't wait for her friend to answer, instead grabbing the nearest flute from the group that stood sentry on the counter. She handed one to Denise and filled them both to nearly overflowing.

Denise licked the foam from the rim of the glass as it threatened to spill down the sides. "Slow down, it's midday. I don't need this much."

"Never stopped us before." Yolanda smiled, holding her glass in the air for Denise to touch to hers.

They clinked glasses. From the red tinge in her eyes, it was apparent that Yolanda had started without her anyway. In the past, the ring of the glassware had told the beginnings of many hours of their escapades. Denise looked around the kitchen, momentarily grateful for Yolanda's friendship. The room had an open floor plan, flowing into the living room ending in a glass wall in the back, overlooking a negative edge pool. Beyond that lay the pond, with its fountain spewing water into the air. "I thought someone was here. I heard laughter."

Yolanda cleared her throat, coughing lightly. "You did. I was on the phone."

"Oh, now that's old-fashioned. Like a house phone? Now who's old?"

"Don't talk about my old-fashioned ways," Yolanda said. "And Darren is back in his office working on Lord knows what." She waved her hand in the air dismissively.

Denise sipped her champagne. "The more things change, the more they stay the same."

"Let's talk about what's changed with you, shall we?" Yolanda cleared her throat. "More than a year has passed so I guess it's okay now?" Yolanda pursed her lips, eyebrows raised like a cat about to pounce. "Your panties were all in a bunch at the thought of it while we were at the cove.

"At the thought of what?" Denise pressed her palm to her cheek. She knew what was coming and was surprised that Yolanda had taken this long to get to it. Even though the air conditioner was on, the room seemed under-cooled.

"You're really going to make me ask? When you met us for lunch, you wanted nothing to do with Trent and even seemed offended at the suggestion. Then the next thing I know, he's over at your house all hours of the night. Which is it?" She gave her friend a knowing look. "I'm supposed to be your bestie and I'm the last to know."

"I already told you." Denise sighed. "I thought there was someone in the house and he came by—"

"And there appeared to be no threat, yet he left hours later? I get it. It's been awhile and you are a grown-ass woman with needs." Yolanda sipped her Prosecco. "I'm not surprised, really."

Denise sat her champagne flute on the counter. "What kind of person do you think I am?" Her face flushed, but she was unsure whether she was mad or embarrassed. She'd actually thought about Trent spending the night and sleeping had not been what was on her mind. "How do you know what time he left anyway?"

"Girl, please. This _is_ an island. News travels fast." She paused. "Well, do you have something to tell me? I totally get it and love the romanticism of it all. Years later, you re-connect." She moved her palms together, then interlocked her fingers. "Sankofa."

"Sankofa? Really? I don't know who you think I am. Like I told you, he searched the house for me, and then I was flustered. He stayed until I felt comfortable. You know how the island can play tricks on you."

"Um hmm." Yolanda paused, lips pursed. "Sure, so nothing happened?"

"Let me repeat. I'm grown and I don't have to tell you anything." Denise lowered her voice. "But nothing happened. Besides, he and I already crossed that bridge back in the day, and that didn't go so well."

Yolanda's eyes narrowed. "Why didn't I know about this?"

"My heart was broken. I don't know… I couldn't find the words to tell you everything."

"You can save that crap for someone who doesn't know you like I do. I still can't believe you never told me about him in college."

"You were gone then," Denise said.

"I took a semester off, Denise. We were still friends. Were you in love?"

Denise shrugged. "It wasn't that kind of party."

"What kind of party was it then, Cher?" She paused, placing her hand on Denise's forearm. "It doesn't matter. It's been almost a year. It's time to move on with your life."

"He is dead, isn't he?" Denise's heart sank. Yolanda was the only one she'd told about her suspicions, but to hear them spoken out loud made them more real than she wanted them to be. "He has to be. There would be no other reason for him to disappear."

"I can think of a few. People disappear. They do it all the time."

"Not my people! Plus, I have his remains now." She spat her words as if there were a bad taste in her mouth. She could barely convince herself that was the truth, so she knew that Yolanda didn't, either.

"A wallet and a shirt don't qualify as remains." Yolanda took a step back, adding some distance between them. "Don't shoot the messenger." She pursed her lips. "I know it was spectacular the way he ended but you seem to forget the reality of things."

Denise spun around. "The reality of things? What are you talking about?"

"C'mon, Denise. Don't act like you don't remember complaining to me about your love life? You stood right here in this kitchen and told me that the two of you had little to no sex in the last six months of your marriage. You deserve to live a little."

"How dare you—"

"How dare I what? Tell the truth? I've been telling you the truth since we were six, I'm not about to stop now. You need to be open to whatever, you understand what I'm saying? You deserve to be happy."

Instead of saying what she wanted to, Denise picked up her champagne glass and emptied it in one, long gulp. She grimaced as she followed the burn down her throat. "It's always the people on the outside that have all the answers," she said, instead. "I'm sure your marriage isn't all that perfect, either." Denise willed back tears and tried to swallow the lump that was suddenly in her throat.

Yolanda wrapped her arms around her friend and gave her a hug. "There's a reason for that, you know."

Denise tensed, pulling away. "I don't want a lecture."

"I'm not giving you one. I'm just going to say one thing. I watched for years as you worshipped that man and he took you for granted.

"What do you mean? He loved me." Denise swallowed hard. He had loved her, right?

Yolanda crossed her arms over her chest. "I'm sure he did. In his own way."

"You're not supposed to speak ill of the dead."

"I'm not speaking ill of anyone." Yolanda paused, searching her friend's face. "Tell me this. Two years ago, remember when you planned that getaway weekend for your anniversary, how did you celebrate?"

Denise turned away as the painful memory came to her. "We didn't."

"Why not?"

"Stop it, Yoli."

"Tell me why not," she demanded.

Denise took a deep breath. "He had to work."

"And for your birthday?"

"Stop it. Why are you treating me like this? I'm already exhausted. I came over here to kick back."

Yolanda walked into the kitchen and pulled a tissue from the box, then handed it to her friend. "I'm sorry. Let's—" Her apology was interrupted by the sound of the doorbell.

Grateful for the interruption, Denise wiped her eyes. "Expecting someone?" She felt her shoulders relax. She'd been saved from more grilling. Why did Yolanda have to be so intense? Ever since they were kids, she'd never been one to hold back her thoughts or feelings. Denise had gotten used to it over the years, but that made it no easier when those feelings were directed at her.

"Sorry, girl." Yolanda unhanded her glass and made her way down the hall back towards the front of the house.

Denise settled into a seat on the nearby sofa, fluffing a pillow as the sound of voices wafted into the living room. There was a lower voice, but still female, that intertwined with that of her friend. It sounded familiar, but she couldn't quite place it.

She didn't have to wait long to find out. "Denise!" the voice boomed as a woman burst into the room. Denise jumped. Yolanda followed close behind, an exasperated look on her face.

"Hey..." Denise said. She tried to sound enthusiastic. Her voice trailed off.

"I was so glad to hear that you had finally come back to the island." The woman's words tumbled from her mouth as she swept around the furniture, her flowy clothes trailing behind her. She was dressed like she was a Bedouin desert resident, stylishly cool, but with enough material to protect her from the sun. The billowy material covered her but hid nothing, strategically highlighting her womanly curves. "I was so surprised."

Denise leaned in to accept the woman's hug, still not quite placing her. She took her in. There was no doubt in her mind that every square-inch of fabric was on the high end of the expensive scale. Nothing that made you look like you were floating was ever cheap.

"Well, you know me, full of surprises." A whiff of expensive perfume caught her nose, and Denise noticed that the woman was absolutely gorgeous. Her makeup was so expertly applied that it appeared as if she were walking around behind an Instagram filter. She quelled the urge to ask her who she was, knowing that if she waited, she would be able to put it all together.

"I told Yolanda, girl, I would be surprised if Denise didn't sell her place." Her words tumbled from her mouth like water over a dam. "It must be so hard without your husband. I mean, I just heard a month or so ago. I was wondering why I didn't see him anymore. I am so sorry to hear of your loss."

Denise's mouth dropped open and her eyes locked on Yolanda's. "See him again?"

"Oh yes. I used to see him all the time, when he came down to the marina to take out that boat. He was so nice. His French was so much better than mine. I noticed the boat is gone from its slip. Did you sell it?" She shooed her words away with a wave of her hand. "I guess it doesn't matter now."

"The boat?" Denise was truly confused now. How often could he have taken out the boat? They lived in Chicago. Denise certainly didn't remember him taking it out when she hadn't known about it. "I'm sorry, you are?"

"Talking too much. I know. I apologize. I can't help it. I was just so excited when Yolanda said you were here. I mean, I came over to drop off some things?" She paused, almost with a question at the end of her sentence. "For the event on the fourth," she continued, practically launching her words, one after the other. "I don't really live here anymore, but I do still keep active on the social scene. And of course, my boat is parked at the marina."

"The marina?"

"Yes, right next to where yours used to be." She paused. "Wait, you don't remember me, do you? I think we only saw each other once or twice, and then from a distance." She looked from Denise to Yolanda.

Yolanda cleared her throat. "I just assumed you two knew each other. Denise, this is Malika Lavigne."

"You got me. But how did you know my husband?" Even if

she didn't recognize her, Denise certainly knew the name. Malika Lavigne was from Charleston, the proprietor of one of the most famous Boutique Hotels in the city, and the only Black female in the city to own one at all.

Malika extended her jeweled hand, and Denise was surprised she could even lift it. The sapphire that adorned her right ring finger was so large it obscured her finger.

"Oh, yes," Denise said. "I do know you. The hotel?"

"I'm glad to re-meet you, although I'm sure you would have seen me at the marina. As I was saying, I often saw your husband when he visited. I like to spend the weekends there, especially in winter when the tourists leave. It is so peaceful on the water, an escape for me from running the inn."

Denise nodded. "I'm sure."

"I just assumed that was you coming and going with him. Remember, I would just wave from my deck?" Malika waved into the air, her head cocked to the side as if doing so would make Denise recognize seeing her before.

The honey color bled from Denise's face. "Oh."

Malika jabbered on, not noticing the change in Denise's demeanor.

"He'd wave back, and a few mornings we had coffee across the decks before you came back to the marina, you know. I guess you're a late sleeper. We all need our rest and I can see yours is doing well by you. You're much prettier from the front. I guess I wouldn't stay on the boat overnight either, if my house were so close." Malika paused, taking a deep inhale. "When the boat didn't come back, I thought you guys had gone elsewhere. People from the north can be so fickle sometimes. They fall in love with Kiawah, and then one day, then sell and the love is gone."

"We're from Chicago." Unable to listen anymore, Denise sat back on the sofa. Malika's voice faded to the background. Why hadn't she known this before?

Yolanda put a hand on her shoulder. "You okay?"

Denise shook her head. "Rough night." Her voice was just above a whisper.

"Oh, sorry. Yes, I heard about that, too." Malika let out a low laugh. "It's funny that I live off-island now, you know, since my Benny died, and I still hear everything that happens. You make sure security looks into that before things get out of hand around here. Yolanda, I'm going to go. I hope to see you both at the party. It's a fundraiser this year. And Denise, when you're in Charleston, come stay at the inn, or at least have dinner. I'll make sure your room is comped." She made a face as if she'd said something awkward.

Yolanda shepherded Malika back towards the door, her face riddled with concern. "We'll put it on the calendar. Thanks for bringing the invitations by. They look great."

"It's the least I can do. Those electronic invitations they use today are so classless. Besides, I needed to take the Bentley out for a spin."

"I bet you did," Yolanda said.

Malika cackled. "Anyhoo, Au revoir." They air kissed in the direction of ear other's cheeks. Malika was barely through the threshold before Yolanda closed the door and actually locked it behind her, making a beeline back to the living room.

Denise was staring into space, still sitting on the sofa. "Girl, what's wrong? I could have sworn you'd met Malika before. She can be a lot."

"That isn't the problem."

"What is it?"

"You know I never come here after the fall. My schedule is too full. So, how did my Charles come here and take the boat out with someone and I not know about it? And who the hell was on the boat with him? It sure as hell wasn't me!"

Trent pulled his truck into the marina parking lot and cut the engine. He started towards the slip that was housing his boat for the summer, enjoying the sound of the lap of the water against the docks. It was one of his favorite sounds and his stress levels immediately dropped like a pressure cooker with an release valve.

As he passed by the small hut that housed the marina office, the attendant slid the window open and yelled to him.

"Hey, there, man. You good?"

Trent paused. That was such a loaded question and could mean a lot of things based on his tone. "Yeah, I'm good." He slowed his walk.

"You know you need to sign in and out of the marina when you come. We keep track of when people are here, ya dig?"

Trent nodded, but then paused. "Have you always done that?" He knew that Charles used to keep his boat at this marina. It really was the only one around that had any services. There were few places actually on the island that you could pull up to, but this place was one where you could actually gas up your boat.

The attendant looked at him as if he'd grown horns. "You're not from around here, huh?" He answered his own

question. "Of course, you're not, or I would have known you.
We sort of used to, but since people have been asking questions,
we're tryna do things the right way." He pursed his lips. "Just
make sure you sign in when you walk past the window, and out
when you leave. That way we know when people are here, and
when they might be hurt."

"I got it."

"Not trying to be a hard ass, but strange things happen in
these waters."

"Strange how?" Trent asked. You never knew who knew
what.

The man shrugged. "Boating can be dangerous. Every couple
of years, someone goes out and doesn't come back."

"Really?"

More shrugs. "It's for your own safety. Is that going to be a
problem?"

"Nah, man. I'm straight."

The man nodded and pushed a worn ledger towards Trent,
pointing at a pen that was attached to the window with red yarn.
Trent signed it, and the attendant slid the window shut with a
thud.

He left the ledger right there, outside the window. Trent
wondered how far back the thing went. He ran his finger over
the outside edges of the book, gauging its thickness. He'd have to
come and check that out later when things were quiet.

8

The Changing Truth

Denise couldn't stop thinking about Malika Deveraux. For the life of her, she couldn't remember her husband mentioning any people with him the times he'd been on the boat without her, and certainly not with other women. More secrets shouldn't surprise her, but they did. This was a new kind of betrayal.

There were only a handful of times she knew of that he'd come to Kiawah without her at all, although he'd taken frequent business trips which he'd claimed were to meet clients and the like. Of course he would leave off that the clients, if they were that, were women.

She thought back to the last time they'd discussed it. Denise remembered looking at the clock on the nightstand in the dim morning light. She remembered the display announcing three AM, the image burning into her eyes. She'd groaned and rolled over, sensing the emptiness of the bed beside her. "Charles?" Her throat had been crazy dry, the heating system in their bedroom had sucked all of the moisture from the air. The heat had still been on; spring in Chicago was winter for another city.

He was but a shadow in the bedroom. "Don't wake up, honey," he'd said. "I'm taking the first flight down to Charleston."

"Charleston," she'd croaked. "It's March. It's not even warm there yet."

"Warmer than here." Charles had leaned over the bed, kissing her on her forehead. That part, Denise presumed, was the truth. Chicago was still frosted over with new snow blanketing the ground. "I'm gonna take the boat out and maybe play a round of golf."

"That sounds nice." She'd just been glad he wasn't asking her to go. It took too much preparation on her part, preparations she hadn't wanted to do, and certainly not for a short trip to not great weather. Packing, outfits. That type of thing was always far less easy for women. She'd rolled over, a thin smile on her face. "Any of the guys going?" The men often met for golf. They'd formed a golf circle over the years that had grown in popularity so much that there were men waiting to be invited.

"Nah. Just me. I need some time to think. I have to work on this presentation for our new client, and the island is relatively free of distractions this time of year. It'll be easier there."

And with that, he was gone. Denise had no more questions for him and he'd stayed about five days. Pretty typical. So what had Malika been talking about?

Denise was somehow sure that she and Malika would cross paths again, even before the fundraiser. It was ten days away and she, like her friends, had already been assigned a job. In the past they'd planned the party together. It used to be much smaller and more intimate, but she'd been pretty much otherwise occupied this past year and didn't get a vote on how the annual event would play out. She'd been grateful for this respite, too. Yoli, along with Samantha and her crew had taken up her slack.

Things had changed and it was much bigger. Denise felt as if she'd been sleeping. In the blink of an eye, the party had moved from someone's house, usually Yolanda's, to a pavilion on the water's edge. It used to be a simple pot luck where the six friends had bought their favorite dishes, to being catered by a group from Charleston.

Trash duty. What kind of a job was that? Denise wasn't even sure how she'd gotten dragged into being part of the committee for this thing. "We wanted to make sure we included you," Yolanda had said. "We know you're busy, but we didn't want you to feel left out, so we did all the heavy lifting."

Denise sighed. "Yeah right." She felt included all right, so much so she would just include her check and hire a professional to take care of the cleanup. There was still too much going on in her world, or at least in the world inside her head and now the Malika mystery had added to it.

A car horn honked outside, reminding her that she was supposed to be throwing things into her bag. Her office manager had summoned her back to the office in Chicago for a reason Denise was sure was nonsense. There wasn't much that couldn't be done remotely nowadays, but Jamel had insisted she come in person, going as far as to book her on the afternoon flight. Denise was perplexed as to the reason. She picked up her phone and re-read the messages.

We need you here for these meetings with the investigators.

That certainly sounded important, but Denise had no idea what he was talking about. Investigators of what? And what was so urgent that it had to be done in person in this day and age of remote working? As it was, most of the employees worked in the field roughly seventy percent of the time. There was never a real accounting emergency when her husband had run things, so what could be different now? She'd had some learning curve since she'd taken over, but she couldn't have been that off base about things.

There was a part of her that felt like she was living Charles's dream. Accounting had been his thing, not hers, although now, after all these years, she was no longer sure what her thing was anymore. She didn't even make enough time to paint or create, that was what he really loved, not this. Her heart lived in pigment and fiber. Her bags thudded across the floor, making an uneven sound every time the wheels hit a spot in the floor joints. Rascal ran behind the bags, his tag making a jingling sound. "Sorry, Boy," Denise said aloud. "Not this time. I'll be back in a few days." She bent down and rubbed the Yorkie Poo in the space behind his ears. He rolled over in response. Normally, she'd fly with the dog, but he'd be okay for this short trip. "I'll bring you something special back. Yolanda will come over and look after you while I'm gone." Denise had no intention of staying in Chicago long.

Denise opened the front door at the sound of footsteps on the veranda, and then turned to drag her bag closer. "Can you help me with this?"

"Of course," Trent's voice responded.

Denise's hand flew to her mouth. "Oh my God. You scared me. What are you doing here?" Why did he keep showing up like this?

"I'm taking you to the airport. Yolanda told me you had to leave. I thought I'd be of service."

She bristled. "She can't keep anything to herself."

"Was she supposed to? Is it a secret?" His eyes seemed to stare right through Denise. "She told me you had to fly back to Chicago and I wanted to be sure to see you before you left."

Denise sighed. "No, it's fine. I just have so much on my mind. There is no reason for me to be short with you. I've already called the car service, though. Thanks anyway."

Trent grabbed her bag, helping her move it over the threshold. "Well, you probably will still need my ride if they were the car I sent away."

She stared at Trent, flabbergasted. "You did what?"

Trent paused, removing his sunglasses. "I'm sorry. Was that presumptuous of me?" He took out his phone. "I can get him back. I'll call the front gate if you want and they'll turn the driver around."

She grit her teeth. Trent had some nerve. What was with him? She inhaled, but then realized Trent was staring straight at her. As handsome as he was, it was hard for her to be too angry at him. He did seem to be genuinely sorry for what he had done. Denise released the breath she hadn't realized she was holding. "No big deal." She had to learn to let things go. Old Denise, the one that had been married to Charles, would overthink things. This new Denise reminded herself to live in the present, and right now, she needed to handle her business and get to her flight.

"I was going to the airport anyway, so it'll save you a few bucks."

"Thanks." It was obvious that Trent meant well. "I hate parking at the airport almost as much as I hate taking a taxi service." What harm would come to accepting a ride from Trent?

The ride from the island to the Charleston airport was forty minutes. She could do anything for that amount of time, and she hated to admit that she halfway enjoyed his company. Maybe more than halfway, Denise thought. As soon as she admitted that to herself, a weight lifted off her shoulders.

A half-crooked smile spread across Trent's face. He reached for her bags again and this time, Denise let him carry them off the small wooden landing in front of her house and out to his truck.

She settled in, but busied herself with email, not wanting to talk. She combed through her memories, trying to remember at least one time where her husband had mentioned taking meetings on his boat, but nothing came to mind. Trent finally broke the silence just as they crossed the narrow two-lane artificial landfill bridge that separated Kiawah Island from John's Island, the longer barrier island that was closest to the mainland and led to Charleston.

"I hope everything is okay." His eyes darted in Denise's direction as he maneuvered the car down the tree-lined road.

Denise let her hands fall to her lap, turning her phone screen-side down. Her neck was beginning to hurt from looking down. "Me, too."

"Is there something I can do?" Trent asked. A look of concern settled on his face.

"Doubtful. It's business. My office manager needs me to come and make some decisions."

"You were in business with your husband, right?" He paused. "Yolanda—"

"Tells everything apparently." Denise sighed heavily. "Not exactly. He ran an accounting consulting firm with a few branches. I would occasionally do some work for him when the client was big enough or they needed what I did."

"What do you do? I always thought you would be an artist or painter of some type."

Denise smiled. "I really am. A painter. And I want to branch off into the fiber arts more. I've been dabbling. He always discouraged that though. He though that was old-fashioned."

"Fiber arts? Like weaving and stuff you used to do in college? You still do that?"

"Exactly that. I'm surprised you remembered. I have this idea that I want to spin wool and cotton and then use that to create mixed media creations, either spinning it and somehow incorporating into my artwork, or create pieces directly from the yarn."

Trent nodded." I think that is fascinating. Not sure how that fits in with, accounting is it?"

Denise giggled "It doesn't. I would occasionally write grants for a client or two if needed. I wouldn't call that being in business together. Charles did everything else. Business development. Everything. I think he was just keeping me close to patronize me and make me feel useful."

"You always were really smart."

Denise chuckled. "I don't feel so smart. I'm still as much of an artist at heart as I was in college. I'm just holding on until I can sell this thing. He also had an office in France. That's nothing but a client list now."

"France? That's fancy." Trent made a silly face.

Denise held back a laugh. "Not really. It was an easy way for him to get some international work, when he needed it.

Clients were more open to hire us if they thought we at least had a presence on the same continent. Made us feel more like we were not foreigners."

"I get that.

"He spoke French?"

"Like a native. He actually would do some meetings and interview in French himself, without a translator. Charles even had a French passport. He is, I mean was, a dual citizen." Denise's face flushed as she corrected herself.

"Dual-citizen?" Trent's eyebrows raised. "How'd that happen?"

"His father was French. Charles was born in Martinique."

"Really? How interesting. I guess that's where the French sounding last name came from."

Denise nodded. "Most Americans just say Martin, instead of Martín. Americans butcher everything, so he added the 'e' at the end so people would say it the way he wanted. Things like that mattered to him."

"Things like what?"

"How things looked."

"And how they sounded?"

"You're still a smarty pants, I see."

Instead of answering her, Trent glanced over and smiled. "You must have been proud."

"I don't know about that." At one point, Charles could get anything he wanted from her if he spoke French. That had just been so sexy to her. "Charles certainly had a way with languages, not just French. It was his thing. He may have had lots of shortcomings, but he always found a way to relate to people and say one or two words to them in their native tongue.

He made them feel comfortable in the language they were most familiar with. It helped him blend in everywhere we went."

Trent nodded, turning his attention back to the road. "So that French office? What's happening there now?"

Denise shook her head. "Not a helluva lot. I basically keep a skeleton crew there. I haven't had time to focus any energy on business development in the states, much less in another country. Like I said, holding on until I can sell."

"And the Chicago office?"

"Thank goodness the employees know what they're doing. Otherwise, this would have been over already. As it stands, we were supposed to be doing due diligence for a sale. I thought it was a go until last night."

"You don't want to continue the company?

"What for?" Denise asked. "This thing was his dream, not mine. Plus, I'm no accountant. He was honoring me by letting me route the occasional commission contract through there."

"What's your dream then?"

"I just told you. You sure have a lot of questions," Denise bristled.

Trent laughed. "I'm just trying to make conversation, Denise. After all this time, of course I'm interested in what has happened in your life." He flashed a smile. "Back in the day, we used to be close. I kinda missed you."

"Did you?" She paused and looked away, focused on the landscape. "You can't go back, Trent."

"No one is saying all that. I just want to catch up." He sighed. "I remember you being very adventurous. Have you changed that much?"

Had she? "There hasn't been a whole lot of time in the past months for me to think about what I want, you know, with my husband disappearing and all."

"So we're here now. What's your dream, Denise? What do you want to do with your life?"

"You want me to figure that out in the next thirty minutes?" Denise's eyes narrowed and she stared out at the roadway. This was really the first time anyone had asked her what she wanted to do in months, and it felt weird. Truth be told, her husband had never cared what she wanted to do. For a long time, everything had been about him and building his business. Now that he was gone, everything had shifted to being about his disappearance and cleaning up his mess.

Denise knew that Trent's question was rhetorical, but she answered anyway. "I'm not sure," she said. That was the truth. Him bringing it up made her realize it was also something she planned to change.

9
The Way People Change You

Trent enjoyed the time he spent riding with Denise, even though he'd spent most of it grilling her under the pretext of catching up. As much as he hated to admit it, it was nice to really get to know her again. He'd meant what he said about missing her, more than he'd first realized. She'd always been easy to talk to and things were no different now. Everyone had that one that got away, and for Trent, that one was Denise. He smiled at her, wondering how much she actually knew about her husband's dealings. It was curious that he'd had a whole separate business in France and she knew nothing about it.

"So, you never learned to speak French?" he asked. "It seemed as if that would be an interesting thing to do and maybe even sexy, if you know what I mean."

Denise smiled. "If I didn't know better, I'd think you were trying to seduce me, Trent. And yes, it was quite sexy." A small smile crossed her face, and from the looks of things, Trent could tell that it was a happy memory for her.

"Me? No, I'd never do anything like that." He smirked. "I was just curious. Seems like you two had such a fairytale life and now it's just gone."

Denise got silent for a minute. His words were grating, though true. The life that she used to know was gone. Some of the things that she and Charles did together, especially in the beginning, were a lot of fun. Adventurous, even. Denise's smile disappeared as suddenly as it had come.

"Did I say anything wrong?" he asked. A twinge of guilt hit him. "I didn't mean to upset you. Since my wife died, I notice things about couples and I know that I miss her as much as you probably miss Charles. From the way you were talking about him, I can tell this is still a tough time. It seems that you had much more in common than my wife and I did. You worked together. You played together. It must have been nice."

Denise looked over at him. "Yeah, for many years, it was."

Trent nodded. "My wife and I barely spent any time together up until the end."

"The end?" Denise looked over at him. "I didn't realize that your wife had died."

"Yes, she did." Trent licked his lips, pausing. "She died several years ago."

"I'm sorry. I've been spending a lot of time talking about me. You must think I'm a terrible person."

He shook his head. "I'm good. We never got to talk about it. There's been so much excitement. First, your friend, Yolanda, was trying to fix me up with someone that I already knew, then you had strangers lurking in your house and all that."

Denise seemed pensive for a minute. "What was she like?" Her lips curved upwards into a smile and the atmosphere in the car lightened.

"My wife? Oh, she was very nice. You might have even been friends," Trent said. "I met her right after we graduated, when I was still playing professional basketball."

"Oh?" Denise said. "Was she like a groupie or anything like that?" She laughed, and pushed Trent in the side of his arm with two fingers.

Trent looked at her, rubbing where she'd touched. "No, I wouldn't say she was a groupie. She used to work in the office and actually was the daughter of one of the coaches. We met and became friends and after that we became lovers. After a few years, we got married."

"Sounds very honorable."

"It was not very Basketball Wives at all," he said, referring to the scandal-riddled television franchise.

Denise looked at her friend, "Aww," she said. "That sounds really cute. It's almost like a fairytale, too. I'm glad you had that. Wasn't that a TV show or something where the girls in the front office of the NBA meet the basketball players and then married them?"

"No, it was nothing like that," Trent chuckled. "Different show. She was really smart and she got an MBA and came back to work at the franchise with her father. We met and connected on a level that I think many of the groupies, as you call them, wouldn't be able to do. She got me, know what I mean?" Trent's face turned dark then.

Denise looked out of the window for a minute, sad maybe, that she'd asked some of the questions that she did. "I could tell that you miss her."

"Yeah, I do." He cleared his throat. "But, that's behind me now."

"Sorry."

"No need to apologize. It was a really bad time for us and breast cancer took her away. She changed my life though and I will always cherish that." He cleared his throat. "But, that was before. There are new things to be done. I'm over it." He pursed his lips then chuckled. This conversation had gone places where he hadn't intended. It had become too much about him. He really was not into sharing this much detail about his life with anyone, especially when he was the one who was supposed to be finding out the details. What was it about Denise?

They were silent for a minute as the road rolled beneath the car.

"I don't know if you're ever over something like that. Would you say that she was the love of your life?"

"Huh," Trent rubbed his goatee. "I never thought about it like that. I don't know if she was the love of my life but I definitely loved her. But like I said, it's time to move on."

"Is it really time to move on? I don't believe people ever really can. Everyone you encounter, and especially someone you spend so much of your life with, changes you one way or the other. It's not possible to move on in the sense of forgetting them or the impact they had on your life."

"That was then. I didn't come here to talk about the past. I came here to talk about you."

"Oh, did you really? Did you think you could just take me to the airport and come back into my life?" She smiled. "Well, I think you should acknowledge the growth that everyone you meet affords you. That is how you move on."

Trent inhaled deeply, then smiled. "I like that. A lot. I think I will think about it that way from now on." His wife had certainly helped him grow. "You helped me grow, too." He was embarrassed as soon as the words left his lips.

Denise's lips parted slightly, and her caramel skin flushed.

"I'm sorry," Trent said. Had he gone too far? "I didn't mean to…"

She shook her head. "It's fine. No need to apologize. We helped each other." She reached over and put her hand on his, patting it. "And look at us, we get to cross paths again and maybe do some more changing. And this time, we are all grown up."

"Thank God for that."

Denise laughed. "I know, right. I'm just sorry things are so crazy right now." Her brow furrowed and she rubbed two fingers across the lines that formed on her forehead. She had a feeling that things were about to get much crazier.

10

Red Circles

Darren finally left the house to play golf, so he would be gone for a while. Yolanda lay in bed and listened to the garage door close, waiting before moving. She wanted to make sure that he was really gone, that he hadn't forgotten anything or had another reason to come back. The sound of her breath was loud inside her head.

Darren hated it when she went into his office, but wasn't his office inside their house? She had as much right to be in there as he did, didn't she? Besides, he clearly was not about to tell her any information so she was going to have to take matters into her own hands.

Even though the house was empty, she practically tiptoed to the back hallway where the office was. Yolanda paused outside the door, underneath Darren's stylized picture of Yoda. Even though it had been hanging there for years, Yolanda grimaced as she glanced at it. This was the only place she'd agreed to let him hang the thing, but Darren loved it.

She turned the doorknob, and the click it made echoed through the empty house. It wasn't until the door swung open that she realized she had actually been holding her breath. She exhaled. Darren would be angry if he knew what she was about to do, but Yolanda had had enough. He usually kept to himself when he was in the middle of a project, but in the last few weeks, something was different. He'd been even more withdrawn than normal and there were deep creases in his forehead that Yolanda didn't often see. Something was going on, for sure.

Yolanda crept into the room and lowered herself into the chair, scooting it closer to the desk. It tilted too far back, almost dumping her on the floor. She paused, stopping the chair by grabbing the sides of Darren's large old-fashioned, mahogany desk. Normally, it was not one of her favorite pieces in the room, really, in the house. Today, she was grateful for its heft.

Yolanda inhaled and sat back in the chair, imagining that she was inside Darren's head. She moved his mouse and the computer screen flickered to life, startling her. She peeked inside the filing drawer, feeling like an intruder in her own home. She rifled through the file folder, realizing that every minute of the last few years had been about her husband and what he was working on, what he wanted, how he was going to invent the next best thing. It didn't feel good.

The silence in the room and house was loud. Yolanda could hear her own breath in her ears, along with the artificial clicking sound that the digital clock across the room made. Why hadn't she thought about this before and why was it so easy to see these things in retrospect? Her phone chimed and Yolanda jumped. A text message from Denise. She could wait a few minutes.

Yolanda ran her fingers across the tips of the folders. Most of them were papers related to the house or bills. Nothing special. If Darren had anything to hide, she knew that he wouldn't do it the old-fashioned, analog way. Darren wasn't the type to leave a paper trail. He'd hide his secrets in the cloud.

She wiggled the mouse again as she contemplated her

next steps. It shouldn't be too hard to figure out her husband's passwords. She did know him better than anyone on earth, other than maybe his mother, after all.

The screensaver came up on the Mac computer and asked for a password. Normally, Yolanda knew that Darren's Apple Watch would unlock the screen, or his fingerprint would make the screen saver disappear. She had neither. She tapped a forefinger on the side of the keyboard while she contemplated, then typed in her husband's grandmother's first name. The curser shook back and forth but didn't unlock. No dice. Two points to Darren for creativity.

Yolanda inhaled, then licked her lips. *Come on, girl,* she thought. Like most men, Darren was not that complicated. He would never think to hide anything because he wouldn't think she'd be snooping. She typed in the first half of his email address.

It worked. *Take back those two points.* The relief she felt was only momentary as Yolanda realized that she had no idea what she was actually looking for. She paused again and moved the mouse to the left so that all of the open windows would be visible. Email. Messenger. Text Messages. A couple of random windows with technical stuff. He'd drawn a lot of circular doodles over and over, with what looked like formulas next to them.

Yolanda held her head in her hands. What had she actually been thinking? Her phone chimed again and she glanced at it. Denise would be calling soon and she'd forgotten that she was supposed to come over. Fate must be with her, because Denise had to suddenly go to Chicago.

One text caught her eye. *I'll pay you soon.* She didn't recognize the number. Her heart jumped. Who had he planned to pay "soon"? Her mind shifted, back to the conversation they'd just had about the credit card bill, but no sooner than she thought it did she realize that she was being ridiculous. No one texted a creditor to promise to pay, at least not anyone legit.

Who was it then? Yolanda wondered. She wiggled the mouse again, waiting for the screen to flicker to life. She put in what she thought her husband's password might be. No luck. She tried a few more times, but as she failed, she finally gave up and pulled out her phone.

She typed the number he'd texted into the search, then scrolled through the results. Nothing made any sense to her. The number was not from a robo call or from any business that came up in the Google search. Who had Darren owed money? And what was he texting about? Yolanda pondered this for a few minutes listening to the sounds in the house. The answer had to be in the computer.

Yolanda tried one more time to put in what she thought might be her husband's password. "I should know this," she mumbled. Her eyes darted around the room, looking for clues, finally settling on a picture of them together, on the beach, several years ago. It had been taken on their anniversary and was just the two of them, enjoying lunch in the sun.

"You dummy." She talked out loud to no one in particular. Why hadn't she started there? She put in both of their birthdates and their initials, the password that they seemed to share between them for everything under the sun. It wasn't the most secure thing in the world, but if anything happened to the other, the idea was they would always be able to get into the things they would need.

She held her breath hoping that Darren had stuck to

their old familiar pattern. The screen glitched and paused before finally springing to life. Her heart jumped. She was in. Thank goodness that Darren was a creature of habit. Relief passed over Yolanda's body and she sat back in the seat.

The Mac computer had several screens open. Darren never closed them. "Macs can handle it." She could hear his voice, clear as day, telling her why his Apple computer was superior to her Windows one. He was a die-hard loyalist.

Yolanda toggled through the windows looking for clues to see if anything would make sense to her. The Mac mirrored most of the windows that he would have been searching on his phone. Even his text messages were open. Most of the files made no sense to her. Numbers. Snippets of sentences. Ideas for future inventions. Darren had quite the mind. It was a wonder she understood anything he said, ever, but there were no surprises there.

A diagram caught her eye. Circles drawn on the page with numbers everywhere. Marks in red. This must be what Darren had been working on for so many months that kept him too busy to spend time with her or do anything else. This was why he looked so worried all the time now. But why?

She looked closer. The name "Charles" was there on the paper bright as day, also circled in red. Yolanda leaned in and started reading the names, squinting to decipher Darren's sprawling writing. Charles and Darren had been great friends for years, almost as long as they had been married. They always talked about the ideas they had, but it looked like they shared more than ideas.

As far as she knew, Charles ran his accounting firm out of Chicago, and she was sure he invested in things, but had he invested or worked with Darren? Did Denise know about this? Yolanda licked her lips. This seemed unlikely, because she and Denise would have talked about it at least once. What if they had both been in the dark? Maybe this was what the money request was about. She would make some time to ask Denise about it to see what she knew.

Her phone chimed again and she looked down. It was time to go. She would catch up with Denise later.

11
Martin's Look

The trip from the airport to the office took forever. The Chicago streets were choked with cars and it was slow going, all the way to midtown. Denise stared out the window and watched the car exhaust rise towards the sky as she rode. It was as if everyone and their mother had decided to drive somewhere and the longer Denise sat in traffic, the more her stress level rose.

By the time they made it to the high rise that housed the offices of Martin's Look, she was grinding her teeth with the memory of why she had run to Kiawah in the first place. Unlike her husband, she hated the grind. She could feel the pull of the island, even all these miles away.

The office was filled with people she didn't recognize, and at first, no one even looked up as she entered. Denise made it to the corner that housed her office without so much as a hello from anyone. The receptionist gasped. "Oh, Mrs. Martine. You're here. I'll tell Jamel."

She was surprised that Jamel, the office manager, hadn't met her at the door. His frantic call was what had gotten her on a plane in the first place. When Charles was alive, Jamel had been his right-hand man, and he'd pretty much been running the Chicago operation single-handedly since.

Denise opened her door and dropped her bag on her chair. She never used it or the office, anyway. She opened the blinds and noticed the thin layer of dust that had accumulated everywhere in the week since she'd last visited. The sunlight revealed finger marks on top of the file cabinets. Denise pulled out the top drawer, curious. The hanging files were no longer there. She frowned. What in the world had happened?

She strode towards the door. The receptionist's head was down.

"Excuse me. Can you tell me who's been in my files? Where are they?"

The receptionist looked dumbfounded, as if Denise spoke another language. "I'm not—"

"It was me." Jamel strode towards her, his Gucci loafers making a clicking sound on the wooden floors. "We've been trying to find records. I'm glad you're here. We have a problem." He walked past her, back into her office and Denise followed.

The receptionist glanced up as Jamel closed the door. "As soon as you left, things went crazy. People started asking all sorts of questions and the Feds asked for our records." The words spilled from Jamel's mouth.

"The Feds? Slow Down," Denise said, leaning back on her desk. Her heart raced. "Start from the beginning." Denise noticed that everything about Jamel was disheveled. His hair stood all over his head and his eyes were rimmed with red. "You look a mess. Have you been sleeping?"

He waved away Denise's comment, his words sounding as if he were out of breath. "We were supposed to be preparing for an audit of the books. I was working on that when we found this." Jamel crossed to the other side of Denise's desk and flopped into her chair. He wiggled the mouse and waited for the monitor to flicker to life.

Denise followed. "What could possibly be wrong? As far as I know, all of the books are in order, right?"

"I thought they were. But look at this." Jamel banged furiously at the keyboard, entering passwords. "We had how many employees last year? 43?"

"On average. Only one or two people left after Charles disappeared, and we didn't hire anyone new."

"So why is it that the retirement accounts have less than three thousand dollars in them?" Jamel pulled up a screen and then pointed to a number on it.

Denise leaned in. "That's impossible. There has to be more than that. Those accounts hold everyone's 401K." Charles hadn't been able to give a whole lot of benefits to his employees, like the bigger companies could, but he'd prided himself on being able to provide a reasonable retirement account and decent health insurance benefits for the people that worked for him.

"That's what I thought, too. But it looks like there was a large transfer out, three months after Charles disappeared."

"Let me see." Denise gently nudged Jamel to the side. "Three months? Transfer to where? Show me."

Denise's heart raced as Jamel explained his forensic accounting. "See, look. Things were fine here. And then, the next month, they were not. The only thing in here are the deposits that happened after that."

"Where'd the money go?" Denise clicked from screen to screen, attempting to make sense of things.

"Best I could tell, to this account." He pointed to a line of numbers.

"Who owns it? I made no transfers. I don't even think I could without the accountant. And why are we just finding this?"

"Well, that's the thing. The bookkeeper really doesn't pay much attention to these accounts. We have an outside administrator for them. I called the brokerage firm, and from what we can tell, the receiving accounts are untraceable Bitcoin accounts."

"Untraceable? Are you sure?"

"Yes. There's no way to tell who owns them. But someone who had intimate knowledge of these accounts imitated these transfers."

"Who could that be? Charles was long gone by the date these were done."

Jamel raised his eyebrows. "He was. I mean, at least he wasn't here. The only other person that knew anything about the accounts was Alma Receda."

At the mention of Alma's name, her heart sank. "Charles fired her." Yolanda remembered her husband talking about having to let Alma go. Denise hadn't seen the woman since, but remembered her well. She'd been striking in an odd kind of way. A pale-skinned black woman with freckles and a discomforting way of staring at everyone in her path with an unnerving look. Awkward, but very smart. Charles had said she was just the kind of person you wanted handling your books.

Jamel's eyebrows rose. "No, she didn't. Alma quit."

"Are you sure about that?"

"Positive. I was in the room when it happened."

Denise exhaled heavily. "When it rains, it pours. Related maybe?"

He shrugged. "You tell me."

Denise fell back onto her office chair, right on top of her bag, all the air sucked from her lungs, her mind racing. This was a lot. What next? "So how did the Feds get involved?"

"The brokerage firm called them. These are people's retirement monies. Now they want to look through everything with a fine-tooth comb. They are bound to find at least one nit. Everything is being audited. Apparently, one is long overdue."

"How does that even happen?" The Charles she remembered was so on top of things. She rubbed the spot between her eyes.

"I think all the accounts are going to be frozen. Even your personal ones." Jamel looked as distraught as she felt.

"Frozen? How am I supposed to live?" Denise's mind raced.

Jamel shrugged. "I hope you have some personal funds elsewhere. Belize? Mexico? We may be in for a long ride."

Suddenly hot, Denise fanned herself with both hands. "I need a minute."

Jamel nodded, gathering up the folders he'd been carrying when he came in. "I'll be in my office when you're ready to talk. An investigator will be here again in three hours. They insisted on interviewing you in person."

"You couldn't tell me that on the phone? I would have had more time to prepare myself."

"I was starting to feel as if this was some true crime scene or something. I had no idea who or what was listening," Jamel said.

He'd always had a flair for the dramatic. "Thanks Jamel. I doubt this is anything like that." Denise's head throbbed now. She rubbed it and sat back in her chair. Was it? She wasn't sure of anything anymore. Charles always told her to plan for a rainy day, but was this what he had in mind? And if there was any doubt before that he was mixed up in something he shouldn't have been, that was a now full-blown certainty in her mind, but what? He was a lot of things, but Charles was not a thief. Why would he empty the retirement accounts?

Denise's thoughts were interrupted by her phone's lights. It was on silent, but the vibrations made it dance across the desk. Denise picked it up and frowned. She didn't recognize the number that displayed on the screen. Normally, she'd let a number she didn't recognize go to voicemail, especially after the strange calls at the Kiawah house. So many calls lately were nothing but robocalls, promising vacations of debt relief or some other such scam. This time though, she took a chance and answered. She didn't have the mental capacity at the moment to think about it.

"Hello?" she held the phone to her ear.

A woman's voice answered. "Hi, um. I might have the wrong number."

Denise waited. "Okay?"

"No, sorry. I'm looking for Charles. Is he around?"

Denise exhaled. "Honey, I don't know who you are, but you're going to have to make one helluva long distance call if you're looking for him."

"Wait, what? Who is this?"

"This is his *wife*. Charles disappeared a year ago, and as far as we know, he's dead."

Silence.

"Can I help you?"

There was a pause. "I, I don't think so. I'm sorry for calling you." The line went dead.

Denise tossed her phone onto the desk. It hit with a thud, then slid a few inches. She leaned back in the chair and spun around, looking out over the city. She let out a deep, cleansing breath, trying to steady her thoughts. Had she suddenly been thrust into the Twilight Zone? Denise breathed in. First, her husband disappears, then months of silence. Just as she'd decided it was time to move on, there were mysterious phone calls, imagined burglars and missing money. She exhaled slowly, letting the breath take some of the stress with it. A television writer couldn't write a better mystery. What next?

The meeting with the investigator lasted about an hour, but by the end, Denise was more confused than ever and convinced she had been of no help. She walked the man to the elevator, feeling confident that, unlike in the movies, she was not being considered a suspect for anything.

"If you remember anything new, please contact me." Agent Jones handed her his card and pressed the elevator button.

"I assure you, I told you everything I know during the investigation about where he went. I'm just as surprised as anyone. And like I told you, I don't know anything about Bitcoin or anything like that." She paused, shaking her head. Denise wished she'd paid more attention to what her husband had been doing, but she'd let herself slide into the trap of letting him handle all of the finances for everything. "I don't know what to do. I have to figure out what I'm going to tell everyone." She took breaths as she digested all of the information.

"I suggest telling them the truth. If you know nothing, say so. The investigation will be going on for a while. If the money is traceable, we'll find it."

"I hope so," Denise said. She accepted the hand that Agent Jones extended and shook it.

"And I'm sorry about this. I'm sure your insurance payments will be held up for some time now. I imagine it's been long enough where you're starting to feel things in the pockets." The look on his face was glum, matching how she felt inside.

"Wait, what? I thought with his remains he would finally be declared dead." Denise's stress level rose again. She'd done okay since Charles had disappeared, but for the most part, she'd barely made it through. Good thing she had always been a saver and had sold a few paintings, but she'd had to live on far less than what she'd been used to. She'd been relieved that the insurance payment was finally going to come through. They'd held it until her husband was officially declared dead, but now here was this stranger telling her otherwise, never mind that it felt as if he was prying into her finances further than he needed to.

"He has. But someone made that transfer from South Carolina—"

"South Carolina? I thought you couldn't tell anything?"

He nodded. "Yeah, it looks like they can triangulate the IP address that initiated the transfer to the coast of South Carolina, but that's all the details we have."

Denise dropped her head. "We have a house there."

The agent's face softened. "We know. And until recently, a boat." He cleared his throat. "And the most likely candidate to have done that was your husband. That will move the official date of his disappearance."

"I'll be okay." Tears flooded Denise's eyes. She dabbed at her face. "I'm sorry." She didn't think she had any tears left. "I mean, how do we know it was him? He worked with a lot of people."

Shrugging, the inspector handed her a tissue. She waited at the elevator bank until the doors slid shut, then went back to her office to grab her things just as Jamel reached her office door.

"So? Did you tell him anything?" Jamel looked as annoyed as Denise felt.

"Anything like what? I'm just as clueless as you are. I learned more today about business retirement accounts than I would have ever thought I'd need to know."

Jamel looked over his glasses at Denise. "Well, good for you, then. There has to be a bright spot in all of this. Tell me this though, what's going to happen with my money? My life savings were in that account."

"Everyone's was." Denise's face felt hot. She didn't want to talk about money with Jamel or anyone else, not like this, not when she had absolutely nothing to offer. They were now all looking to her for answers, as if she and Charles were one and the same. They had to know that she was as much a victim as they were.

Her phone buzzed and she glanced at the screen, exhaling a bit. "They'll let us know as soon as they have a lead." Distractions were good.

"Any idea when that will be? I feel as if we all have been held hostage by Charles's disappearance for months now," Jamel huffed.

Denise shook her head. "None."

"I'm tired of being helpless." Jamel ran his hand across his forehead. "I know this will all work out, but hell, I gotta feed my family."

Jamel's words struck Denise like a pilot light. She was absolutely tired of waiting and being helpless, too. She felt a little ashamed; she'd only been thinking of herself being in limbo, but everyone associated with the company was in the same boat. Yes, she was not sad and angry at her husband for leaving and for the debris he'd left behind, whether he was dead or not, but she wanted some control back in her life, too. She owed it to the people that had been loyal to them through all of this.

"What do we know about all this, really?" Her eyes narrowed as she muttered the words.

"I thought we just said we knew nothing? Are you even listening?"

"I'm sorry. I was thinking out loud." She thought about her conversation with the investigator. The money was transferred to untraceable Bitcoin accounts, weeks after Charles disappeared. That was true. They can't tell who made the transfers, and they can't tell where they went. The only information was that they were made from a computer in South Carolina.

"I've got to go back to Kiawah."

"What?" Jamel said. "We really don't need you to be on vacation right now. Even if you know nothing, it makes everyone feel better if you're here and not running off burying your head in the sand. They need to know that you are in this with them."

Denise sat down at her computer, waking it. "Oh, I'm in it, but I'm tired of waiting for things to magically sort themselves out. Aren't you?" Her typing made loud thuds on her keyboard.

"What are you doing? Beating your keyboard to death isn't going to make things <u>sort</u>." He made quotes in the air with his fingers.

She ignored his sarcasm. "I'm booking a ticket back to Kiawah. The transfer was made from there. I know Charles visited without me, but it seems there was a lot more happening there than I was aware of." She paused as she mulled things over in her head. "I need to go figure out what's at the root of this and something tells me that's where the answer is. I'm tired of being helpless."

"Are you sure you don't want to leave this to the

professionals? What if it gets dangerous?"

"No, I'm not sure. But no one is going to be more than an expert on Charles than I am."

Jamel shrugged. "I don't know…"

"I do. It's time for me to help myself."

Jamel looked at Denise with a new admiration. "Help all of us, will you?"

12
Slide to the Left

All night long, Yolanda had tossed and turned, imagining the worst about Darren. If she'd had any doubt something was going on before, after snooping around his office, she was sure of it. Her imagination took her on a ride that got even wilder when Darren slept in his office after returning far too late last night. How had she missed the signs that something was wrong? He'd always buried himself in his inventions, sure, but this felt bigger than that.

She tried, but couldn't remember the last time they'd actually done anything together, including have sex. Was she that unattractive? Yolanda sighed. She tried to keep herself together, but Darren didn't seem to notice anything she did. And now he was neglecting the bills, too. That was hard for her. She hadn't actually worked as an accountant in a while, but old habits die hard. He'd blown her off, but Yolanda knew a bill collector call when she heard one.

By morning, she'd developed a new resolve. The only way to figure out what was going on was to put herself right in the middle things, and that was exactly what she planned to do. Darren would be playing golf first thing, so he could get it in before it got too hot. The only question was which one of the seven golf courses on the island he would be teeing off on.

It was easy to get out of bed since she was already awake.

Yolanda had lain there listening to the sounds of the house. Her breathing had grown quiet with every creak, her ears straining to hear the footsteps that never came. By morning, Darren had not come to bed, but Yolanda had heard when he'd started moving around, so she at least had known he was in the house. The pump that moved the water to the house hummed loud and clear when Darren had turned on the water, presumably to shower. Yolanda listened as the house alarm announced when he'd finally opened the door that led to the garage.

The sun was just starting to peek over the alligator lake behind their house and Yolanda was already in her clothes and dressed for golf. Darren had gone into the garage twenty minutes before. He was not one to be late for tee time. He'd get there early to warm up. When they were on the island, he would spend time on one of the golf courses in the vicinity several times per week.

Yolanda opened the family calendar on her phone to see if she could tell which of the courses Darren was headed for. She knew that he would normally enter the tee time on the calendar. There it was plain as day. 6:40 AM. She opened the calendar entry and scrolled down, but the notes were blank. There was no details and this time, he hadn't entered which course he'd be playing on. She smiled, as the wife of a man that invented things and was probably the king of the techies in Low Country, Yolanda had a few tricks up her sleeve.

She paused, feeling just a twinge of guilt. Tracking her husband was not the nicest thing to do, but it certainly wasn't hard. Yolanda's hesitation didn't last long. Darren was driving her car, so she opened the Tesla app on her phone and scrolled down to the location section.

He was headed to the Ocean Course, located at the far end of the island. Yolanda shook her head. Of course it made sense to him to pay almost four hundred dollars in green fees for a round of golf, yet he couldn't remember to pay their credit card bills. They'd come from modest beginnings but had somehow ascended into madness.

Yolanda grabbed her keys and headed for the garage. She wasn't really sure what her plan was past getting her hands on her golf clubs and showing up to play with her husband. She used to do that all the time, but hadn't recently. He'd be surprised. Yolanda knew the old adage that said that much business was conducted on the golf course still rang true. Darren might not be doing big deals out on the links, but if anything was going on, she'd probably overhear it out there or at least catch a glimpse of it.

The garage was still warm from where her car used to be. Yolanda glanced around the managed clutter of the space, noting that things were just as she'd imagined they should be. Her car and his golf clubs were gone. Her clubs normally sat right next to his. She picked up her bag and slung it over her shoulder, almost stumbling backwards. She was out of practice and the bag felt much heavier than she remembered.

She missed golf. She'd been so caught up in planning the upcoming party, she hadn't had much time for it like she used to. A lifetime ago, she'd been an avid golf player and she and Darren had played together all the time. Yolanda smiled. In fact, she'd been a damn good golf player, better than most of the men that Darren played with on a regular basis. There were few of the men that he played with that could even hold a candle to Yolanda on the golf course. Playing golf next to Darren used to feel amazing to her. Why didn't she make it a priority anymore? What happened?

It was only a fifteen-minute drive for Yolanda to make it to the Ocean Course. As she drove, the trees filtered the early morning light, creating shadows inside the car. Yolanda put on her sunglasses and let her car windows down. The salty ocean smells hung in the air and the breeze still felt cool, at least for the minute. She turned a corner and large sand dunes came into view, eclipsing the light of the orange-hued sunrise. Yolanda shielded her eyes and pulled into the parking lot where all of the other golfers were parked.

No matter how many times Yolanda came to the course, the view always took her breath away. She paused for a minute to take it all in. The course itself was huge, but the view from where she sat at that moment was a microcosm of the beauty of the place. Ocean, sand and greens met just outside the clubhouse. The contrast of colors was startling but somehow felt right all the way to her core.

Darren would be surprised to see her, but she wasn't sure if he would be thrilled that she was adding herself to their foursome. Yolanda had a lot of skills but top among them were her golf, and she just didn't know how Darren would feel about that today, not with the way he'd been acting. He barely seemed to want her around. How might he feel when she bested him in the game he imagined himself to be good at?

Her arms were normally sun kissed from being on the golf course or tennis court so much, but today, they seemed pale. A feeling of familiarity swept over her as she retrieved her golf clubs from her trunk. She'd missed it. Too bad that this time she was actually playing a game of revenge golf or maybe it was golf to put her back in the mix of things. Most people had babies to bring spice back in their marriages. She would use her golf game to try and fix hers.

A caddy ran over to her, and greeted her by name. "Hello Mrs. McAlister," he said. "I'm glad you're joining us today. My apologies. I didn't realize you were coming in. When's your tee time?"

This caddy had helped her with her game many times before. A good one was indispensable to your golf game. "Hi, Reed. It's good to see you," she said. "I actually don't have one. I'm just gonna join my husband's foursome."

Michael smiled. "Well, you're in luck then because he just checked in and I believe he only has two people in his group."

"That's great, then," Yolanda said, trying her best to look relieved. She'd done her homework. She already knew who Darren had been playing with lately, and at least one was off island this week, so she'd been reasonably sure there would be a space for her. "I'll meet you inside."

Reed nodded and took her clubs. "I'll take care of these."

Yolanda slipped the young man a tip and strolled away from her car and into the building that made up the small clubhouse. She weaved her way through the front of it. They forced you to walk through the retail space like it was an Ikea rather than the one thousand square foot building it was. The racks she passed held many variations of the men's golf shirts and golf pants that barely registered for Yolanda.

She'd come prepared. She was smartly attired and was ready for anything the course had to offer today. Yolanda had learned a long time ago that being appropriately dressed was part of the game. It made her feel great, and it showed in her strut.

Yolanda barely looked to the side as she strode through the pro shop to the small check-in desk at the back. "McAllister," Yolanda said.

The clerk smiled at her and murmured a greeting, checked her in without questioning her, then handed her a slip to sign. Yolanda returned the woman's smile and checked the bottom for the exact tee time. 6:42. She had twenty minutes to catch up with Darren.

There was a small café just on the other side of the pro shop. Many golfers stopped there to have a cup of coffee or pick up a snack for later when they would be midway through their golf game, invariably waiting for the young woman that would drive the snack truck across the greens. She never came when you wanted her to, and any golfer worth their salt knew they had to be prepared. There was no rushing through eighteen holes of golf and it took sustenance to last for the entire four hours it could take, depending on the skill of the people you played with.

Yolanda strolled in and looked around. Not bothering to sit, she ordered her coffee at the counter, added her two Splenda and some almond milk to it until it was the color of her light cocoa skin. She smiled and then dropped her normal pack of butter into the coffee.

The clerk was stunned. "I have never seen anyone do that," he said.

"Hmm. Well, you learn something new every day. It's bulletproof. Makes me strong."

The clerk raised his eyebrow and smiled, raking his eyes up and down her five-foot-two frame. "Well it's obviously doing something because you look quite strong to me." He did not hide his admiration of her arms, fixating on her strong shoulders and biceps. "You have Michelle Obama arms."

Yolanda laughed, "No, Michelle had Yolanda McAllister arms."

They laughed together for a minute and Yolanda turned to exit the building. The caddy would already be waiting with her bag outside the door, no doubt removing the dust from her clubs so expertly it would be as if they'd been licked clean. They could certainly use it. Yolanda couldn't remember the last time she'd given them any attention.

Just as she got to the door, she glanced to the right and spied a familiar silhouette she knew well. She took a few steps to the side to make sure the light wasn't playing tricks on her. Yolanda was paralyzed by what she saw. Darren was sitting in the corner. His back was to the door and he was not alone.

Yolanda inhaled deeply. That was certainly unusual for Darren. Whenever they were together, Darren would refuse to sit where he couldn't see the door. He claimed that he always needed to see what was going on and who was coming into a place, and you couldn't do that with your back to the door. Wasn't that some gangster knowledge or something?

She kissed her teeth, guessing that argument went out the window when he was hiding. She couldn't tell for sure, but that was certainly what it felt like now. He was sitting in a corner that most people would miss if they didn't look twice, and he was there with a woman.

Yolanda squinted and paused for a minute. Should she go over and say something? Or should she act like she hadn't seen him and meet him outside at the first tee as she'd planned? She wasn't sure. Frustration rose inside her. At times like this, Yolanda was more aware than ever that marriage had no playbook. There was no manual that had rules on how to proceed or that laid out the right thing to do at times like these.

The woman Darren was with threw her head back in a throaty laugh and Yolanda cringed. They seemed to be in deep conversation. Where were his buddies? The people that Yolanda had expected to find her husband with? She glanced around the room looking for Darren's other friends, but they were nowhere to be found. The roller coaster of emotions inside her made her feel weak; her heart raced and then dropped to the pit of her stomach. What in the world was going on?

Yolanda tried to get everything back under control. Where was the steely resolve that had her taking charge of things just a few short hours ago? She put her sunglasses on and then glanced in Darren's direction again. Neither he nor his companion looked up and it appeared that whatever they were discussing was important. They both leaned towards the other, maybe coming close so no one else could hear them. Yolanda wanted to believe this was a business meeting, but the time of day made that unlikely.

She watched a few more seconds. Her brain didn't want to believe what she was seeing, but it felt like she was witnessing some canoodling rather than any kind of business transaction. She opened and closed her fists as a few beads of sweat popped onto her forehead. Yolanda started in their direction but thought better of it, instead going out the back door as she had originally intended. The caddy was waiting with her bag and newly shined shoes, just as she knew he would be. She swallowed hard, forcing a smile. At least she could count on one thing to be a constant. She struggled to maintain her composure and took a towel from the young man, wiping her forehead with it, then gulped from her coffee cup.

"Hello Mrs. McAllister. Good to see you. I'm glad you finally made it out. I cleaned all your clubs and you're ready to go. Will you be walking or riding this time?"

"I think I'm riding. I think I'm riding," she repeated herself, too flustered to concentrate on anything. The picture of Darren in the café glared in her head. Here she was thinking that her husband was playing golf with his friends and he was with a woman who was not dressed for golf at all. She ran through what she had seen in her head, over and over again.

It was just past dawn. Strange woman with long brown hair that was a stark contrast to Yolanda's short natural. Slim thick, from what Yolanda could tell. Even across the room Yolanda could tell she had been fully made up with red lips, long legs that had stuck out from under the table and heels that were not unlike what you would see on the stripper pole on any given day. It would all be forever etched in her memory. Darren had some explaining to do.

Yolanda hit the driving range while she waited, just a few steps from the staging area for the first hole. She hit several balls in a row, the thwack sound of the club contacting the ball comforted her.

It took an eternity for Darren to finally come out of the café. Yolanda had gone through a whole bucket of practice balls. He paused as he spotted her, a smile frozen on his face.

"Hey, Babe. You should have told me you were playing today."

Yolanda looked around Darren for his lady friend, her eyes sweeping the landscape. "How could I have done that when I haven't laid eyes on you since yesterday?" Her eyes bored holes through him.

The smile left Darren's face. He didn't have a chance to speak.

"Hey, good people!" Two of Darren's friends, the two Yolanda had thought he'd be playing golf with, strode across the field towards them.

Darren greeted them, the smile returning to his face, as he keep glancing at Yolanda.

She noticed that the corners of his mouth twitched and that his voice was just a little higher than it had been a few minutes before. She would let him slide, for now.

13

Swimming Upstream

Yolanda boiled with anger. It was going to take everything she had not to ask Darren about his golf game. By the time he'd come out of the café, the woman was gone. As far as Yolanda could tell, she must have gone back out the front, to the parking lot. He'd never mentioned the woman and she was nowhere in sight for the rest of the morning.

After they played, she'd excused herself, leaving Darren to have lunch with his friends. Now, she paced her kitchen thinking about what she would do next. Part of her wanted to let Darren walk through the door and then start throwing different things at his head. She poured herself a drink from an open bottle of wine in her refrigerator, then leaned on the counter as she tried to calm herself down.

If she resorted to the violence her emotions were telling her was necessary, it wouldn't be good. She would certainly get nothing from Darren that way. He'd claim she was crazy and then would clam up and storm away. She'd seen that scenario many times over the past few years. Her feelings would be dismissed and chalked up to histrionics. It had become an unspoken thing in their relationship that she not question him about things, and that included his inventions or what he did when he was away from her. She'd gotten used to not asking about his work, and had no reason, at least not before this past week, to think that any of his actions while they were apart needed examination. Until now. When and how had they gotten to a place where she didn't care and didn't ask questions? It felt like a lonely place Yolanda didn't care to be.

The rumble of the garage door as it opened shook the house and she wiped her eyes. She had been fuming so hard that she'd been crying, and there was certainly no way in hell she would let Darren see her like that. Yolanda wiped her hands on a napkin and then proceeded to remove things from the refrigerator as if she were going to make herself lunch, even though she didn't have much of an appetite.

Darren came in and grunted his hello from the mudroom. She heard the water turn on. He'd be using the bathroom, then washing his hands and face. He'd stop in the hallway and run his hands down his face. She knew his routine like it was her own. Right on time, he joined her in the great room.

"Oh, hey!" He picked up the tablet that he used to read the newspaper. "I was surprised to see you at the golf course today, honey. You should come more."

"Should I?" She held back the urge to blurt out what she had seen and ask him what she really wanted to know. She'd known Darren long enough to learn that patience would serve her much better. "I would have gone with you but you left kind of early for your tee time. Was there something going on?"

Yolanda hoped that her husband would take the bait.

"No," he said. "I just needed to get there early to practice my shot and I wanted to get some coffee. You know I like how they make that fresh brewed coffee at the café."

"Umm huh." It was just too easy for him to come clean. "Oh yeah. I know. It is kind of good."

Her heart sank to the floor. She was highly disappointed in Darren. She was also highly disappointed in herself for letting him become so distant. And really disappointed in his friends because they didn't raise an eyebrow that she had joined their foursome and she knew that they must have seen that woman, too. She deserved an explanation. And there was no doubt in her mind that he was definitely hiding something or he would have told her about the meeting. If nothing else, Darren liked to talk about himself. She'd give him a few hours to come clean and maybe it would come out in regular conversation.

"Do you want something to drink, honey?" Yolanda asked. In the movie in her mind she poisoned him as she poured him a beverage. Instead, she just opened a can of Diet Coke before he asked.

"A diet." She poured it into a glass and brought it to him in the living room, like normal, then sat on the chair opposite him. Her mind raced. Was her husband cheating on her? She imagined the worst. Who was the woman? Was this why he hadn't paid the bills? Because he'd spent it on some random woman she didn't know? Yolanda clenched her fist, then opened it.

She made it her business to know everyone on the island and she'd never seen this woman at all. And she'd been really overdressed for a morning meeting. Overdressed for Kiawah at all, really, obviously an outsider. So, what gives? Was she the reason Darren had been acting so strangely lately?

Yolanda stared into her husband's eyes and her internal dialogue raced ahead of her. She imagined Darren leaving her for someone else, someone younger, someone who looked like that woman.

"It was a beautiful day for golf," he said. "It didn't get hot until we were almost at the end of the eighteenth hole."

"Umm huh. It wasn't hot at all." Although she said it wasn't hot, she was steaming inside. In fact, her internal fire was burning so hot, the air-conditioning had little effect. Yolanda was burning up from not knowing what was going on.

She watched Darren reach for the remote and begin flipping through the channels. Why did he do that anyway? For some reason, his incessant channel surfing annoyed Yolanda more than usual. Her fingers dug into the armrests. Finally, she couldn't take it anymore. "So, you're just not going to say anything?"

Darren barely looked up. "About what?"

"Darren!" Yolanda shouted. "Look at me, please."

"Huh?"

"Look at me." Yolanda's voice was lower and uncharacteristically calm.

Darren's eyes shot up. "What is it? Why are you acting like this?" He stood up. "All cryptic and strange? If you have something to say or ask, spit it out."

Yolanda recoiled, unprepared for the shortness in his voice. All the anger she was feeling drained from her body. She blinked back tears. Why did it feel like she was the one who had done something wrong? "I'm sorry. It's nothing." Her lip quivered.

Darren softened. "I'm sorry. I didn't mean to upset you." He paced the living room, stopping again in front of his wife. "I've just been so stressed out lately, and I know it's been hard on us." He pulled her close.

She sniffled, unable to speak. Feelings rushed at her like she was swimming upstream.

"I'm sorry, baby." Darren wrapped his arms around Yolanda. "Do you forgive me?"

Yolanda wanted to forgive Darren, to believe every lie he hadn't told her yet. She let her body melt into his, then nodded. Maybe she'd been wrong about things. She missed him and this felt a little like he might be coming back to being the Darren she loved.

14
The Life Changing Power of Produce

From the time he'd watched her walk through the doors at
Charleston's airport, Trent couldn't stop thinking about Denise.
In college, he'd been as in love with her as he had been capable
of at the time, which wasn't saying much, really. At that age, who
knew anything about love? He tapped his fingers on the table as
he thought about Young Trent and how he'd left things. He'd
been too busy basking in the glow of being an athlete and taking
advantage of all the perks that went with that to really care about
anyone besides himself. This was certainly one of those times
that he'd wished he hadn't burned bridges.

Most of the details had faded. They'd both matured, and now
it was clear that Denise was an amazing person that had been
dealt a bad hand. Their history was ancient now, and he wanted
Denise to feel as he did. College and his immaturity just didn't
matter anymore, or at least he hoped it didn't.

Trent hadn't imagined how he'd react seeing Denise
again. He sighed as he thought about it and began to feel just a
little badly about deceiving her. Yes, it was his job, and yes, he
had agreed to follow up on the leads he had on the island, but it
still felt as if they were starting things off on the wrong foot
again, even if he hadn't directly deceived her. Trent held his
fingers to the bridge of his nose, as if steadying his head would

somehow steady the turmoil he felt inside.

        Now he could see that once he'd realized they knew each other, he should have walked away. Then he should have walked away again when Yolanda re-introduced him. None of that had actually been planned. He'd come to the island, went into Fresh Fields to pick up a few groceries and next thing he knew, he'd been practically stalked by Yolanda in the produce aisle.

The more he thought about how it went down, the more he realized that Denise probably wouldn't believe that he hadn't engineered the situation once she'd found out the truth. Hell, he would have a hard time believing it himself.

It had all been because of the spinach. He'd picked up a bag of pre-washed spinach and then paused when he felt a presence behind him, and then heard Yolanda's voice. "You're new."

He'd looked over his shoulder. "Excuse me?" She'd been standing so close he could practically taste her perfume. He couldn't have gotten around her if he tried.

"You're new," she said again. "Are you renting? I know because I know all of the brothers on the island and I have never seen you before."

He'd hesitated, but he hadn't been surprised. She'd been quite forward but this type of encounter was all too common. Black person, white space, and you learn to greet each other whenever the opportunity presented itself. Usually, it was just a nod, though. "That can't be true. I'm on the island and you don't know me." He'd smiled. He should have just said yes, he was and then walked away. "I'm Trent." He'd offered his hand. "Visiting, yes."

Yolanda had grabbed just his fingertip and barely shook it. She'd been smiling ear to ear. A blue skinny scarf hung around her slender neck and he remembered that it had reminded him of Goofy's ears. "Are you renting? Buying?"

"I feel like I'm on trial." He dropped his spinach into his small, red basket, then looked up. "Am I?"

She'd paused then and her face had flushed. "I'm sorry. I'm just so excited to see people of color when they're here. We have a small, tight knit community." She'd paused. "I bet we know someone in common. Most people don't just *come* to Kiawah, you know? The masses prefer Hilton Head or places like that." The words tumbled from her mouth, and she seemed oblivious that she'd actually just referred to people as "the masses."

"No self-respecting South Carolinian goes to Hilton Head. That's for amateurs." He'd chuckled, remembering all the times his wife had said those words.

She'd seemed surprised at his comment. It probably had sounded as ludicrous and condescending to her as her comment about the masses had to him.

"Are you from the Carolinas then? Where?" Intrigue had flashed in her eyes.

"Still an inquisition." He'd raised his eyebrows but had a hard time keeping his smirk at bay. "My wife was."

"Was?" Her eyebrows reached towards the ceiling. Trent could tell he'd put his foot in his mouth when he'd said that. Just as he was used to being greeted by other Black people in public spaces, Trent had become accustomed to the ladies swarming around as soon as they'd found out that yes, he was single, and yes, he had ten fingers and ten toes and both eyes still worked.

There was no way out, so he might as well go down the path he'd started on. "Yes, she's gone now."

Yolanda crossed her arms across her body. One hand held

onto her sunglasses and for a moment, he'd thought she'd chew on the end. "Divorced?"

"No, she died." Trent sighed, prepared for what was next.

That only slowed Yolanda down for a minute. "I'm so sorry."

He shook his head, wanting to let her off the hook. "It's been a long time. It's fine."

"Are you here visiting friends, then?"

"You don't get side-tracked, do you?" Trent remembered feeling interrogated. "Well, actually, I'm staying on my boat. Over at the marina. Just thought I'd explore."

"*Well,*" she'd drawn out the word in a sing-songy way that made it into a multisyllabic word. "Nice to meet you. I'm Yolanda. I don't know how long you're staying, but maybe you can join us for lunch tomorrow. How long <u>are</u> you staying?"

"That's nice, but I wouldn't want to intrude."

Yolanda had been almost grinning at this point. "No intrusion, I promise." She reached into her bag and scribbled information on a piece of paper she found there. "I have some people you absolutely must meet." She handed it to him. "Maybe you'll consider making this more than a visit then. Mm'kay, cher?"

Trent had known that he wasn't supposed to answer her question and it probably didn't matter if he resisted her invitation. He'd met Yolanda's kind. She'd persist and insist. Yolanda was the type with an agenda, but he appreciated her retreat into the colloquialisms of the Low Country. It actually reminded him of better times. He'd taken the paper she offered, holding it with both hands as carefully as he could muster.

"Well?" Yolanda put her shades back on.

Trent sighed, then smiled, pulling out some colloquialisms of his own. "If I'ma be there, I'ma be there. If I'm not gon' be there, I'm not gon' be there."

Yolanda had grinned, tapping him on the side of his shoulder with her left hand. "Alright now!" she'd said.

"Ow. I think I'll have a bruise. You need to watch it with that thing." The rock that lived on her hand was hard to miss.

Yolanda had laughed. "I think I like you. You take care."

And just like that, she'd swept away into the supermarket.

He'd had no idea that the encounter, which had been amusing at the time, would lead him to where he sat today, literally and figuratively; outside an airport, waiting for a woman he used to date, full of feelings like a pimply-faced teen.

Even as he thought of it now, a small inner conflict continued. It was too late now. He was all in. He'd come to do a job; find out about Denise's husband by following the paper trail. When this all started, he hadn't even known that the man they were looking for was married to Denise. The only problem was he didn't want to investigate her. He wanted to date her.

He'd surprised himself when he realized that he was actually happy to have heard from her. "Sure," he said. "No problem." Trent hung up his phone, making a note of her flight information. He'd gladly pick her up from the airport. In fact, he couldn't wait.

Trent was waiting, air conditioner at full-blast and thankful or small favors, when Denise came to the curb. Charleston's airport was an old military airfield wrapped in a shiny commercial wrapper, so it took no time at all for her to get from the plane to the small curbside pickup area. When she came through the automatic doors Trent was by the side of the car, standing with the trunk open to receive her rolling bag.

As soon as she left the climate-controlled comfort of the terminal, Trent could see that she was hit with an impenetrable wall of air, thick with summer heat. Denise wiped at the sweat that had popped onto her forehead in the few steps she'd taken.

"Damn. How could I forget?"

"Chicago in the summer is hot, isn't is?"

"Yeah, but South Carolina heat? This mess is a whole 'nother level. And it only gets worse when you go further inland."

Trent smiled. "I guess it's a good thing we are going the other way, then. The car is nice and cool. The heat is a beast." He held the door open for her and waited for Denise to slid inside the truck.

"It's hot, but I like it." His stomach lurched as soon as the words were out of his mouth. He did like it, but the weather had nothing to do with it. "Good flight?" He was almost at a loss for words.

"As good as can be. Thanks for this." Denise barely looked up. "I could have taken a car."

"My pleasure, M'lady." He closed the door with a flourish and walked around the vehicle to join her inside. "You shouldn't have to, though. And it's not like I had a ton to do."

"Wow, that feels special." No one had held a door for her in quite some time. Denise tried to hide her surprise, a small smile playing at the corner of her mouth, despite how she felt inside. She'd been deep in thought for the entire flight.

"Is there any doubt that you're special?" The words slipped through Trent's lips before he could stop them. He cringed. Thankfully, Denise either ignored him, or was just very eager to escape the heat. "Where to?"

"Just home. I don't want to interrupt your vacation any more than I have."

Trent licked his lips as a small pang of guilt hit him. "It's fine. I'm not too good at doing nothing. And this little drive to get you was very relaxing. It fits in with the reason I came." He waited for her to put on her seatbelt and pulled away from the curb.

"The reason you came? I thought you were just hanging out on your boat?"

Things slowed down. His brain was clicking. A more perfect time to come clean could not present itself. His eyes narrowed as Trent contemplated his options. He could throw caution to the wind and tell Denise everything, including how he was feeling. Or not. He could put it all out there and hope for the best, or he could keep lying to her. One choice surely left him jobless. The other might leave him with Denise never talking to him again.

"Trent." Denise called him back to the present. "Are you okay?" she asked.

He cleared his throat. "Yeah, I'm fine." His heart raced. Which was it going to be?

"Did you hear what I said? It feels like you went somewhere."

'I'm sorry, I'm just a little preoccupied."

"I can relate. There are so many things going on in my life. You wouldn't believe it. So many things to think about."

"Yeah, I can only imagine." Trent bit his lip. He could imagine, but he didn't have to since he was sure that he knew most of the details.

"I found out today that the company 401K money is missing."

Trent looked over at Denise. "Like all of it?"

"Might as well be. I need to find out what happened. Everything is being investigated. All of those people. What am I going to do?" She dropped her head back onto the headrest.

Guilt hit Trent like a ton of bricks. How could he not tell her? "Denise—"

She held up her hand, cutting him off. "Don't, Trent. You can't fix this, even if you tried. I have to be the one to do this."

"You don't understand." He did want to fix things, just not what she thought. He already hated seeing her so conflicted. She might be involved or somehow responsible, but he doubted it. In his gut, he knew she was unaware of what her husband had been up to. In fact, he was confident that she knew less than he did.

"I know I don't understand any of this. I don't understand how money is missing. I don't understand all the people snooping around in my husband, I mean, Charles's business. He's gone. I just want to confirm that he's dead or he left me or something, anything that would make more sense than having absolutely no information and a person missing with no trace whatsoever."

Trent pulled the car over to the side of the highway.

"What are you doing?" she asked.

"Listen to me." He paused. "I have something to tell you and I just hope you won't hate me when I'm done." Trent took a deep breath, closed his eyes for a minute to clear his thoughts, and began.

15
The Tea

Denise had Trent drop her at Yolanda's house instead of
at home. She just wanted to be out of the car and away from
him. After his confession, their ride had been virtually silent,
with Denise looking at her phone and Trent staring at the road,
mesmerized. He slowed in front of the house. He'd barely
stopped and she'd hopped out, slamming the door too hard
behind her.

He leaned over and opened the window, "Wait, your
bags."

Denise barely looked back. "Just bring them by later. I
can't deal with that right now." She stormed away and walked
into Yolanda's house without so much as a knock on the door.
Denise was still fuming. Was no one who they said they were?
She was angry at herself more than anything. She'd misread
Trent, and fell into him feeling familiar too quickly. Everyone
had an agenda. She should have gone with her first instinct, and
that had been to stay as far away from Trent as possible. Her life
was still splayed wide open like chicken legs separated from the
carcass. Her heart didn't need to be that way, too.

"Well, hello," Yolanda said. "Nice to see you. I didn't

think you'd be back so quickly."

"Me either but, I had to get back. There are some things here that I had to take care of and besides I didn't want to leave Rascal on your hands too long. Where is he?" She made kissing sounds with her mouth and the dog bounded to her and jumped into her arms. She put her nose in his fur.

"You've only been gone twenty-four hours," Yolanda said. "It's not like you haven't seen him in weeks."

Something about holding him in her arms gave Denise comfort. "Uhm. I think we need to talk," Denise said.

Yolanda looked concerned. "Is everything okay?"

Denise paced the room. "So, is there anything you need to tell me about Trent?"

"What are you talking about? I know he's a hottie. He seems to have a thing for you." She grinned.

"Well, you didn't know that we knew each other before?"

"Actually," Yolanda said, "No, I didn't. I told you I was surprised to hear that."

"And how did you meet him?"

"I told you, in the supermarket. Why do I feel like I'm being grilled? Can I expect to be waterboarded next?"

Denise ignored her quip. "And you didn't know that he was actually here to investigate where Charles was for the insurance company?"

"What are you talking about? He was shopping. That's how we met. Thumping melons."

"Melons, huh? I'm not sure I buy all that yet. And I want to trust him, but I don't think I can afford to. It's a weird coincidence that Trent, my ex-boyfriend from college is hired by an insurance company to investigate the disappearance of my ex-husband and runs into you, my best friend, in the supermarket."

"I think you need to slow your roll and take one day at a at time. How did you find all this out?"

"He told me."

"That's positive. Who tells you stuff like that if they mean you harm?"

Denise's pacing slowed. "I guess you're right."

"That would not be new. What were you saying about Charles, though?"

"I'm not sure, but I'm just finding out things about Charles that I didn't know." She sighed, shaking her head.

"Aww sookie cookie. Things like what? Good things? Bad things? Spill the tea." She laughed. "I'm supposed to meet Samantha for dinner in a few. But which one of those things would you like to talk about first?"

Denise paced the room, speaking too quickly. "Okay. That's good. Do you think we can all go?"

"Of course. You're always welcome. You know that. What's up?"

"That works, but first I think we need to go down to the police headquarters on the island. Do you think you can take me there?"

"Police? Wait, what? You gonna have to fill me in," Yolanda grabbed her keys from the counter. "I'm ready when you are. I somehow think this is going to be good."

It didn't take long for them to get back to the front of the island where the police security building and headquarters were located. The dimly lit building was sleepy this time of day, with only a receptionist and one policeman visible. He didn't even look up when the two women walked in. Yolanda cleared her throat, then pushed the bell on the counter to get someone's attention.

Denise crossed her arms across her chest, bouncing on of her feet as they waited. "Hello?" she said to the empty room. There was no sound, other than from something that sounded like a television in the back room. They waited for too long before the receptionist noticed them.

"Can I help you?" the woman asked.

Denise nodded, "I need to see the detective that is normally on duty here. I have some questions."

"Do you have an appointment?" The woman looked at them over the reading glasses perched on the end of her nose.

Denise shook her head. "I don't, but I don't think it will take a long time. "She softened her voice. "It's imperative that I talk to him. Is he in?"

The receptionist eyed them both. "Let me see if he's available." Instead of calling back or using an intercom, she got up and walked towards the back of the building, her kitten heels clicking on the tiles as she left. They watched as she disappeared around the corner.

Yolanda moved closer to her friend. "You want to tell me what this is about?" Her voice was hushed.

Denise sighed. "You're not going to believe this, but I found out that all the money is missing from my the business 401k."

"Uh-oh. I can't believe you're just telling me this." Yolanda replied.

"It gets worse. It was transferred after he died. While he was down here in Kiawah. I'm not sure if he was at the house or the boat or what. I need to figure things out before my accounts are seized, and the only way for me to do that is to know what the police know."

"You sure you want to do this?" Yolanda asked. "You know they're professionals and they'll find out something eventually."

"Will they? You sound just like Jamel," Denise said. "It's been months, almost a year, and we know nothing and I just found out today things that I didn't know before. Things that make it look like Charles was not the person I knew him to be. Did you know that he's being independently investigated? That's news to me." Tears sprung to her eyes. "I'm so angry. I feel so stupid. He was supposed to take care of things, not steal other people's money. I feel like I didn't know him at all."

"Let's not jump the gun," Yolanda said. She knew all about what secrets felt like in a marriage, but it didn't feel like something her friend needed to hear right then. "Okay. Let's see what they have. Maybe they can tell you something that would clear this up. You'd think they would already know these things. I mean, they did look into his death or whatever it was."

"You'd think so, but then again, look where we are. Half of these people aren't even really cops, you know?" She bit her lip. "This place is crazy. It's so beautiful on one hand, and the rest is an enigma. They don't really care about the details about what happened to Charles. They care that the island appears safe for tourists."

"It's okay." Yolanda rubbed her friend's back. "There's no use in getting all bent out of shape. Let's see what they have to say about things."

After a few minutes, a policeman came from the back and motioned towards them. They walked in his direction and followed him into a small office. He closed the door behind them and pointed towards some chairs. "Have a seat. How can I help you ladies?" He walked around to his desk. "I got the report about someone being in your house, Mrs. Martine but we didn't find any evidence of a break-in, plus they are very unusual around here. If someone did manage to get inside, we think they had a key or the door was unlocked. That's all I got."

"I'm not here about that," Denise said.

"Oh." He sat back in his chair. "So how can I help you then?"

"I want to find out all you know about my husband's disappearance and maybe, if you can check the logs, the last time he was here. When did he enter the island for the last time? Aren't there cameras? Can you tell me that?"

"Sure, I'll see what I can do. But hasn't he been missing for quite some time now?"

Denise's stomach was in knots. There was a part of her that wanted to be told that Charles actually had been there after the date he was supposed to have disappeared. That he's been hiding from her and had come here and made the transfers himself. Denise nodded, "Yes, he has, but I just found out that someone transferred money from an IP address down here from our business accounts. The money was sent to Bitcoin accounts somewhere else. I want to see if we can trace them."

The policeman looked up at her, "I'm not sure I can help you with that. We're just a small-time security office and this certainly seems above my pay grade or ability." He paused, shaking his head. "Look, most of us are just retired police officers. I'm the only person that is active law enforcement here, and I cover Kiawah and the island next door.

"You need to talk to the real police in Charleston or see what you can find out from the Chicago police. They should be able to tell you something."

Denise's heart sank. A dead end. "Look, I'm just trying to get to the bottom of things. No one seems to be able to tell me anything useful and the folks in Chicago are as in the dark as I am. I really just want to help the people whose money is missing and make things right for them, you know?"

The officer crossed his arms over his chest, "I bet you do and I understand that it's really admirable, but you know, people down here, we kind of take it easy, and I think you should, too. There are professionals that take care of these kinds of things."

"I thought you might say that." Denise sighed. She was tired of people telling her what she shouldn't do.

The policeman stood up and without speaking, let them know that they were being dismissed. Yolanda and Denise followed suit and stood up and walked through the office door that he held open for them. They passed in silence, not even answering the receptionist's perfunctory "Have a good day" as they walked, not stopping until they were safely away from the building and back in the parking lot.

Yolanda finally spoke. "Cher, I'm sorry. Let's go meet Samantha. She'll be waiting. We have some things to talk about."

16
High Time for a Visit

There were eight messages on her house phone, and four of them were blank. Denise dialed into the voicemail and listened twice, double-checking that she hadn't inadvertently cut them off or something. "What in the world?" She slammed the phone back onto the hook with a little too much force. "It's either someone selling something or a wrong number. Every time."

"Where do you want me to put your bags?" Trent came into view with a bag in each hand. He moved like he was walking on eggshells, a sheepish look on his face. He'd come right over with her bags when she'd texted.

Denise motioned towards the front room of the house. "Anywhere over there is fine." Her words were clipped. She watched him for a minute, standing with her hands on her hips. "I can't believe you could think for one minute that I had anything to do with whatever Charles got himself wrapped up in, if there's anything." The words erupted from her mouth. If she'd had any doubt before she'd gone to Chicago, she knew now that things weren't right, all the way down to the center of her soul.

"To be fair, I hadn't talked to you in years. How would I know anything at all about what you would or would not do, Denise?" Trent looked away.

She tilted her head to the side, but didn't answer, biting her lip. Now she had mixed feelings about Trent, too. "I'm just not sure who to trust, you know? You marry someone and you think you know them. I thought I knew him. Nothing makes sense anymore. Why do I even have a phone here?" Tears stung her eyes.

Trent exhaled heavily. "Are you mad at me? Or at him?" He ran his hand down his goatee. "Because I'm not him. I needed to come clean with you, Denise. I care about you, can't you see that? It was not my intention to upset you anymore than you must already be. This is a lot. For anybody. If I had known what I know now, I would've excused myself from the job."

Denise's eyes shot daggers at Trent and he recoiled as if they were physical objects. "Is that what I am to you now? A job?"

"You're not hearing me, Denise. You're much more than a job. I'm removing myself from the case. I'll be telling them I can't continue and giving them back their deposit. Your friendship means much more than that to me."

Denise looked at Trent, her head cocked to the side. She wanted to trust him. She felt like she should. "You're so good it's making me hurt."

"Is there any other way to be?"

She chuckled. "I suppose not. I just have so much on my mind. It's hard. And who gives back money?" Samantha and Yolanda had really talked her down. She was in a totally different place than she had been when he'd dropped her off.

"You've had a rough couple of months, so I get it." Trent paused. "Care to unload?"

"Do you, Trent?" She rubbed the lines that had formed on her forehead.

He turned towards her and put one hand on each of her arms, rubbing them. "I'm sorry if I made anything worse."

She froze in place for a second and then relaxed. She might have been angry at Trent, or annoyed, she wasn't sure which, but the chemistry was still there between them. There was a certain amount of electricity in his touch.

"I want to help you."

"You can't, can you? I mean, you'll lose your job."

"I'm self-employed. I'll lose a client maybe, but I decide what I'm going to do. And I think you need some help here." He paused. "I owe you."

Their eyes locked for a minute, and then Denise broke the silence with a laugh. "Yeah, you kinda do."

Trent joined her in the laughter and the mood in the room lightened.

"What I need is a drink, you know?"

"I do." He paused. "I know you're tired from your flight, but we should go to the hotel and have one. On me. We can leave this discussion right here. Just be done with it and move on."

"We could," Denise said. "Do you mean The Sanctuary? Or the new little Inn? Because I just came from there."

"You know I mean The Sanctuary. Who do you think I am? I would never take you to the Andell Inn. It's not special enough for you." He raised his eyebrows and Denise smiled.

The Sanctuary sat in the middle of the island, at a prime spot overlooking the ocean. It was old-fashioned and grand, with the houses that had been built up around it forming a moat between it and the condos and rental homes on the mainland-facing side of the island. "Oh, fancy," Denise teased. The

Sanctuary was where many tourists came to stay when they wanted to stay on the island less than a week, and they paid dearly for it. "Have you been there before?"

"Just once. Very quickly. What are the alternatives?" Trent asked. "I just know that I couldn't get a hotel room there."

Denise shook her head. "Yeah, that would be hard time this time of year. The hotel is the center of the holiday festivities. There aren't a lot of alternatives for the likes of you."

"The likes of me?"

Denise grinned. "Yes, the likes of you. You summer people."

Trent nodded. "I see." He really could see why she and Yolanda were friends.

Denise's face lit up. "Unless we go off island."

"I want to know more about these likes of me..." Trent stared at her intently.

Denise squirmed, wetting her lips. She felt pinned down by his eyes. "Well, you know they put that Andell Inn near Fresh Fields not too long ago."

"That barely feels like it's on the island." Trent had seen the new hotel. It was small, and though the outside looked like it tried to blend with its surroundings, from what Trent could tell, the place was very modern on the inside. "It's not even inside the gates."

Denise was intrigued. "That's true. And it's new and fancy. I have only been there once, but the bar felt nice." She had no reason to really go there. "You like being inside the gates?"

"I like being in the <u>middle</u> of things." He laughed. "Tell me about the other options you mentioned."

"You know, the clubs?"

"Clubs?"

"There are a few. Most are members-only unless invited by guests. Like the Beach Club. I know Yolanda invited you to the party there on the fourth."

"She did." Trent nodded. "She was quite insistent."

"And the others you can go to if you're playing golf. Again, with a member."

"I'm thinking somewhere calm and relaxing and easy right now, to help you unwind. And somewhere inside with air-conditioning."

Denise chuckled. "Yes, the beach is beautiful, but I do need to be inside right now. The heat is killer." Now that they'd mentioned it, she was acutely aware of the heat as the air conditioning struggled to keep up, even though they were inside.

"The romance of The Sanctuary feels good to me. Won't it be the most private?" He stumbled over his words a bit. He didn't want to play his hand too soon. They'd just gotten past a hurdle and he didn't want to be up against another one.

Denise gabbed her phone, a lightbulb coming on in her head. "You know what, drinks feel good to me, too. You're driving."

"Works for me." Trent, shrugged, relieved.

Just as she touched the phone, it chimed with a text message. Denise unlocked it and read the text.

"Everything okay?"

She nodded. "It's Yolanda. Party stuff. I want to freshen up a little." She thought about meeting Malika Lavigne at Yolanda's. "I think I have a better place for us to go. Are you down for an adventure?"

Trent smiled. "I'm always up for adventure."

"Let me feed Rascal real quick." The heels of her sandals clicked on the hardwood floor as she walked towards the laundry room. "This place is sort of midway between here and Charleston."

"Didn't we just come from Charleston?" He raised his voice slightly. He stepped closer to the window, moving the curtains aside.

"Sort of." Denise closed the laundry room door, leaving the dog inside. "Are you okay?"

Trent nodded, moving the curtains to the side. "Think so. I thought I saw something. "

"Probably just a golfer. They sometimes lose their balls close to the house, especially the bad ones."

"You're probably right." Trent squinted as he gazed out onto the golf course.

Denise joined him for a minute, looking in the same direction. "I don't see anything. Stop creeping me out, please. If anyone is on edge now, it's me." She stepped around him and checked the patio door locks anyway. "Just in case."

"I approve of that message," Trent said.

Denise chuckled. "So, are you up for my adventure or not?"

Trent moved the light curtain, watching as the golfer appeared to pick up a ball and leave. "I assure you, I'm all in. Anywhere you want to go, I'm there."

Denise smiled. That was exactly the answer she was hoping for. "Good," she said. "I know a place." As much as she enjoyed visiting The Sanctuary, it was high time she took Malika Lavigne up on her offer and paid her Inn a visit.

17
The Planter's Club

Planter's Inn sat in the center of the historic Charleston District, just across from Market Street. The busier feeling of downtown assaulted Denise and Trent as the landscape changed, leaving them feeling as if the islands had coughed them up and spit them out into the business center of colonial South Carolina.

Denise had told Trent that she only got to town maybe once or twice a season, preferring instead to avoid the influx of tourists that came with the summertime. They were easy to spot as they milled around in groups or ignored traffic, navigating their way through the downtown streets. Many explored the Slave Mart and other museums, choosing horse-drawn carriages instead of cars as their means of transport around the history-steeped city center. The carriages and police on horseback made the cars as out of place as Denise felt every time she came there.

Trent navigated the narrow streets as Denise suggested. She directed him to park at the lot that was part of St Philip's Church. The lot was surrounded by an old fashioned-stone wall, and was about a block away from the Main Street in downtown Charleston. High decorative grass spouted just inside the wall, hiding most of the cars from view of passers-by.

"Are you sure?" Trent said. "Maybe we should have driven your car?" His hands tensed on the steering wheel. His car seemed overly large now as he maneuvered the small, cobblestone-lined streets, and he felt more like an outsider as he navigated them.

Denise held back her 'I told you so' about the truck, recalling her first encounter with it in the parking lot of Buster's Place. "Positive," she said instead. "The tourist revenue from the parking really helps support the church." She pointed to a faded parking sign, half hidden by a small shrub and bent to the side.

If tourism was seeping into Kiawah Island, it had completely taken over the historic district of Charleston. The market that the street was named for neatly divided into two ends; one air-conditioned and enclosed and full of marked-up tourist items, and the other more old-fashioned and open to the air, overflowing with goods from local farmers and craftspeople. The market straddled the median and divided Market Street in half, running its length for several blocks. During the day the market was filled with all sorts of people exploring the historic area, leaving the streets teeming with throngs of people and parking, scarce.

A patrolman on horseback stood sentry just outside the small stone hedge that marked the perimeter of the church grounds. "How's crime around here?" Trent asked. The sight of the policeman made him uneasy.

"If you're asking if the policeman will be able to protect your car, don't worry. His horse will gallop anyone to death if they get too close." Denise rolled her eyes.

"Jokes, huh?" He sighed. "I'm just checking. Downtowns everywhere are notoriously the worst places in town."

"Maybe. But look at this place. The worst that might happen is someone may get pick-pocketed."

"You're amused, aren't you?"

"Just a little. No one wants your truck. This big old thing sticks out too much. It's getting late anyway, so things will start clearing out soon, you'll see. There'll be a short lull and then all the nightlife will come alive. It's awesome, actually."

"I'll just have to trust what you say."

'You don't have much of a choice." She paused. "I can't believe that I'm actually enjoying how you're reacting to this place.

Trent smiled. "Maybe that's because you don't come down here that much."

"Could be. It wasn't always that way. There was a point when Charles and I would not hesitate to come down here for dinner or maybe to take in some live music."

"That must have been nice for the two of you. What happened?" Trent asked.

The smile disappeared from Denise's face. She shrugged, not exactly able to articulate it.

"Don't worry about your car. Security is always high here. Tourism brings in a lot of money. Crime wouldn't bring good publicity."

"I guess I can't argue with that." Trent pulled his car into a small space in the rear of the church lot. "I get the feeling that you came down here to take in all of this awesomeness you speak about."

"I didn't." Denise shook her head. "I came here to see what my husband was up to before he died." Her eyes darkened. "After we stopped coming to Downton Charleston together, Charles apparently came by himself, both when I was on the island, and when I wasn't. He'd been so outgoing, I couldn't imagine that he hadn't met and hung out with lots of people during that time.

"That doesn't sound good." Trent pressed his car remote and waited for the chirp.

"Yeah, and for some reason, sharing information about my husband with you feels like cheating."

Trent smiled. "It shouldn't. For so many reasons."

Denise's face felt warm. She knew he was right.

Planter's Inn was classic Charleston, its green awning flanked on either side by neat window boxes overflowing with native ivy. Old-fashioned lamp lights framed it all, their flames long-since replaced by modern lightbulbs.

Trent stepped forward to open the door for Denise. "And you picked this place because?"

"I know the owner." She stepped through the door into the darker entryway, pausing a minute to let her eyes adjust. "I thought I'd come explore." She let her gaze sweep the room, quickly landing on a sign pointing towards the bar.

Trent followed without being asked. "I guess it's bad time to mention that you had us come to a place that practically made us back track all the way to the airport?"

Denise glanced at him, then looked away without answering.

He cleared his throat. "It does smell nice in here. Is the owner one of the ladies I met at Buster's place?"

"No. " Denise shook her head. "Malika Lavigne is a local socialite, for lack of a better word. Our circles overlap, but no, she was not there. "

"This reminds me of a speakeasy. Like the Twenties."

"She did a very good job of making sure it does. That

seems to be her brand. Details. Every little thing on purpose."

Trent stepped to the side and Denise lead him inside.

"I saw her the other day at Yolanda's house, the owner, and I felt like I met her before. Now that I'm here, I realize that that place was featured in an article in *Charleston Now* Magazine, and she was on the cover. That's why she'd looked so familiar.

"That's nice for her," Trent said. "Good publicity."

"Maybe. She used to keep her boat next to Charles's and apparently saw him much more than I realized."

"Ruh-oh," he said, imitating Scooby-Doo.

Denise shot a glance at him. "Funny guy." She paused. "I'm just not sure what level of ruh-oh I'm dealing with. I think she knows something I should know." The booth was private but allowed enough visibility that they could see everything and anyone that came through the velvet curtain that marked the entryway. Denise slid into it, patting the seat next to her. "Come over here."

Trent's pulse quickened. "Wouldn't you rather me sit across from you so that I can look into your eyes?" He smirked.

"Ha!" she said. "I'm actually cold in this air-conditioning and I want you to sit next to me so I can take advantage of your body heat."

Trent sunk into the chair. "Really? Cold? Weren't you just begging for some AC?"

"I know, right? But this way we can watch things in the room, too.

"Right. That makes sense.

"And I wouldn't have to look around you to see what's going on."

"Always an ulterior motive with you. I get it. People

watching." He scooted closer to Denise.

Denise crossed her arms and rubbed herself, the hairs on her skin standing from the chill in the room. "We need to get a waiter's attention."

"I got you," Trent said, raising his hand just as the waiter rounded a corner from what he presumed was the kitchen.

It wasn't hard to spot Malika Lavigne. As soon as she stepped into the small bar area, she drew everyone's focus. Denise lifted her hand to wave. Trent looked at Malika, his mouth dropping open just a bit.

He dropped the hand he'd been using to summon the waiter. He'd already started towards the table. At the same time, Malika squinted, and then seemed to recognize Denise. She stopped the waiter in his tracks by pulling on his arm.

Denise and Trent were unable to hear what she said, but it looked like "I've got this one." The waiter stopped, then turned back around to what he'd been doing. Malika ran her hands over the front of her dress as if to compose herself, finally waving in their direction.

Like when she'd met Denise at Yolanda's house, Malika wore yet another balletic outfit. The blue silk billowed around her slender figure as she floated about the room, smiling and nodding to each table. Malika took her time, asking each patron if things were okay. She shared a joke with several of the tables as if they all contained old friends.

Trent turned in the direction that Denise was staring, then back around. "She's something, huh?" Like everyone else in the room, he couldn't take his eyes off Malika.

Denise studied how she worked the room. "Oh, sorry. She is. That's Malika." She stumbled over her words as if they were hard to get out.

"I've heard of people taking your breath away, but—"

Clearing her throat, Denise let out a small laugh. She felt a twinge of something, but couldn't quite put her finger on it. Was it jealousy? Denise shook it off. She would have to unpack that later. "Tell me about it. She's just so…interesting. And different than the last time I saw her, but at the same time, not." Malika was slowly making her way back towards them. The other day, in Yoli's living room, Malika had seemed unsophisticated and the most interesting thing about her had been that she'd somehow known Charles. Now, she appeared to know everyone and everyone wanted to know her. She was absolutely the center of this space and she knew it. Seeing her in her element, Denise could imagine Charles being drawn to Malika, too. The more she watched, the more she was certain that he would've been under her spell, just like everyone else.

Malika locked eyes with Denise and smiled, but didn't stop talking with the gentleman she was currently engaged with. She motioned towards the bar. The bartender immediately stopped doing whatever he had been doing and grabbed a bottle from behind the bar. Denise watched as he deftly added three glasses from under the counter and opened what she could only imagine to be a small fridge of some type. He removed perfectly round ice cubes, each the size of a softball. The clink they made as they hit the glass was perceptible all the way across the room.

Trent rubbed Denise's hand and she momentarily looked away, glancing back just in time to see the bartender pour an inch of a clear brown liquid over each ice cube, leaving them spinning in the glasses like a river boat wheel as the liquid cascaded over the ice.

That looks amazing, doesn't it?" Denise had been watching the bartender so closely, she failed to notice when Malika had finally made it to the side of their table. She startled at the sound of Malika's voice, her raspy tone heavy with a lilt only the Deep South could cultivate.

"Oh," she said. "It does look amazing."

Trent leapt to his feet as Malika motioned over her shoulder. The barkeep immediately placed all three glasses on a round tray and made his way to the table. Malika nodded and he slid each glass in front of them in the booth. He nodded, then backed away almost as quickly as he appeared.

"Allow me to share some of my finest scotch with you. I reserve it for my best customers." Malika's voice reminded Denise of Eartha Kitt's, the original Cat woman.

"You don't have to do that," Trent protested.

"But I do. I don't know if you've heard, but I own the place." Malika winked.

Trent and Denise made eye contact. The presentation was certainly loaded with drama, but it didn't get any better than this. She didn't have to chase down Malika as she'd originally thought. She'd come right to them, almost as if she'd been expecting her. Trent motioned towards the spot he'd been sitting in and waited as Malika sat down, then sat back down next to Denise.

Just as she had the front of the room, Malika's presence filled up the small space and the musky smell of her perfume caressed Denise's nose. She glanced at Trent. He seemed as taken with Malika as she was. She inhaled involuntarily.

Malika cleared her throat. "I'm just so glad you decided to come down and visit me. I thought it would take you longer to get here. And I know how it is for islanders, especially when you're a seasonal person."

"I've been coming to Kiawah Island for years now," Denise added. "I'm hardly a seasonal person." Her defensiveness slipped through with her words.

"Oh, how is that, exactly?" Trent asked. "You said you know how it is for seasonal people?" He leaned in as if he were under a spell.

Malika wet her lips. "The island is like a sanctuary, right, Denise? Once you're there, you almost don't want to go off-island. Ever. Even to experience a place like The Planter's Inn."

"Is that so?" he said. "You do. Apparently every day."

Malika nodded in agreement. "It's true. I do. But I didn't always. I used to live on the island full time. Sometimes it feels as if there are magical gates keeping you there. Separating you from the real world."

"You don't anymore?" This was news to Denise and almost contradictory to what Yolanda had told her. If she remembered correctly, the story was that Malika had married old Man Lavigne on his deathbed. She had been something like thirty years his junior.

"No, not since I sold that house, my husband's house. I'm mainly there on my boat now, and that's technically right outside the island." The only true marina, other than the one on Bohicket Road, was at the Beach Club, and only members used that.

"Of course everyone includes me like I still live there, out of courtesy." She paused. "And I love that about the place. I don't mean to sound like a cliché, but it is magical."

"I get it, " Denise said. It was true. The island was the kind of place that was hard to break into, but once you were in, you were in, even if you sold your house. The people made the place. Sure, it was beautiful, too, and most people came for that, at least initially, but they stayed for the family they made there.

Malika continued. "I used to be on the island all the time. It was our primary residence, but when my husband died, I couldn't bear to be there anymore. The house and the place reminded me of him too much."

"I'm sorry," Denise said. "I didn't know." She wasn't aware that they shared that much in common. She looked so young to be a widow. Probably just as young as she looked herself. Denise didn't have to try too hard to put herself in Malika's place. She knew exactly what she was feeling and part of her hated that she did. She'd come prepared to grill the woman and actually felt some kind of way that she'd shared something with her husband that Denise wasn't privy to. Now, she felt a little silly.

"It's okay, honey. Why would you know? You're a summer person."

Denise cringed. There it was again. *Summer person.* She got the distinct feeling that Malika was trying really hard to separate herself from the rest of them, or at least from Denise. Any empathy she was feeling towards the woman left.

"Our paths rarely crossed." She patted Denise's hand with her own. "Our husbands knew each other, though."

"What?" Confusion flowed through Denise. On one hand, she felt as if Malika was trying to set herself apart from Denise by reminding her how different they were, but then she threw in tidbits like this that pulled them back together again.

"Oh yes. My Damien, he was also an investor in that company." She waved her hand in the air as if trying to find the words. "The one that made the thing."

Denise narrowed her eyes. "What thing?"

"I don't know. I didn't pay too much attention to that. I've never had much of a head for technology. Damien made it so I never had to worry about things like that."

Trent's eyes narrowed and he leaned in. "Things like what?"

Denise put her hand on Trent's knee as if to hold him back.

"You know. Money, and such. I was a different person before him, and my life is forever changed after him." Malika looked down at her glass.

So many questions swirled inside Denise's head. "That could be said of so many others we cross paths with in life." She bit her lip. Malika was going to be a harder nut to crack than she'd anticipated. Denise lifted her glass.

"Toast?"

Both Denise and Trent lifted theirs to the air and the three of them clinked them together, pausing when they met. There was a glint in Malika's eyes. "To love," she said.

They all nodded as they repeated Malika's toast and then took small sips from their glasses. The heat from the scotch spread across Denise's tongue and spilled down her throat. She swallowed, struggling not to cough. "I'm not much of a scotch drinker."

Malika cleared her throat. "I never used to be, Damien taught me about scotch. It's an older man's drink and when I met him, he'd been drinking it for years. I was just a girl."

Trent and Denise locked eyes again, but didn't speak. It was clear that the woman had things to get off her chest, and Denise wanted to know it all, even if she had to endure Malika's melodrama. She had no idea how much Denise actually knew about her.

"He was almost thirty years older than I am." She laughed. "People had so much to say, you know? When we got married, I was called all sorts of names, as you might imagine. Opportunist. Gold Digger. But I didn't care. He was brilliant, and he wanted me."

Denise smiled. She remembered what it had felt like, to be wanted like that. Every new relationship felt that way. Now that Malika mentioned it, she did remember some of the whispers that had gone around the island about the Lavigne's, but this was the first time she was able to put a name with a face.

Malika continued as if reading her mind. "Yes, he was a strange, strange man." She shook her head. "But he was good to me."

"Sounds like he was quite a man," Trent said.

"Oh, he was." Malika seemed to come back to herself. "You don't know the half of it." She lifted her head. "Would you like a tour?"

"A tour?" Denise was baffled. What was there to tour? She glanced around the room for a clue.

"Let me show you what my Damien enabled me to create."

Denise had no idea where this was going, but if it was going to get her closer to any of the answers she was looking for, she was all for it. Malika motioned towards the bar again and the same bartender appeared instantly, whisking away their glasses.

Malika stood abruptly. "Come on. Let me show you the property."

The property?" Denise said.

"I *am* speaking English." Her chuckle sounded much like she was purring. "I know that sometimes when I've had a few drinks I switch to French without thinking, but the evening is young and this is my first." She paused. "Come. I want to show you what I fell in love with and tell you the story of how I got here."

Trent and Denise glanced at each other. "Here?" Denise said.

"You don't think I was always this way, do you? Damien allowed me to make this place what it is today." She was back to being amused. "I mean, not allowed me, exactly, but his death was quite lucrative for me, as you might imagine. I was able to buy this place with the insurance money."

She looked at them. "Don't look so surprised. He had a heart attack. There was insurance money. People don't accuse people of being a gold digger in a May-December marriage if there's no money." She chuckled, amused with herself. "But he did help me create Malika Lavigne. I was just Mandy Johnson from Sweet Fork, South Carolina, when I met him. What kind of name is that for a little Black girl?" She laughed again. "He named me Malika. I married the Lavigne. He created me in the image of the fantasy he had, and in his death, enabled me to create a fantasy for others. That's what I do here. Let me show you."

Not feeling as if there were really a choice, both Denise and Trent stood, and followed Malika towards the corner of the room. Malika greeted a few more people as they made their way through the tables, but this time, she didn't dawdle, instead smiling politely and touching a few hands on the way past.

Malika led them through a dark curtain that Denise had been unable to see from where they'd been sitting. Their way was blocked by an unmarked wooden door. An electronic keypad sat where the key hole should have been, and Denise watched as Malika quickly entered in a five-digit code and a red light blinked. The door clicked and released open immediately. "This keeps the bar separate and lets the people that stay here feel more comfortable, like they have some privacy. That's what they come here for. Follow me."

She led them up a narrow stairwell, which was painted a bright orange and it seemed more modern and in stark contrast to the bar area. At the top, they were spilled into an open loft-like area. Denise gasped and the much brighter light momentarily blinded her.

They paused. "I know, right?" Malika said, beaming. "I hired the best decorators. I wanted to create the feeling of a sanctuary miles away from everything, even though we are right here in the center of town."

"I love that it is so incognito."

"Yes, it is isn't it? " Malika said.

Their gaze followed Malika's. The conical room culminated in a glass, cathedral-like ceiling, a window that revealed a large atrium that was filled with vegetation, giving the feeling that they were suspended in a room nestled in the trees. "I'd say you succeeded. It's wonderful." Trent took it all in, appreciating the effect that bringing the nature inside had on the room.

"So this is—" Denise looked around the room, noticing

that a feeling of calm came over her. The decorators had done a great job because she, along with Trent, automatically felt at ease. "—amazing."

"Oh, I'm sure. This," she spread her arms wide in a dramatic flair that reminded Denise of something out of a Las Vegas show, "is the Planter's Club. An exclusive, invitation-only establishment."

"Invitation only?" A quizzical look spread across Denise's face.

Trent ran his fingers across the tip of a sleek stone credenza. "That type of thing is popular in these parts? Like at Beach Club on Kiawah? Don't you need an invitation for that, too?"

"Not quite. For that, you need a deed. Here, members get in by referral only. And then only if they can pay the fee. In cash. Not unlike how many social clubs work. This one is primarily for people who sometimes want to get away to a discrete place to conduct business. Or just to relax. Someplace where they know their comings and goings won't be talked about."

"That would be kind of hard in this town," Denise said.

"Damn near impossible in most places." Malika motioned for them to follow and they did. "It's laid out like a cross, so there is privacy for anyone staying here. Unless they want to use the landing. That's the area where we were just in." Malika gestured around the room towards the various features. Denise looked where she indicated, but Trent was fixated on the woman's long, slender fingers. And the monstrous ring that sat there.

The hallway was as narrow as the stairwell had been. It was painted in a blue, slightly deeper than the sky, and ended in a single door almost hidden by a very skillfully painted mural of a tree. The whole thing evoked a memory of the road from Charleston to Kiawah.

"This is the blue wing," Malika said. Denise raised her eyebrows as she watched their host. She was in her element and relishing the idea that she'd been able to surprise them.

"Creative name." A smirk played about Trent's lips.

Denise tapped him on the back. She didn't want to piss Malika off, and the tour was fascinating. It was as if they'd stepped into one of the novels Yoli liked to read.

"I like to keep things simple for both myself and the guests. Each wing is furnished slightly differently and have differing purposes. I find that it makes it easy for members to request what they want by color. We chose the color schemes from the natural landscapes of the Low Country to make people feel like they're here, but not here at the same time."

"What's the purpose of the blue room?" Denise asked.

"Blue Wing," she corrected. "It's a whole wing." Malika opened the double doors that blocked the way with a dramatic flourish. "Its purpose is whatever the guest needs it to be. We try to cater to our members' every desire."

Both Denise and Trent gasped at the sight in front of them. The door revealed a beautiful series of rooms, bathed, again, in the fading natural sunlight.

Malika smirked. "I know, right? This suite of rooms is meant for entertaining. A guest could host a small party here if they liked, complete with its own entrance and courtyard. Or, they could have an intimate dinner for two."

Denise closed her mouth. "You really have quite the vision." The rooms they strolled through now were absolutely breathtaking, more of an apartment than a hotel room. She could see how guests would come back again and again.

"Thank you. I tried to raise the bar on club membership and Bed & Breakfasts combined."

"I think you succeeded," Trent said. "I could really like this room."

"Could you?" Malika reached up and straightened a painting that hung above the sofa. "This one had many people that visited regularly. Denise, you'd be interested to know that your husband liked these rooms, too. At least your men seem to have similar tastes."

Malika's words hit Denise like a double slap to the face. She recoiled as if the wind had been knocked out of her. "Excuse me?" She was reminded of the real reason she had come to Charleston and it certainly hadn't been to get a tour of some rich widow's pet project.

"I'm sorry? My husband?"

"Wait," Malika continued. "I knew I should have been surprised when you acted as if you didn't know about the club. There aren't many times that people drop the kind of money it costs to belong here and their spouses not know."

"What?" Denise's heart raced. Was this yet another thing she didn't know about her husband?

A soft laugh escaped Malika's lips, almost as if she were somehow getting pleasure about Denise being caught off guard. "I thought that's why you'd come. Memberships in the Planter's Club are deedable. That means that as Charles's wife, your husband's membership passed to you."

18
The Blue Wing

Trent's eyes followed Denise as she strode from end to end of the main living room of the Planter's Club's Blue Wing. "You gonna be okay?"

Denise didn't answer him. She knew she should be angry, but after a few minutes of silence, all she could do was laugh even though nothing was funny. The past few months had gotten more and more unbelievable. "For months no one knew anything about what happened to Charles and then, in just a short time, I find out all this stuff about the man I thought I knew. It's like someone opened a closet and all of our skeletons came tumbling out." She rubbed her temples with her index fingers.

"I don't think you can ever know anyone completely." Trent's voice was low. He didn't want to do anything but soothe Denise. He couldn't help her and comfort was the only thing he could offer at this point.

"Obviously." Denise stopped in her tracks and stared at Trent. Did he even get it? she wondered. "I mean, look. I thought I was married to a mild-mannered accountant, and now

I find out my dead husband, if he really is dead, was maybe not an accountant at all. Or, maybe he was and he just had some over-the-top side hustle. I don't know." She laughed nervously. "He had a secret apartment, women that I didn't know on his boat, business investments with my friends' husbands. Did I leave anything out?"

"Secret Bitcoin accounts that may have received the proceeds to all of his employees' 401Ks?"

The room was silent for a moment as they locked eyes. Trent held his breath, and then suddenly Denise burst into full-fledged laughter. After a few seconds Trent joined in. "I'm living in a spy novel." Denise doubled over, holding her stomach.

She laughed so hard that tears ran down Denise's cheeks. She flopped onto the couch, next to where Trent was now sitting, and continued laughing until she was exhausted and her stomach hurt.

"So, this is amusing to you, huh?"

"It's not to you?" Denise asked. "It can't get much stranger."

"If you say so. I see some pretty strange things in my line of work." Trent shrugged. "Now what? A drink maybe?"

"That is a damned good idea. You mind?"

He shook his head. "Malika said she'd left us some champagne up here."

"I bet there's scotch. Or vodka. I think I need something stronger. Don't you?"

Trent nodded and strode towards the credenza. The frosted glass on the front revealed the silhouettes of several bottles. "There has to be something suitable in here." He pushed back and the top of the credenza slid open. "This is fancy."

"I know, right? Another thing I didn't know about Charles. He was all into *the simple things*, or so I thought." She made air quotes with fingers. "So much for what I thought I knew about the man I was married to for over ten years."

"There's a lot of expensive looking liquor in here. Do you think it's okay?" Trent picked up a few bottles and read the label, then carefully placed them back into their spots. "I don't recognize half of this stuff."

"Well, since I'm a member in this fucker, we might as well." Denise kicked off her shoes and leaned back into the well-cushioned sofa.

Trent opened the heavy doors further, selecting a bottle from the myriad he found here. He removed two glasses from the cabinet and held them up for Denise's approval. "These are nice. They have some heft to them." He weighed the glasses with his hands.

She nodded. "Bring the whole bottle. Nice glassware makes everything taste better."

"Oh," he paused. "It's like that?" He waved the bottle in front of his nose, inhaling. It was nice to catch a glimpse of the Denise he remembered. It might be a little strange since she was under a bit of stress, but he was enjoying spending time with her even though he probably shouldn't be. The things she was going through would be a lot for anyone.

She nodded. "Most certainly is."

Trent turned around and paused, his face suddenly serious. "Have you given any thought to the idea that maybe your husband's death was not an accident?"

"What are you saying?"

"Let's look at it for a moment." Trent paused, leaning

back onto the credenza. "He is working on some inventions with a whole bunch of investors with a lot to lose. Has anything been delivered?"

"Truthfully, I don't know, but it doesn't seem so."

"Okay, so, nothing. Let's say nothing. Behind schedule. Maybe they need more money to make it happen. So, then the 401K money goes missing, right?"

"My husband was a lot of things, but he wasn't a thief." Denise folded her arms across her chest.

"Stay with me. I'm not saying he was. I'm just helping you to take an objective look at where we are now. Maybe he thought he could take that money and use it and put it back before anyone knew it was gone."

"There are a whole lot of scenarios that could have happened. Maybe he borrowed money or pissed off the wrong person or—"

"Now you see what I'm saying."

A heavy sigh escaped Denise's lips. "All this time, I refused to believe that he was actually dead." She shrugged. "Who knows? Maybe he's run off or something." She patted the spot next to her on the couch. "Nothing I know to be true seems to be. It's all absurd."

"Real talk." Trent handed her the class of scotch and put the bottle on the coffee table, then eased down onto the sofa next to Denise.

"I thought you were off the case. You sure sound like you're still looking for answers."

"I *am* looking for answers, but only so you can find the peace of mind you deserve."

She nodded. Denise turned her glass up and emptied it,

making a face as the brown liquid slid down her throat and ignited a fire in her chest. She cleared her throat and extended the empty vessel in Trent's direction for a refill, not sure if what she was feeling was due to the scotch or Trent.

He paused "Whoa."

"Don't whoa me," she snapped. "I deserve another drink."

He couldn't argue with her. She deserved more than another drink. Trent nodded and poured another two fingers of scotch into her glass. "Okay." He already knew that he was all in and at this point there was very little he could deny her if she asked.

"Nothing I know is truth. I wonder what else Charles lied to me about. This is some bizarre shit." She waved her glass in the air like it was a pointer. "The only thing real is that he abandoned me." She tossed back the second drink just as fast as she had the first, then held up her finger for Trent to be silent.

Trent ignored her signal. "I don't think he abandoned you. I believe he was trying to protect you." His glass made a thud as he put it down on the heavy coffee table.

"Isn't that a pleasant fairytale? All I can do is look at the facts, and that's not what they're saying." Denise needn't have said anything to him. Trent could feel the hurt and confusion emanating from her body. "And you can't project what you think you might do in a situation onto someone else. I don't see why you would. It's not like you can or should protect him."

Denise had more than enough to work through and Trent just felt grateful to be around her while she did it. He nodded as he considered her comment. She was right. How could he protect someone that could do what Charles had done?

On one hand he might have been messed up in some shady shit which meant, of course, that he was planning to leave his wife high and dry when he ultimately either was caught or killed. On the other hand, there was the possibility that he'd walked off, which was just plain wrong. Neither made Charles look like a person who would be worthy of a defense from Trent or anyone else. How could Denise have fallen in love with someone like that? Neither scenario was good.

Trent looked on as Denise drained her glass. "If you keep knocking drinks back like this, you're going to be very drunk, very fast."

"What are you, the drunk police? I can handle my firewater, okay?"

He smiled, almost feeling honored that he would be able to be the one to keep her safe while she did it. "Alright then, You got this."

She nodded. "That's what I thought." Denise put her glass down with a thud. Trent's eyes followed her motions. "I guess I should ask if you're okay. You don't have to hang out for any of this."

He looked up, realizing that Denise was much closer than she had been just a moment earlier. "Why wouldn't I be?" His throat was suddenly dry.

They paused, locking eyes again. Trent was surprised at what he saw in Denise's gaze, and before he could sort it out, she pressed her lips to his. He did the only thing he could do. He sat back and went with it, parting his lips to let their tongues touch. He was drawn in and kissed her back.

For a split second, a fleeting idea of guilt entered Trent's mind, but then the part of him that had been feeling Denise from the moment he'd helped her at her house brushed it away. He might allow himself to feel guilty later, but now was absolutely not the time.

The sound of Malika's shoes clicking on the hardwood floors made them both freeze and they pulled back, putting a respectable distance between them. Denise smoothed her clothes and sat back. Trent tried to look as if nothing was going on even though he felt like a fourteen-year-old that had gotten caught kissing in the back of a classroom.

"I'm sorry about that." Malika entered the room talking. "I needed to sign for a shipment." She paused, looking from Denise to Trent. "I see you started without me."

They both looked at the floor. "You told us to go ahead," Trent said.

"No worries. That's what I intended for you to do but thankfully there's enough to go around." Malika walked to the credenza where Trent had gotten the scotch and helped herself to a glass from a different bottle without waiting for one of them to offer. She turned and joined them, sitting in the accent chair across from the sofa.

"So Denise, as I was saying, you're welcome here anytime. The membership in the Planter's Club goes with the surviving spouse, and that means you. I didn't get to mention it to you when I saw you the other day. But I thought it was something you might not want me to say in front of Yolanda."

Denise put her glass down on the table. "Yolanda and I have no secrets between us. We've been friends since we were children."

Malika cocked her head back. "Is that so? In my experience, You never know what secrets people keep from their friends, but I didn't want to be in the middle of any of it. People either didn't want to make their friends feel bad or they don't want to embarrass them."

They didn't know each other well, but once again Malika had found a way to make Denise feel small, as if she was an outsider, oblivious to everything going on in her own life. "You don't know anything about my relationship with Yolanda." The terseness in her voice made both Trent and Malika pause.

"Don't get offended," Malika said. "I'm sure I don't. I apologize if I said something to upset you."

Trent cleared his throat. "Ladies, let's find out more about why we're here. You don't need to quibble over something that won't matter in the long run."

Malika smiled graciously. "Trent, you're obviously a gentleman and completely right. Let's talk. You have some questions for me Denise, I presume? I know you didn't come here to take me up on my offer for a casual visit."

Denise swallowed, grateful that Trent helped avert the argument she'd been about to start. "You're right. I didn't." Acting otherwise would've been unfair to Malika, and that was something she had no desire to be, no matter how nice-nasty Malika was. The jumble of emotion inside her was ready to erupt, but it didn't make sense to take it out on people that really had nothing to do with things, especially when they might be able to help you.

She sat forward on the couch. There was no reason to beat around the bush. "Yes, I do actually. You said that there are a lot of things people do here at the Planter's Club. What did you mean? And can you tell me exactly what my Charles did here?" She flinched as soon as she said it. She'd referred to Charles as her Charles. She was going to have to move on especially since she'd just been kissing another man not ten minutes before.

"Oh yes," Malika said. "Some people come here because they want to meet their mistress." Malika's face lit up with surprise, "I mean, not your Charles. That was a joke, of course."

Denise nodded.

"Actually, not many people. Most of the time the Planter's Club is a discreet place for businessmen to take care of things not far from the airport and then get out of town. People can fly private planes in and out of Charleston and they often do. It's not too far from many places on the east coast and the Midwest. We get a lot of people from Chicago coming down to do things."

Denise took a sip of her scotch. "I see." Her mind racing. What exactly had Charles been doing here? "You said that you saw my husband on the boat several times and you thought you saw me?"

"I thought I did."

"I was never here." Denise crossed her arms over her chest.

"Really?" Malika sipped her drink. "I guess that explains it."

Denise continued. "I found out recently that Charles had been coming to the island without me quite a few times and I'm really confused as to what he was doing here. I thought we had no secrets between us, but I'm learning differently."

Malika continued, "Yep, that's exactly what I mean." She paused. "I see a lot of that in my business."

"But can you tell me why he was here?" she asked again.

Malika locked eyes with Denise. "Are you sure you want to know?"

The question surprised Denise. She thought she did. If nothing else, it would answer some questions for her. She deserved some closure. The full force of the last few months came to her, all in that moment. She really didn't care what Charles had been doing. What was important was that she <u>know</u>. She wanted to know where the money had gone so she could at least help the people that'd trusted them all these years. Denise had to know that there had been no real secrets between them. A small sob escaped her lips.

Trent leaned in, rubbing her back. "We don't have to do this."

Malika looked on, and the smile she gave them appeared to have so much behind it that had nothing to do with being happy.

"I do, I mean, I want to do this. You have no idea what the past few months have been like." She looked over at Malika. "If you know anything, please tell me. At least tell me why he came here." She looked from Malika to Trent and then back to Malika again. "Anything to help me make sense of things. I need to reach some kind of understanding. I really want to know."

Malika stood up, then walked to the other side of the room. "I'm not sure I should tell you anything. I should have known that wasn't you on that boat. I mean, that woman looked nothing like you. I can see that now, but people trust me and

Planter's because, well, it's discreet. You know what I mean?"

"And if you tell her what you know, you think people might not trust you anymore?" Trent asked.

"Correct."

Denise's eyes darkened. "Who will know, Malika? Charles isn't here to tell."

Malika sighed, shaking her head. "Yes, I guess that's true." She paused. "Your husband wasn't coming here to have an affair. I really want you to know that." They locked eyes then. "And I don't know everything."

Denise suddenly felt knocked backwards. Conflicted. On one hand, an affair would have been a relief. At least she would have an idea of what Charles had been up to, a twisted certainty about something. She would have some reasons to really hate him versus the nothing she had now. But it was good to know that some part of her old life had been the truth. Under the current circumstances, was there really any way for her to know what Charles had been up to while he was there? It wasn't like she could just ask him.

Malika put her hand on Denise's shoulder as she tried to comfort her. "If it makes you feel any better, I do understand what you're going through and I know it's not the same. At least I had solemn finality to the truth in front of my eyes. I watched as my husband died."

Denise nodded. "That would have been too much like right. Charles always had a flair for the dramatic." She shook her head. "A disappearance is actually perfectly over the top. People would be talking about him for months. Years even. If nothing else, he was consistent." She rubbed her forehead. "Charles was a man that quietly loved drama."

"Looks like he got it," Trent said.

They nodded in agreement and Malika stood up to go. "I have to get back to the bar. You make yourself comfortable though. You may find some comfort in spending some time in this space. As you already know, it's fully stocked. And of course, like I said before, Charles's membership is yours now."

Denise nodded. "I still have one question. How do you know for sure he wasn't having an affair? Were you always here when he came? Did you keep some kind of record of his visitors? How do you know? Unless you do know what he was doing and it wasn't that?"

Malika's face flushed and she stumbled over her words. "What are you saying? Are you accusing me of something?"

"Not at all. I just feel like something is missing."

Trent stood. "she has a point. Seems like you are working really hard to make sure she understands what Charles wasn't doing here, but do you know what he actually was? Or are you trying to take attention away from yourself, maybe?"

"And this is why I stay out of people's business." Malika's eyes were filled with fire. "I am trying to help you, that is the only thing I am guilty of."

"While I appreciate that, the only thing you are giving me is more unanswered questions. I think you knew full well that wasn't me you were seeing in the Marina. Are you sure you have nothing else you can tell me?"

Trent and Denise locked eyes, and she immediately calmed. If she pissed Malika off, she would most certainly not help her then.

"Nothing that I think will give you the answers you seek. Stay as long as you like." Malika's lips were drawn into a thin line as she extended her hand for Denise to shake.

Denise paused, staring down at the long slender fingers that Malika had extended. Why was she so angry? This was nowhere near this poor woman's fault. Finally, she shook Malika's outstretched hand.

A new lightness took over the room as the two released their grips and an unspoken understanding passed between them.

"I'm sorry," Malika said. "I wish I could be more helpful." Her lips were punctuated by a thin smile. "Oh, and every member has a small locker. I almost forgot. I brought you a spare key."

Denise's eyes lit up. "A locker?"

"Don't get too excited. It's nothing more than a safe deposit box of sorts. They're in the back of the closet through the small safe room."

"Safe room?" Trent said. "Why would they need that?"

Malika shrugged. "Part of what I'm selling here is the illusion. It doesn't matter why, just that our patrons thought they might, and that they thought they could feel safe under any circumstances. I'll show you."

Trent and Denise followed Malika as she strode from the front room, down a long hallway and into the bedroom. She threw open the doors to a massive closet.

Denise gasped. "Wow, this is something. This is better than the closet I have at home."

"It is a good one. None of the guests really ever use it." She got to the back of the closet and pushed the door and then released it. It sprung open.

"Wow." Trent said.

They might have missed it had she not pointed it out.

The opening to the room was hidden in a fold of the wall.

"Safe room," she said. Malika struggled to pull the heavy door forward, then stepped though it into darkness.

She fumbled along a wall. The small space was windowless and pitch black. Malika finally located a switch and flipped it, flooding the small space with light.

"Wow," Denise said. "I have never—"

"I thought this would be a nice touch. As it turned out, no one was really interested so I turned it into out-of-sight storage, making it a place where the members could file important papers and things." She gestured towards the side wall. The room was lined floor-to-ceiling with built-in metal lockers.

"Why would anyone use this instead of a normal safe deposit box in a bank?" Denise asked as she looked around, filled with disbelief.

Trent answered. "So they could fly under the radar."

19
Old Times

There were still quite a few people left in the dimly-lit area when Denise and Trent got back downstairs at The Planter's Inn. Normally, Charleston was an early town, with most things closing by midnight, but there were a few venues that had a speakeasy vibe to them. The Inn seemed to be one of them.

There was a different bartender now, but his back was to the counter. He didn't look up as they rounded the end of the bar, instead busying himself with wiping around the alcohol bottoms with a green towel that matched the color of the awning outside the entrance. Instead of going back to their table, they bellied up at the bar. Trent pulled out a stool and the rubber feet bumped along the floor. He kept it from sliding as Denise climbed onto it, then signaled to the man to get him to come over.

"Scotch," he said. "McAllen." He smiled at Denise.

She fluffed her curly mane back to its almost pristine state. No one would be able to tell that he'd had his fingers in it less than an hour before.

They were silent as the barkeep poured just the right amount of liquor into just the right glass. Trent's face was blank, and it felt like even the air had paused. He slid the glass a few inches closer to Denise and she wrapped both hands around it, interlocking her fingers. She'd long since lost track of the number of drinks she had.

"You feeling okay?" Trent asked.

"I am." The time they'd spent together had helped her tremendously. "Very clear actually. Probably more clear than I have been in days." She licked her lips, leaning to the side enough so that her shoulder touched Trent's. She wasn't exactly drunk, but she was absolutely more relaxed than when she'd left Kiawah, and infinitely better than when she'd flown back from Chicago. With the aid of the alcohol, she'd let her guard down and had actually enjoyed a few laughs with Trent. Almost like old times, she thought, remembering how much fun they used to have together.

Denise blinked, catching herself. Her smile waned. Am I crazy? She knew better than anyone how the past always looked rosier in a rear view mirror. What exactly was she doing besides letting herself get sidetracked from what she really needed to do.

Trent put his hand on Denise's shoulders. Denise looked into his eyes, noticing the size of his pupils. He was feeling the tequila, too. "Can you believe her? Malika?"

Trent shook his head. Neither one of them was ready to mention the time they had just spent together. "She's something else. That's for sure." He leaned in close. "I hope you found out what you needed to know."

"I think I did."

"I know for me at least, the day turned out much better than I could have imagined it."

They laughed together. Denise's body was warm from the spirits and the friendship she was feeling. And she was thinking about sex. It had been so long. Her ears were still ringing and just from the short time they had spent together, she could tell that Trent had matured and he must have refined his skills over the years.

"Malika is a lot. This place is a lot."

"It is," Denise said. She lowered her voice, leaning into Trent again. "I want to know what she is withholding."

"Me too. But I'm not sure if she is holding back a secret, or if she believes her own hype." He paused. "At first, I thought she was joking, but then, when she didn't crack a smile at all, I realized she was serious about all this."

Trent raised his glass. "To helping people achieve their fantasies." He mimicked Malika's drawn out southern-sounding accent.

"With discretion." Denise clinked her glass to his and they rose into another fit of uncontrollable laughter.

Trent's chair tipped backward and a look of surprise came over both of their faces. "Careful!" Denise shouted, just as the gentleman sitting next to them stopped the chair from falling over totally.

"Whoa," Trent said, catching himself on the bar. "Thanks, man. Appreciate it."

The man nodded and immediately turned back to what he'd been doing on his phone.

Denise looked towards Trent and raised her eyebrows. "I think someone has had too much to drink."

"Someone, who?"

"That would be the one who is falling over in the bar." She paused. "You know, you never could hold your liquor. Not much has changed in twenty years."

Trent laughed. "You're not right."

"But I am. I don't think you could pass a sobriety test right now." She sipped her glass.

"If I can't, neither can you." Trent raised his eyebrows now, mimicking the same look that Denise had given him just a few moments before.

"What are we, two? I wasn't aware this was a competition."

Trent got quiet. "I don't want to compete with you, Denise." He ran his tongue across his lips.

Denise's eyes followed Trent's tongue. The air in the room seemed still as they locked eyes. Finally, after what seemed like an eternity, Denise cleared her throat. "Okay," she said, immediately regretting the word as soon as it left her lips. What did that even mean? Denise felt exposed and as awkward as a teenager.

Trent's face brightened. "We have a problem to solve. You were always good at that, if I recall."

"A problem? My only problem is I still have no idea who that woman was with my husband on the boat."

"That's not what I meant." Trent nodded slowly. His face gave no clue to the tumult he felt inside. "We are 47 miles from home, and neither one of us is fit to drive. South Carolina cops don't play."

Denise's brow furrowed. "They do not." She could see and feel what was happening, and she didn't want to let herself care. For the first time in months, Denise just wanted to relax and let things go wherever they wanted to go. "So what should we do?"

"I know this place we could hang out for a few hours."

His eyes were wide.

"Oh?" Denise could barely hide the smile that had crept into her face. "You really are going for it, aren't you?" She drained her glass, then opened the small purse she was carrying, removing the key that Malika gave her. She held it up between them. "Doesn't seem like we have much choice, I mean, if neither one of us can drive."

Trent took the key from between her fingers and grabbed her hand. "I'm glad we're on the same page." There was nothing left for her to say.

20

Dick Tracy Powers

Denise blushed as she thought about the evening she'd spent with Trent. It had been a lot. She was acutely aware of the rise and fall of her chest as she ran through the evening's events in slow motion. It had been a night full of embraces and kisses that took her back many years and filled her up, making her keenly aware of what had been lacking in her relationship and missing from her life for longer than she'd realized.

Denise was positive what she'd learned was just the tip of the iceberg. Even thinking about it made her head ache. She juxtaposed the whole secret meeting space thing against now having to admit that she'd enjoyed the time she spent with Trent, even if the only person she had to admit it to was herself.

Had it been long enough? Denise wasn't sure. Did the rule that a woman had to stay in mourning for her dead husband for a year still exist, or was she just being old-fashioned and ridiculous? Yolanda had been right. Their marriage had not been great for a long time. They'd been more like roommates than the lovers they used to be. She sighed. She and Charles had barely done anything together so it was no wonder she had no idea where he'd been going and who he was with, and it hadn't been all his fault. She could hide the truth from her friends, but she had to at least be honest with herself.

Malika hadn't turned out to be as much of a dead end as
Denise had originally thought, but that was a good thing. She
was still not sure how much or if she could trust Malika at all.
She wanted to like her, but this was hard. It might not have been
intentional as Malika had claimed, but Denise was positive that
there was something that was not being said, and she didn't
know why.

She looked over at Trent as he drove them back towards
the island. His hand rested on hers, its sinewy strength
highlighted by his melanin-rich skin. It was just before dawn, and
Denise had a mixture of feelings storming inside her. She'd
thought she was taking just a few hours trip into town to have
maybe a drink or two, tops. Instead, what she'd gotten was earth
shattering revelations, a mind-blowing evening, and a sense of
freedom unlike any she'd had in a while. At her core, she felt
good about it, even if she still had no answers.

The familiar tunnels of trees filtered the early morning
light, making it dance inside the car. They were both silent as
they traveled. The land bridge that was the last stretch to the
island was covered with a light fog. As they got closer, it felt as if
they were on a journey back to real life. Like Denise, Trent was
practically glowing.

"You okay?" Denise asked.

He looked at her. "How could I not be?" Was it
appropriate to thank her? His face was riddled with uncertainty.

The security gate came into sight and Trent pulled his
hand back. He slowed and approached the gate, pointing to the
credentials that would let him on the island. He drove forward
but didn't stop. The guard leaned outside the gate house,
squinting to see inside the car. He finally caught a glimpse of

Denise in the passenger seat and waved them through as if it mattered, and she nodded in return.

"I thought he wasn't going to let us through for a minute."

"He might not have now, given the events of the past few days." Denise said.

"All this extra security got a brother uptight."

Denise nodded. No words were necessary.

"I guess I can get used to this. If you're here. I think I can like this place."

Her head snapped left towards Trent. "I thought you already did."

"Well, you're giving me a reason to come back. I really do want to help you find out what happened to your husband and I'm sorry I didn't tell you earlier why I was here."

"Are you going to be okay without that job? I'm the last person to get between a brother and honest employment."

"Yeah, I will be. There's no way I can keep that money now. That feels somehow dishonest. Frankly, My motive for getting to know you has totally changed. I didn't expect this." He paused. "I don't normally let work and play get intertwined."

"I understand that."

"It happened kind of fast. I'm curious now to understand what Charles was into and about what we found in that safe deposit box."

"Yeah, me too." Denise said. "As far as I can tell, it feels pretty worthless. It doesn't make any sense."

"I can't think of any reason why two simple steel rings would need to be inside of a safe. You knew him best though. Maybe they were somehow sentimental to him?

She shook her head. "If that was the case I would've seen them before. And they don't look old or anything." Denise pulled the two rings from her bag turning them over in her hands. "In fact, this one is kind of shiny, almost like it's never been worn."

"Assuming it's jewelry."

Denise nodded in agreement. "Right." Her brows furrowed as she contemplated the small metal rings. "Truthfully, I only paid as much attention to the various things he was working on as I needed to. Maybe these rings are part of something else." She shrugged. "I can't imagine how this ties into what we know. All those people are that much further from their retirement because of something Charles was wrapped up in."

"You don't know that. We still have no proof that he took the money. He'd been gone awhile when that money disappeared."

Denise contemplated Trent's words. "That's true, he had. But my gut says this is all connected."

"Your gut, huh?" Trent smirked. "So, you're some kind of super sleuth now?"

"Make fun if you must. I'm not claiming Dick Tracey powers or anything, I have to be right about some things." She paused. "Besides, even if these things are two worthless washers, they're connected to this. Think about it. He had them in a safe-deposit box in a secret apartment! How was he paying for that place? I saw no money out of any account that could cover what that must have cost."

"True. Not a small chunk of change, but I doubt it was millions in 401K cash." Trent raised his eyebrows as he pulled into Denise's driveway. "All things done in the dark come to the light."

Denise smiled. "Now you're sounding like my grandmother."

"Mine, too. She must have been one wise woman."

They pulled up to Denise's garage but didn't go in. Unlike the managed chaos of Yolanda's garage, Denise's served more like storage for summer people than a functional part of the house. No one could really park there because it was filled with a bunch of junk; things they didn't use when they were not on the island.

She hopped out of the car and climbed the few steps to her front door. Her heart almost jumped out of her chest. The door was ajar. And this time she wasn't imagining it. She replayed leaving the house in her head. She'd locked the door when they left, she was sure of it. She'd checked it, too.

"Trent—"

"I'm right behind you." He stepped in front of her as if he were a human shield. "Do you want to wait out here?"

She looked over her shoulder, sweeping the yard with her eyes. What had she missed? "You know I'm not doing that."

He nodded then put his finger to his lips before gently pushing the door open. The creaking sound echoed inside the house. They paused and Trent put his hand on the door to steady it.

Denise followed him into the house, more closely this time. Their bodies were separated by a margin so small, Trent could feel Denise's breath on the back on his neck. She held his shirt tail like she might a lifeline. They both gasped as the room came into view. Denise screamed and suddenly felt lightheaded. She grasped the handrail on the stairway. The house had been ransacked.

Denise's free hand flew to cover her mouth. "Oh my God." Tears sprung to her eyes and she fell back on the steps, steadying herself.

"Shh," Trent said. "They may still be in here."

"They probably already heard us. We weren't exactly quiet."

Drawers had been opened and papers dumped on the floor. The curtains had been torn from the windows and cushions had been removed from the couch and chairs. They had been cut open and were strewn about the floor with the filling everywhere. Even the paintings had been ripped from the walls.

"We weren't gone that long." Denise couldn't believe what she was seeing.

"Well, looks like maybe our friends from before returned. I thought I'd seen someone outside last time. Remember when you told me that it was golfers? Maybe people had been casing the place all along."

She shrugged. "I don't understand why. It's not like I have any major secrets in this place or even anything valuable." Denise rarely left anything at the house when she was there. Normally, she travelled with very little.

Trent's footsteps echoed on the now seemingly empty house. Denise listened to his progress from the bottom of the staircase, unable to move. Trent rounded the corner and she could hear banging as he opened and closed the cabinets.

"I don't think anybody is here, Trent," she yelled so he could hear her.

"Well, you can never be too sure."

"I'm sure. I can feel it in my bones. They took everything they wanted and left."

"From the looks of things, they threw everything they didn't want on the floor. They were looking for something. I bet upstairs is the same."

"You just sit here and let me check out the house, okay? Where's the dog?"

"He's still with Yolanda. I don't leave him alone here if I'm gone overnight." Denise had an empty feeling in the pit of her stomach. Her eyes surveyed the floor, littered with all of her belongings. Her toiletries were strewn about. Her stomach suddenly felt queasy. Denise had never been physically assaulted herself, even all the years she'd spent growing up in what some would consider a not-so-nice area of Chicago, but she couldn't imagine the aftermath feeling any different than she did right then.

Trent opened and closed more cabinets back in the pantry. "Is it bad?"

"We'll discuss it later," Trent said. "I'm going upstairs." Denise soon heard his footsteps over her head, walking from the rear of the house to the front. She fidgeted. It felt like Trent had been gone forever even though five minutes hadn't even passed. He came back down the front steps to where she was sitting and put his hand on her shoulder.

"There's no one here. It's all clear."

Denise broke into sobs, her whole body trembling. Who had done this, and why? "Things keep getting worse. This is what I get. It's my punishment."

Trent wrapped his arms around her and she buried her face in his neck. "You haven't done anything to deserve this."

"Maybe not that I realize. I feel guilty about so many
things. For enjoying last night..."

"Oh, Denise," Trent softened. "You couldn't be
punished for anything like that. You're a grown woman and I
would hope you enjoyed it as much as I did."

His words made her feel a tiny bit better. She bit her lip.
"Maybe I'm being punished for the things Charles did."

"C'mon. What kind of messed up karma would that be?
Who gets punished for the sins of their spouses? This is
traumatic. I get it, but let's not go down that road. No one
deserves what happened here and I don't believe in
coincidences." He paused, looking around. "Don't you have an
alarm on the house?"

She nodded her head. "I do. We also have a Ring
doorbell. There was no alert or anything, though."

"Hmph. That's mighty funny. Can we look at the footage
on your phone? Any motion alerts outside the door at all last
night?"

It took three seconds for Denise to unlock her phone
and open the Ring Doorbell app. Trent looked over her
shoulder.   "See, the last alert was from when we left and walked
out the front door." She pointed to the indicator that declared
there had been motion at her front door at the time they'd left.

"Well, they probably came in from the back." He walked
over to the oversized glass wall that faced the golf course. "I
don't suppose you have a sensor on this door?"

"I thought I did."

Trent opened the door and fumbled around near the top.
"Looks like the sensor that was installed here is gone." He ran his
finger over the spot where the sensor used to be. "The system

wouldn't be able to know that the door had ever been opened."

"What? How does that even happen?

Trent shrugged. "Someone must have by-passed it before and disconnected the rest of the system, including the Ring."

"Actually, all they would have to do is cut the internet and there would be no signal to either system, and no notification at the guardhouse. We should probably call the police."

Denise shook her head in amazement. Whoever had been there had given some thought to what they were doing. "I need to look around first."

"Don't touch anything. There may be fingerprints."

"Fingerprints? As if the police will do anything."

"Oh they'll do something. In this high-price zip code they'll be out here looking for people before you hang up the phone," Trent said.

Denise's sigh belied the weariness she felt. "If you say so. They pretty much dismissed me before." She found the strength to stand up and walk through the house, Trent trailing behind her. Every drawer, every cabinet had been opened and overturned. All of her clothes were thrown on the floor. The memorabilia she had in the back room from the early days of she and Charles's marriage was all destroyed. Some even torn up. "I don't understand."

"They were looking for something," Trent said.

"They were just trying to be mean."

"No, I think they were looking for something. They would've destroyed more if they were trying to be mean."

They'd destroyed enough. Denise couldn't even see the floor in her bedroom. Every stitch of clothing had been taken from the drawers and closet and thrown on the floor, even the chest she kept her bags in was overturned. She picked up a tote bag and then dropped it back down onto the pile. They'd even dumped out all of the bags she'd been collecting from the conferences she'd been to.

"Can you tell if anything is missing?" Trent asked.

She shook her head. "I can't tell." They stared at the pile of bags.

"You've gone to a lot of conferences that use these colors, I see."

"It's all the same organization, my sorority."

Trent nodded. He remembered when Denise had pledged Alpha Kappa Alpha Sorority in college. She'd walked around in the same black dress carrying a plant forever. "You're still carrying plants?"

His joke fell flat. "You know I'm not, but my chapter in Chicago does a lot of community service and I help out." Denise paused. "I think you're right. It doesn't seem like anything is missing here. If this was a thief, they would have at least taken the little jewelry I have here instead of dumping it in the corner like they did."

Her entire jewelry box and its contents were overturned in a corner. Denise walked over and started picking up the pieces.

"Any ideas?" Trent said.

"I'm not sure but I'm guessing it has something to do with what we found in the safe deposit box." Denise removed the metal rings from her pocket again. "You think they were after these?"

Trent shrugged. "Anything is possible."

"I bet there's more to these than we thought, I mean, Charles did hide them for a reason. He must have known they would be valuable to someone." She juggled the rings up and down in her hand, turned them around and looked closer. Trent peered in to.

"I know a few people who can assess them."

"People?"

"I have a few connections." Trent smiled. "And it won't hurt to see what we can find. Might be nothing, but might also be what we are looking for."

"You think so?"

"Yes, I believe so. And we need to leave and wait for the police outside. If these people didn't find what they needed, they might be back."

Denise's eyes were wide. She hadn't thought of that. "I can clean this stuff up later. I think I need some air. Let's go."

21
Nothing is as Simple as it Seems

Like everything else on the island, the Beach Club was unusually crowded this time of the year. There was even a line down the road that led to the club. Located on the far end of Kiawah, it was another favorite place for the regulars in their crew to gather. Any other time, it would be a reasonably peaceful place to get some sun and catch up on the latest island gossip, but the impending holiday made it a madhouse. Like The Sanctuary, the Beach Club was only open to members and their guests. Unfortunately, those same members would have a ton of guests for the July holiday.

Yolanda drove into the parking lot, swearing under her breath as she circled a few times, until she was able to find a spot. She wedged her car into a corner, closer to the door of the club than she imagined she'd be able to. Just as she stepped out of the car, Denise walked past her, a floppy hat and sunglasses covering her face. The beach tote on her shoulder was packed to the brim. Her gauzy coverup just grazed her knees.

"Don't you look fancy," Yolanda said. "You're so incognito in that getup that I might not have known who you were." Denise's sunglasses covered most of her face. "Very

Miranda Priestly." She referenced the villain from *The Devil Wears Prada.*

They exchanged air kisses, one in the vicinity of each cheek, in proper *les bise* style. Denise held onto her hat to make sure it stayed on her head. "You know me and you know that I'm not okay with this harsh sun."

"I know you like looking like a movie star, cher." Yolanda wound her arm through her friend's. It felt good to see her, even though it had only been a day since they'd last seen each other.

"How are things going?"

Denise shrugged, "As well as can be expected. I've had a lot to deal with."

Yolanda laughed, "Yeah, you and me both."

"The police are asking questions I can't answer."

"Ooh, girl. Thank goodness that is one problem that I don't have right now. I can't imagine what you're going through."

"Although nothing at the house was particularly valuable, I still feel violated."

"Sentimental value is still value."

Denise managed a smile. "Thank you for saying that. It's true, but some redecorating will help me move on."

"And redecorating is fun! Just say the word and I'm there to help you."

The attendant at the door smiled warmly at the duo. The fan blowing above her head barely moved her blonde hair and her hairline was moist from sweat. "Are you having any guests today?"

Yolanda said nothing as she shook her head.

Denise cleared her throat. "I have one." Her small voice

was almost a whisper.

Yolanda turned to look at her friend. "Oh really?"

"Name, please." Both the attendant and Yolanda waited expectantly.

Denise took the pen from the woman's hand. "I'll just write it in, okay?"

Yolanda kissed her teeth. "Are you trying to hide it from me? I'm gonna find out eventually." She folded her arms across her chest. "But I already know."

"Know what?" Denise grabbed two towels from just inside the door.

The attendant gave Denise her membership card back and smiled. "Thank you. We're only allowing each member to have two guests this time of year because it's so busy. You ladies enjoy your day. I'll let you know when he gets here."

"Thank you," Denise replied. She smirked at Yolanda and they both walked across the veranda to The Beach Club. "Aren't you going to get towels?" she asked.

"You know we don't really need any towels. We're not actually going onto the sand nor are we getting into the pool. It's not what we do."

It was Denise's turn to laugh. "You're right." Her swim heels clicked on the wooden veranda as they made their way over to the adult pool on the far side of the club. They passed the children's pool, filled with families who were either renting or visiting someone who actually owned a home on the island. Denise sighed as a child squealed and jumped into the water, splashing all over her. She cringed.

"Maybe we do need towels," Yolanda said.

She bit her lip. "I know that some people love kids. But

when you are past that or you don't have any, that pool doesn't look attractive at all. I guess the bright side is that splash cooled me down."

"I know that's right," Yolanda said. "But it's like you've been splashed by toilet water."

"Thanks for that." She scowled. "Not all kids pee in the pool."

"I aim to serve." Yolanda smirked, but walked further away from the pool's edge.

The adult pool was on the other side of the beach club and its negative edge drew the eyes, making you focus on the coastal grass and beyond that, the ocean. The view was stunning and certainly more sophisticated than that of the kiddie pool which evoked the image of a concrete bathtub.

"So, you're not going to say anything? Don't play games with me, Denise Martine." Yolanda followed her, a few steps behind, scurrying to keep up with Denise's stride.

"Wow. I get my whole name." Denise ignored her question and smiled. She knew full well what Yolanda really wanted to know, but wasn't ready to get into that discussion with her just yet. She was still processing it herself.

"Oh, I see it's like that now. First, you didn't want to see him, know him or anything and now you're bringing him into the beach club as a guest? Things change quickly, don't they?"

"Don't look so smug, Miss Thing." Denise looked at her friend, "You think too much. It's no big deal. He's been so kind to me. He helped me halfway put my house back together." She paused. "And yes, things do change much too quickly. Look at my life. Look at what's changed for me. A year ago, I was in the perfect marriage and had the perfect almost-beach house and now that's all gone to hell, hasn't it?"

Yolanda's mouth dropped open. That was not the reaction she'd been expecting. "I—"

An attendant reached out to greet them, interrupting her, just as they got to the gate between the two pools. "Would you like two chairs?" the young man asked. "And it is nice to see you, Mrs. McAllister. We haven't seen you in a while."

"Yes, that's true, Milton." Yolanda looked at his name tag. She vaguely remembered the young man from last season. Normally, she would come to the beach club almost daily, but she'd been too preoccupied in the past week or so, handling the details for the fourth of July event. "And we'll need some shade," she added.

"Right away, Mrs. McAllister. I'll roll over a few umbrellas. Will that area over there work for you?" He pointed to a cluster of chairs in the far corner.

"That will be fine," Yolanda said. The two women were grateful that it was as far as they could get from the noise coming from the family pool. There were other people on the pool deck, sure, but when the rest of the gang arrived, they'd almost have a private corner to themselves.

The young man scurried off in the direction of the hut that housed all of the pool supplies, and they made their way to two chairs in the corner in the direction that he'd indicated. It was a great spot, giving then the vantage point to see who would enter and leave the pool. And since they would bring them any drink they wanted, they wouldn't have to get up until it was actually time for lunch.

As much as Yolanda wanted to confide in Denise about her suspicions about her husband, she hesitated. Denise had so much going on that she didn't want to burden her with anything else, and she wanted to be sure before she got her friend up in arms. Right now, she knew nothing, just a gut feeling that something was off. She'd learned from experience that it would be impossible for anyone to unhear what she told them. Yolanda mulled things over as they settled into their chairs.

"So, Denise," she began. "Do you know anything about what my husband was working on?"

Denise spread her towels out on her chair. "Anything like what?"

"What the project was, maybe? He never tells me anything."

"Might be better that way."

"What do you mean?"

Denise shrugged. "I don't know. Seems as if all kinds of skeletons are tumbling of the closet lately. You knew as much as I did. Have you thought to ask?"

"C'mon. You know I'll just get the brush-off like I have been for years." She paused. "And do you know if Charles was involved in it?"

A second attendant came over with two drinks on a serving platter. Denise strained to read her nametag. "So nice to see you ladies. How are you, Mrs. McAlister?"

"Why does everyone know your name and not mine?"

"You go home to Chicago. I come here almost every day. I'm fine, LaShauna. Is this my regular?"

She sat the drinks on the small table between the deck chairs. "They are. You enjoy and just give a wave if you need anything else."

Yolanda lowered herself down onto her chair as the

attendant walked away. They settled in and sipped their drinks before Yolanda continued. "As I was saying. Do you know if Darren and Charles were working on anything together?"

"Uhm no. I really don't know." Her brow furrowed. It bothered her to no end that she had been so in the dark. "I'm still trying to figure it all out. There's a lot I need to make sense of, but if I find out anything, I'll certainly let you know. You should ask him before it's too late."

"I think he's cheating on me." The words erupted from Yolanda's mouth.

Denise's mouth dropped open. "Girl, stop. You're being crazy. Are we talking about the same man?"

"I know. But I saw him at the golf course, all cozy with a woman."

"He could have been working. You never know. You told me yourself that he was trying to get some forward momentum on things. Don't jump to conclusions."

"Something wasn't right about it," Yolanda said. "I can tell."

Just as Yolanda was about to elaborate, they heard their names being called from across the pool. They both cringed. "Oh, here comes the rest of the gang." She heard voices that she knew to be those of Samantha and Jillian.

"Yes, and apparently they don't know that this is supposed to be a dignified pool area." She snorted with laughter.

Yolanda waved and put her finger to her lips, shushing the two women as they approached. She pointed to the quiet area sign that hung on the gate.

"Loosen up. This is supposed to be fun," Denise said.

"No one expects us to take a vow of silence when we

come up in here," Samantha said. She led, as usual, with Jillian a close second, her face shrouded almost completely by her oversized sunglasses and floppy sun hat.

"I know, but that doesn't mean they have to sound like a pod of Sperm Whales. We come here to avoid the riff raff, so we shouldn't <u>be</u> the riff raff."

Jillian and Samantha surrounded them, sharing air kisses all around. They juggled chairs to rearranged them as Samantha pulled out her cell phone.

"No, Ma'am," Yolanda said. "You know the rules."

Samantha paused with her phone in midair. "Indeed, I do. What's got a stick up your butt all of a sudden?" The Beach Club had a strict no cell phone rule that they were all familiar with. To use your phone, it was common practice to step down off the pool veranda and onto the sand. They were supposed to talk in hushed tones at the adult pool to avoid disturbing the other members that had come to soak up the sun and just enjoy the serenity that the beach club provided, but they ignored that, too.

"It's nice to see you, too." Samantha's mouth was drawn into a thin line. "I'll be right back." She glared at Yolanda, heading for the steps that led off the veranda and onto the white hard-packed sand. She stood just on the other side of the barrier that ran the length of the massive deck, but still in earshot.

Before they could ask, the pool attendant rolled another umbrella into place.

"Excuse me, can I have a Mississippi Mudslinger?" Samantha yelled over her shoulder. "I'm going to take a call and I'll be back."

Yolanda laughed, "Not wasting any time, are you?"

"Nope, no need to. I only have a short time here."
Samantha's voice was loud, her phone still to her ear. "What are
you guys drinking?"

Denise rubbed her forehead that was still tight from her
shenanigans the night before. "I'm not sure but it won't be that. I
can't take the dairy."

"I hear you," Samantha said.

"Are your husbands joining us?" Yolanda asked.

Samantha shrugged, "I'm not sure what that man is going
to do. If he ever gets off the golf course, we may see him. I think
they played twenty-seven holes today. How about Darren?"

"He should be over shortly. He always likes to come."
The group immediately broke into laughter.

"Y'all are dumb." Samantha re-joined them, talking lower
as she got closer. She looked at Denise, flinching. "Oh, I'm sorry.
I hope that's not a soft spot."

"No, it's fine." She sipped her drink, wiping the sweat
from the glass on a beach towel. "I actually do have a guest. A
friend from college is going to join us."

Samantha nodded, "Oh I see. I know what time it is. Is it
that tall man with the great big boat, right." She elbowed
Yolanda.

Denise glared at Yolanda. "You can stop acting like you
have some news. You were there, remember? And there is
nothing more to it."

"What?" Yolanda replied, a sheepish grin on her face. "I
didn't say anything about your business. I'm not the only one
who was there, and people are talking about your break-ins all
the way to Charleston."

"Uhm huh, they are." She laid back on her chair, ready to

take anything they dished out. "His boat is quite large." A snicker travelled through the group. Samantha's phone buzzed and she jumped up again.

"Dang," Yolanda said. "You're pretty busy for this to technically be a non-work day."

"Well, technically, it's not work," Samantha replied, "But I have stuff to do, you know what I'm saying?"

Denise laughed. "It seems like none of us can have peace here anymore. What is it about this place?"

"We make it hard on ourselves," Yolanda said. "We keep our days packed full."

Denise wasn't sure who made it hard, but they all seemed to have something complicating going on in their lives lately, and she couldn't help but wonder how much of that was their own doing.

22
The Duchess of Delegation

In contrast to the melee taking place in the family pool, The Beach Club dining room was cool and serene. The room itself seemed sound-proofed from the children's screams, and soft music wafted through the air. The dress code was relaxed here. There were no jackets required and shorts were allowed, provided they came to mid-thigh or longer. Bathing suits had to be covered with a non-transparent outer garment. Combined, those two things helped to maintain the dignity that The Sanctuary properties were known for.

From any table in the room, the diners had an unobstructed view out over the white sands, dotted with beachcombers, and the Atlantic Ocean beyond. Although the room was air conditioned, large, slow moving fans suspended from the ceiling gave the illusion of air being circulated the old-fashioned, southern plantation way. Every time Denise was in the room, she imagined some old-soul standing over her and fanning with a feather fan on the end of a long stick, just far enough back to make one feel as if they were out of earshot and part of the decor.

It was easy to find the men. They were seated in the corner, where two of the glass walls intersected and due to an architecturally genius bend in the room, almost out of sight from the front door. As Denise and her friends rounded the corner,

Trent stood and pulled out a chair. Darren and Samantha's husband, Tino, looked on, but didn't stand. They nodded a dignified acknowledgment in the women's direction.

"I see you've met everyone," Denise said. She tried as hard as she could to control her face, but failed miserably. Her grin practically lit up the room. She couldn't help herself. The sight of Trent made her whole body feel warm like a shot of tequila. She blushed at the thought of feeling as much like a school girl as she did.

Trent nodded. "They were kind enough to welcome me in with no problem. We're just having a scotch."

Yolanda looked around, as if surveying the scene in front of her. "Or two. Looks like you all have been here awhile." She locked eyes with Darren. He was silent, sheepish even, and didn't stand or offer to pull out her chair as Trent had done for Denise.

Denise tried to keep a poker face as she watched the exchange between Yolanda and her husband. "Everything okay?" It was obvious that something was off between them.

"Everything is fine." Yolanda replied without taking here eyes away from Darren's. "Some of us do go to bed angry."

Darren cleared his throat. "Everything *is* fine.

Yolanda's mouth dropped open, then just as suddenly, she snapper her lips back together, closing it. She plastered a photoshoot smile on her face, then walked around the table to join her husband as if nothing were at all awkward.

"Hey, baby," she said. Her kiss only got as far as his cheek.

"I hope your game was good." Yolanda held his shoulder a little too tightly.

"It was," Darren said, glaring. "As expected."

What in the world was going on between the two of them? Denise wondered as she watched them. She looked from Yolanda to Darren, trying to see something in their faces that could clue her in. She'd seen more warmth in a Chicago snow drift, and for them, that was a change. Every other time she'd been around them, they at least acted like a couple, but this was an exchange between two people who were barely cordial to each other.

Denise sat in the chair that Trent was poised behind and let him push it in as the other men looked on. She flashed a smile. Courtesy was definitely a turn on.

"You're making us look bad, man," Tino said, laughing. The other men joined in.

"Nah," Trent said. "I'm just being a gentleman. You guys could take a lesson. You forget that you have to do something to keep 'em once you've got 'em."

"What?" Denise dropped her head to conceal her blushing. "That implies you've got me, whatever that means, and I think you should check with me first and not get too cocky."

Trent didn't have a chance to answer her.

"Where's my wife?" Tino interrupted. He looked past Yolanda and Denise. "Wasn't she with you?"

Yolanda motioned over her shoulder. "She's behind us. You know she can't stay off her phone, like a millennial." She rolled her eyes. A darkness passed over Tino.

They could hear the commotion before Samantha had rounded the corner. "Here she comes now. Can't you hear her?" They all turned to look towards the front door, just in time to see Samantha come in. She was laughing as loud as she had been outside, but this time, she was talking to someone they couldn't see.

"Hey, everybody. Have you ordered already?" Her heavy voice seemed to bounce off the walls. Samantha made her way around the table, leaving her friend standing on the other side.

"Samantha, can you please—"

"Okay, Yolanda, I get it. I'll do better." Samantha kissed her husband. He stared straight ahead, past his wife.

"Doubtful." Yolanda made a face at Denise, who suppressed a smile.

Samantha sneered in Yolanda's direction. "You should be grateful. I'm working on your party." She waved her phone at Yolanda.

"Since when is it my party? It's everyone's party. Maybe it used to be—"

"Really?" Samantha said. "It may no longer be at your house, but it's still your party. You're the one who's the 'Grand Duchess' of this island." She made quotes in the air with her fingers.

Everyone's heads whipped around.

"The what?" Denise said.

"C'mon, woman. Don't play innocent," Samantha said. "I know I'm only on the outskirts of your little group, but I know what time it is. Y'all are making me crazy. I'm glad to be included but it feels like I am doing all the work. That's what these phone calls are. Your vendors." She tapped on the table with every word. "Whatever happened to just a fun, summer get-together at someone's house? That's what used to happen when we first started coming here."

"It has gotten out of hand," Yolanda replied. "But I had

nothing to do with that. It's just too big for my house now."

"You ladies invite everyone for miles," Darren said. "We had to clean up for days after that party." He barely looked up from his phone screen.

"Sounds like something," Trent said.

"It <u>was</u> something when it was at our place," Yolanda smiled.

"You're not fooling anyone, Yolanda," Samantha said. "You're still pulling all the strings. Do you know how many times Malika Lavigne has called me in the last three hours? You've got her running--"

"Malika?" Denise asked.

"Oh, honey," Samantha said. "Don't you know about your friend, here?" She turned to her husband. "Babe, please get me a drink." She paused just long enough to get the words out. "Yolanda is a task master. She gave us a to-do list a mile long. The Duchess of Delegation. She didn't give you a job?"

"My job is day of," Denise said. "Trash duty."

Samantha guffawed. "Oh, girl, I'm sorry." She looked from Denise to Yolanda. "I thought y'all were friends? Or maybe I'm not. You won't be running yourself crazy trying to get things together. I mean, it's not like there are trash emergencies, right? You'd think this party was the wedding of the century instead of just a simple Southern Barbecue."

"Simple?" Yolanda sorted. "Nothing about my parties are simple."

Samantha slammed the table with her palm so hard that all of the silverware jumped. "See what I'm saying? <u>Her</u> party. She said it and y'all heard it. Just wait until Malika gets here."

"Malika?" Darren suddenly looked interested in the

conversation.

Denise took in the exchange, her eyes grazing from face to face. Darren put his phone down and seemed like he might actually engage with the group for the first time since they'd arrived.

"What about me?"

They all turned to look towards the voice that had interjected itself into their conversation.

In the midst of all the commotion, Malika had floated in so quietly that none of them had noticed. "Are there any seats left? Not planning on staying long."

Samantha stood. "I'm so glad you could join us." She air kissed at Malika, first one cheek, then the other. "I asked Malika to come. I thought it would be easier than the hundreds of phone calls, you know, since the phone police have taken up residence on this end of Kiawah and all." She glared at Yolanda, then winked. "I hope that's okay with everyone."

"Why wouldn't it be?" Yolanda hugged Malika. "The more, the merrier. I'm glad you were on the island so you could come over. I know how busy you are."

Malika smiled. "Busier at night. And I have a good team. I was actually here at Fresh Fields meeting a client." The Fresh Fields shopping center was right outside the entrance to the island.

A waiter brought a chair over and Malika shimmied it up to the table, next to Samantha. "Can you bring me a glass of Prosecco, please? Separate tab, okay?"

Yolanda smiled. "So, you still keep a membership here?"

"Of course. I didn't sell it with the house. That way, I get to meet clients here if I need to."

"I thought you had to be a homeowner to be a member?" Samantha asked.

Malika flashed a smile. "There are ways around everything, my dear."

"Wouldn't most of your clients meet you at the Inn?" Denise frowned.

"You'd be surprised." Malika turned towards Darren. "Hey, you're awfully quiet."

"I have nothing to say when all of you ladies are around. It takes everything I have just to speak up." He fidgeted in his seat, then stood. "Excuse me a minute, please?" He waved his phone back and forth in the air.

Denise and Trent exchanged glances. *That was odd*, Denise thought. Darren had damn near run out of the room.

"Was it something I said?" Malika chuckled. "Oh well. Can we talk party? I have to get back into town early."

Yolanda stared in the direction her husband had gone, a look of confusion on her face. She shrugged. "I have no idea why he would be in such a hurry. He's been acting a little strange lately. Who knows?"

Samantha was too oblivious to be concerned with Darren's exit. She leaned in, her head almost touching Malika's. They poured over their planning list together and were immediately engaged in deep thought.

Denise looked from Yolanda to Malika and finally to Samantha, trying to make sense of things. She noted the look of pain on her friend's face and the way that Tino was alternating between staring down at his phone and scowling in his wife's direction. He was completely disengaged from what was going on around him and Denise could read every emotion that flashed across his face. Watching now, it felt like everyone in the room was fighting some kind of private battle. She tapped Yolanda on the arm. "You good?"

Denise's touch activated Yolanda as if it were electricity, causing her to jump. "Oh, yeah, girl. I'm fine. Why wouldn't I be?"

Denise shrugged. "You tell me. Did we do something to offend Darren? He left so fast."

Yolanda shook her head. "I barely have time to figure out what is going on inside that man's head. As a matter of fact, I'm surprised he's here at all."

"As long as you're good." She used her head to motion in the direction of Samantha and Malika. "They seem to be very invested in the party. You got yourself a good committee."

"I guess." She shrugged. "My head wasn't in it as much this year, and those two volunteered to handle it. I was just giving Samantha a hard time earlier. I'm grateful for her help."

"Nice for you," Denise said. "We all've had a rough year."

"Tell me about it. And they go way back, so they work well together."

"Way back?"

"I don't know, they just seem real tight. It's good."

Denise nodded. "A win-win all around, but I see how I got trash duty."

"You're still there? I thought you were past that." Yolanda laughed. "Just remember you were here first, okay. This is going to be the best party yet."

"Can't wait," Denise said. She had a feeling that it would be.

23
A Bit of A Barge

They circled the parking lot at the marina looking for a space. Denise sighed. She leaned against the car door, one hand touching the temple as if in pain as she watched Trent maneuver. She couldn't believe that she'd let Trent actually convince her to go to his boat. She hadn't been to the marina nor on a boat since her husband died and the memories were flooding back the closer they got. She rubbed her stomach, trying to quell the queasiness she was feeling.

Trent glanced over at her, narrowing his eyes. "If you'd rather go home—"

"No. I'm good," she lied. She was far from good. She dreaded stepping foot on Trent's boat, or any boat, but she needed to focus. It felt like she was already being side-tracked from her main goal of finding what happened to the missing money. There were people that were depending on her, so she was just going to have to get over herself. Trent was trying to help her. The past was the past, right? Denise had a feeling that if she didn't figure out what had happened to Charles, no one else would. She'd forever feel responsible for having ruined the retirement dreams of at least twenty-three people.

"Are you sure you're ready to do this? We don't have to, you know," Trent asked again.

Denise shook her head, "No, it's fine really. I have to do this. I really am grateful that you want to help. Plus, you said you have access to the internet on that barge of yours."

"Barge? I might be offended." Trent smiled and Denise's anxiety abated just a little bit. "But yes, I have internet access and my screen will be much bigger than the one on that phone of yours. We're too old to try and do anything serious on those tiny screens.

Denise took a deep breath. Humor hadn't failed her yet. "As I was saying...your boat has internet service, so I think this is where I need to be right now to find out what I need to know. Besides, I'm not ready to go back to my house yet. Nothing is back up and running. I have no internet, no phone. Nothing." Denise paused, amazed at herself for even being able to voice that so soon. The break-in at her house had left her feeling violated. "It doesn't feel like the police are actually doing anything to help, you know?"

Trent did know. The feeling of being abandoned was not uncommon in victims. "You never can tell. They usually don't tell you every step they're taking. Sometimes they have to act first and explain later."

"I'm supposed to trust that? This island was supposed to be a safe place, Trent." Her voice caught in her throat.

"Being safe and being your sanctuary aren't the same thing."

Denise nodded. "I've never thought of it that way before. This has always been a special place to me."

"I can tell that," Trent said. "But not everyone may feel

that way. It's clear they don't. My gut says there's an agenda here that has nothing to do with this place being a Sanctuary or anything like that."

"Our guts are in agreement, then," Denise said. They had been on the same wave length all night.

Earlier, they'd sat back and watched the other people leave the Beach Club. They stayed until they were the last two of their party left. Her friends thought it was because they were love birds, but really they'd been observing everyone else. They'd both noticed how uncomfortable Darren had become when Malika arrived. "What do you think was the deal with Darren?" Denise asked. "And did you see how weird Samantha and Tino were together?"

Trent shrugged. "Yeah, it was strange. All of them were."

"And that thing with Samantha. Obvious tension. I feel like an outsider with Malika and Samantha together. That certainly isn't the way I am used to Yolanda and Darren acting. He's often distant, but they are definitely into each other."

"I'm sure you would have liked to be a fly on that wall."

"Yolanda did say she thought he might be cheating on her, but I doubt it. There's a story there. We're having dinner, so hopefully I will get more insight. It's too much of a coincidence that everyone is acting weird at the same time."

Trent pulled into a parking spot finally and came around to Denise's side of the truck to open her door. He held her hand as she tried to hop down, practically throwing herself out.

"I'm never going to get used to that."

"Hmph. Yeah, in hindsight it's probably not the most practical vehicle. I don't use it for anything. I don't work on a farm and I really can't even pull my boat with this truck."

"Boys will be boys."

"Who would you rather them be?"

Denise blushed. "As much as I want to take that bait, we need to be serious now."

The gate that separated the floating pier and the marina clicked shut behind them as they walked through. Although it was supposed to be high season, the place was eerily peaceful. The click of Denise's shoes resounded on the wooden deck. There was no one at the marina window. Trent stopped, knocking on it with his knuckles. After a few seconds, it slid open and the guy that he'd met before stuck his head out.

"Hey. Good to see you again, guy. Got a guest I see." He titled his head towards Denise.

"Yeah, I do." Trent's mouth was drawn into a thin line. He wasn't about to offer any more information than that.

Trent signed himself in and handed the pen to Denise to follow suit. As they made their way to the end of the pier, the sound of water sloshing against the hull grew louder. "This looks a lot bigger close up," Denise said. "It must be the biggest one here."

Trent shrugged. "I didn't notice. It might be though. Most of the people that keep their boats here have houses nearby. I don't imagine they have much need for a big boat when they live up the street."

"And do you live on yours?"

"Whenever I need to." Trent grew silent.

"Okay." Denise raised an eyebrow. "That's cryptic. So you're a like a pubescent couch surfer?"

"I follow the job. Sometimes I'm on the boat, sometimes I'm in a hotel."

"Must be nice. Sounds like an expensive way to live."

"Yeah, it is. I got a huge settlement when my wife died. I needed some toys and I have no other responsibilities. So now you have *The Timber Wolf*." He motioned towards the words painted on the stern of the boat.

"Oh really? The Timber Wolf? That's uh creative. Not." The wolf was the mascot of their alma mater, Loyola.

Trent shrugged, "It was a good time in my life so it made sense to me. I was lacking in creativity that day." He chuckled. "Besides, wolves are loners and you know they survived a lot of change. So, I figured it made sense for me to name my boat after my spirit animal."

"Your spirit what? You're really trying to relive the college glory days, huh?" A memory of Trent on the basketball court flashed in her head. Back in the day, the crowd used to cheer for him, especially since their team had been a winning one. Denise walked from end to end of the deck admiring the boat from all sides. "This is a huge undertaking and has to be expensive to maintain."

"Yeah, it's sort of a money pit," Trent agreed. "But since I live on it a lot of the time it serves its purpose. I get a tax write-off and major relaxation." He made way for her to get onto the boat. "After you. You can leave your shoes at the back end."

Denise had already started removing them. She remembered the boat etiquette quite well. She'd seen Charles nearly lose his mind when a visitor wearing hard-soled shoes hadn't taken them off as they boarded his boat.

She followed Trent across the deck and down the four steps into the cabin. Denise took it all in. The interior was masculine and nicely appointed. The modern colors were juxtaposed with burl wood, not unlike the inside of a classic Jaguar. He grunted her approval of Trent's taste. The control room was in the bow of the boat. Trent moved a sliding door to the right and stepped inside.

Denise looked around. "Wow, this is something." The triangular room was flanked with several different kinds of machines, satellite, more than one computer and one radio.

"It looks like you are preparing for the Apocalypse."

"Yeah, something like that." Trent moved forward and flipped a switch. "I admit I've become a bit of a prepper. If you look hard you'll find disaster supplies on here, too."

"I can tell. I bet you could survive for weeks on here without leaving."

"Maybe." He paused. "Let's just say that all of this hardware is not standard issue. I've got friends in high places."

"You must have something because I have not seen anything like this outside of a surveillance van on TV." She reached her hand forward towards the console. Trent stopped her by resting his hand on hers.

"Not exactly standard issue, I know. But in many cases, I get hired to figure out all sorts of things and I need to be able to listen to systems, do a little hacking."

"So, break into stuff?"

He smirked. "That sounds so illegal." He paused. "But yeah."

"Look at this," Trent said. Denise walked over to him. "She told us that she was born Mandy Johnson. What else do we know about Mrs. Lavigne?" he asked.

Denise snuggled in behind him looking over his shoulder to view the computer screen. "Not much. I think she said she was from some little town in South Carolina. Traveler's Rest, or something like that."

Trent nodded, "Yeah, that's it." He typed in Traveler's Rest into his browser and also added Mandy Johnson to the search. A few articles popped up but nothing seemed really important at first. He scrolled down the page.

"Look at this. *Preacher's Daughter Taken in By Authorities.* He clicked on the headline. A picture appeared.

"Oh look. This looks like her. It's an old picture and she's not wearing any make-up but it's certainly her. She was much, much younger here."

Trent leaned in. "Yes. You're right. I think that's her." He opened the article and they read it together. "Apparently she was taken into foster care at an early age."

"Wow, that's sad," Denise said.

"Yeah, those types of things always leave their marks on people."

"What do you think her marks are?" she asked.

"Not sure. "He paused." Whatever it is, I think it has something to do with Charles."

"She's shady. I can feel it in my bones." Denise paused, tapping her finger to her temple.

"What?"

"Something is missing." She shrugged. "It'll come out. It always does. She made a point of telling us that she created this

whole new persona of Malika Lavigne. And that her husband,
Damian helped her do it. What was she running from?"

"People are always running from something."

"Search her current name now," Denise said.

Trent nodded, then typed in the woman's name. Unlike
the first time, pages and pages of search results came back. "She's
been busy." He scrolled down the page.

"Apparently so," Denise agreed. "Switch to the images
tab. Maybe that will help us see something that makes sense."

Trent clicked over to the images that had come up and
scrolled through. There wasn't much that either of them
recognized at first.

"Wait," Denise grabbed his arm. "Click on that one." She
pointed to a thumbnail that had no caption. There looked to be a
crowd of people at a formal event in the picture.

Trent enlarged the image. They stared at a group of men
in tuxedos posing for the camera.

"Can you make it bigger?" Denise asked. Her heart
missed a beat.

Trent double-clicked to enlarge the photo. Off to the left,
Malika Lavigne came into view. "In the second line it says
'Malika Lavigne in the background.' Doesn't say anything else
though."

"Can we tell where this was?" Denise asked. "Who's she
with?" She didn't expect a caption to tell her everything. As she
searched the picture, she tried to quell the unease in her stomach.

"Some charity event in Charleston," Trent said. "I'll make
it bigger." He clicked on the picture.

Malika Lavigne was standing between two men. Denise
strained to make out the details. She tapped on the screen with

her fingernail. "I'm pretty sure this is Charles next to her." Her heart sank. More secrets.

"Do you remember ever going to an event like this?"

Dense shook her head. "I can say with certainty that I was not at whatever this is. This looks to be a Red and White ball. I've never been to one of these in Charleston. I would have remembered, especially if my husband was hugged up with some woman. I had only just heard of Malika before this weekend and had never met her in person."

"Don't let your imagination get away from you. There's three of them." He leaned in. "This looks like Darren to me. Take a look."

"Me, too. Try adding Planter's Inn to the search."

He did, then added the name of Malika's husband. A whole new crop of hits came up. "Look here," Trent said. "Damien Lavigne owned a string of small hotels all across the south just like The Planter's Inn."

"Wow. He must have been loaded."

Trent continued. "Apparently he was. There were 32 of them in all. None of them really big or affiliated with any chains or anything."

"That's a lot of properties to look after. Wasn't he older than her?"

"He was," Denise said. "I didn't know her well, but I know they talked about it all the time on the Island. Their May-December relationship. What are you getting at?"

"Well, seems like with that many hotels, he would have had a business partner, or he would have been very busy, don't you think?"

The buzz of Denise's' phone punctuated their exchange.

"One second. Hold that thought." She held up her finger like she was in church, asking for forgiveness for walking around during the sermon. "I have to take this." Denise put her phone on speaker. She hadn't spoken to Jamel in a day or so and she really needed to know what was going on back at the office.

"What's up?" she asked.

"Well, we've been doing some digging and found out some things you need to know," Jamel said.

Trent leaned in, listening intently.

"Oh really?" Denise could feel a headache coming on. Just being removed from the Chicago office had helped her make that part of the whole thing feel less personal. "Tell me." She really didn't want to hear any more bad news.

"Well, as it turns out, that transfer that we saw, it wasn't the first one."

"It wasn't?"

"No. There were a series of transfers going back a number of months, four to be exact. They were exactly eight weeks apart."

"Huh. That's interesting. So, were they all going to the same place?"

"We're not really sure. It looks like they were but you know with Bitcoin accounts you can never tell who's the sender and who's the receiver. That's why people do this. It makes them hard to find.

"All we know is that they all went out from the retirement account, to accounts that your husband had and then gone - poof. We followed the trail of money until we lost it."

Denise's heart sank. This was more complicated than she expected.

Jamel's voice was strained as he repeated the facts. "Seems like Charles was in deep."

Denise and Trent's eyes locked.

Jamel continued. "I don't know. I don't want to accuse anybody. I loved Charles like a brother. I just can't believe he would do this to us all. I mean, I'm young but what about some of the older people in this place? They had transferred their retirement funds here and it was everything they had. I don't know what I'm going to do. Just yesterday I had to talk someone off the ledge."

"What? What are you saying? Talk someone off the ledge?"

"Yeah. Sam down in marketing. He was ready to jump in front of a train. He still hadn't told his wife what happened and now they don't know what they're going to do. He was ready to retire and he'll have to work until he dies now."

His words were like a punch to the gut. "Okay, Jamel. Thank you for the update. We're working on it here and hopefully we'll have some news soon."

"Oh, one more thing."

What now? Denise thought.

He hesitated. "You might want to sit down for this. That detective came by. The investigator? The one who was here earlier. He had more questions. Apparently that finger that they found? It did belong to Charles."

24
Straight to the Source

Yolanda perused the menu alone while she waited for Denise.

"Are there going to be four of you?" the waiter asked.

Yolanda shook her head. "Just three." She was looking forward to having dinner with her friends. She needed the respite they provided. She was supposed to be having fun planning the summer party of the year and instead she was tied up in knots as she tried to figure out what in the hell her husband was up to.

She looked up just as Denise walked through the door. Yolanda waved, and a broad smile spread across Denise's face. She waved back and made her way through the tables, heading in Yolanda's direction.

"Hey, girl," Denise said. "Sorry, I'm late."

They hugged, air kissing each other's cheeks. "No worries, cher," Yolanda said. "You know we could have come together."

"I know, but I had some things to take care of."

"I'm sure I'll hear all about it."

Denise's face flushed, but she didn't respond. "Why are you staring at me?"

"Am I? Not my intentions to stare, cher. I'm just making sure you're good, you know. I'm here when you need to talk."

Denise nodded. "I will. When I'm ready. I'm not there

yet."

Samantha called to them from across the room, saving her from explanations. "Hey. Sorry," she said. "I couldn't get myself together this morning."

Yolanda looked her up and down. "You seem to have done just fine. I'm flattered that you did so much just to get together with us. You look like you're getting ready to go out on a date or something."

Denise laughed. "Yeah, she sure does."

Samantha waved away their comments. "You know sometimes date night is the way to go. Tino and I have some special plans later. You know how he can be." She made her rounds, exchanging air kisses with each of them before she finally pulled out her chair to join them at the table.

Denise and Yolanda glanced at each other. "Yes, we do. He doesn't let you get far, does he?"

Samantha waved her away again, "You know. Same old, same old. He's got to be a part of everything in my life and when he's not, he thinks I'm up to something."

"Well, in my experience, a man is only jealous when he has a reason to be," Yolanda said.

Denise and Yolanda exchanged glances again. "<u>Does</u> he have a reason to be?"

Samantha laughed, looking from one friend to the other. "You guys have too active an imagination. What would he have to be jealous of? He's my boo, you know that."

Denise shrugged. "I don't know. You tell us."

A hint of a smile appeared on Samantha's face. "I'm telling you, there's nothing. He's always been the way he is."

"Really?" Denise said. "I don't remember him being so

clingy last summer."

"Yeah, well. You know how it is as men get older. Maybe this is part of his midlife crisis or something."

The waiter returned, interrupting them. "Here you go, ladies. I hope these will work for you." He placed a glass of wine in front of each of them.

"Oh, good," Yolanda said. "I hope you don't mind that I ordered some drinks for us. I knew it would take you both awhile to settle in."

The conversations stopped as they touched their glasses to each other's. Samantha's face relaxed, seemingly relieved to be out from under the spotlight. "How's Darren?" she asked.

"I don't know. You know, ups and downs. Some days I actually think he may be cheating on me." Yolanda took a big gulp of her wine. She had no intention of sharing all of that information when she'd come in, but now that she said it, it felt as if a weight was lifted off of her.

Both Samantha and Denise gasped, training their eyes on her.

"What are you saying?" Samantha asked. "I can't imagine that Darren is cheating on you at all. He's so committed to you in every way. I think you're over reacting."

"I don't know." Yolanda shook her head. "He's been really secretive lately."

Denise interrupted, "He's always secretive about his work."

Yolanda shrugged. "Maybe. But this time it's really bad. My gut says there's something going on that shouldn't be."

"How'd you get from something going on to cheating?" Denise asked. "Maybe if this was zero to one hundred, but how far off is his behavior from normal for you? You said you never have an idea what's going on."

"This is worse. This is different. Bill collectors are calling and he says they're not. He claims that he's on top of things and then he's not. And then..." Both ladies turned to their friend, quiet. Yolanda paused and sighed heavily. "I saw him with another woman."

Samantha almost choked on her drink. She grabbed her napkin and dabbed at the sides of her mouth, trying to wipe away the spills. "What do you mean? Who was it?"

Yolanda tried to hold back the tears that had come to her eyes. "I don't know. I couldn't really see her. They were across the room. I just know I didn't know who she was."

"Then how do you know he's cheating if you didn't see him?" Denise asked. "I mean, saying you *saw* him cheating means he was butt-naked in a room making the beast with two backs. What you saw was lunch."

Yolanda shook her head. "Maybe, but I have a feeling I saw a whole lot more than just a meal. It was before seven in the morning, at the golf club."

Samantha's eyebrows raised.

"You know he likes to play golf at dawn. It was very early in the morning. His back was to me so he didn't see me. I know it was him, though. He was seated with her in a corner."

Denise cleared her throat. "Could you see her? What can you tell me about her? Are you sure you didn't recognize her? Between the three of us, we know everybody."

"Exactly. And she didn't even look vaguely familiar. That's just it," Yolanda said. "I can't tell you anything. I didn't know who she was. It was too far away but I know he normally doesn't do things like that. He doesn't meet a woman first thing in the morning who has on heels and not golf clothes at the golf club. What's going on with that?"

"Where were his friends?" asked Denise. "He wasn't playing alone."

"No, he wasn't," Yolanda replied. "I actually was planning to play with him. But, that's just it. They all acted like nothing happened. If that's not proof in itself that something is going on, I don't know what else would be."

"Maybe it was a business meeting. Maybe he's just preoccupied with whatever he's working on. You know it has been tough on him since Charles disappeared."

Yolanda shook her head. "I hope you're right, Denise. I really do." She wanted to believe in the good, too.

"Well, speaking of that. I have some news." Denise said.

"Oh, you're going to tell us more about you and Trent?" Samantha asked.

"You know that is really not your business and no that's not it."

"Oh, it's like that?" Yolanda said, her mouth turned up in a half-smile.

Denise rolled her eyes. "I promise if there is something worth telling there, you will be the first to know." There was a glint of sparkle in her eyes for a moment. "Actually, I have news about Charles."

"What is it?"

"Well, they found a finger and the finger belongs to him. To top it off, yes, the money that has been missing from his business was transferred by him, and it's not the first time. So, now I'm not even sure if his last transfer was planned before he died - before he left, or whatever happened. It could have been a recurring transfer." For a minute all three ladies were silent.

"Do you have any idea where the money was going?" Samantha asked.

"None at all." She paused. "All I know is that it's gone and I also found out that he had a place at The Planter's Inn. Did you even know about the Inn?"

"The Planter's Inn," Yolanda replied. "What? You mean that place that Malika owns?"

"Yes, but apparently there's a whole social club upstairs."

They were silent for a minute again and finally Samantha said, "I knew about it."

Both Yolanda and Denise's heads whipped around in her direction. "You knew what?" Denise asked.

"I knew that there was a social club there. I didn't know anything about Charles, of course, but I knew that there was something going on. You know that Malika and I are friends. I've actually been to a party there."

"You're kidding," Denise said. "You didn't share any of that with us before."

Samantha shrugged. "I had no reason to. I went once and I've never been back. I'm surprised that you guys didn't know about it."

"Why would we?" Yolanda asked.

Samantha sipped her drink. "The time I was there, I saw both Darren and Charles there. They were together."

"You saw <u>my</u> Darren there?" Yolanda's face darkened. "Are you sure? Why would he be there without me?"

"I can't tell you that," Samantha said. "I didn't talk to them."

"Was this a ball of some type?"

Samantha nodded. "It was. I think they were trying to raise funds or something. I didn't talk to either of them that night. They spent a lot of time with Malika. She was introducing them to people, if I remember correctly."

"And you didn't think to mention this to either of us?" There was more than a hint of annoyance in Denise's voice.

"Don't be upset with me." Samantha said. "We didn't see each other, and then Charles disappeared. A lot was happening. We just kept moving forward and in the scheme of things, it no longer seemed important. I'm sorry."

"We'll have to deal with that part later. Denise, please finish your story." Yolanda's nose flared. "Let's not get sidetracked."

"I see," Denise said. "So, in addition to being at the social club for a party I didn't get invited to, he was a member there and had a secret locker. And in this secret locker, I found these rings."

"Wait, what?" Yolanda said. "Rings? What kind of rings? Engagement rings?" Her breath quickened.

"They just looked like metal rings." Denise looked perplexed. "It didn't look like there was much more to it than that."

Yolanda's eyes narrowed. "Did you look closely? I know that when I was looking in Darren's computer, he had lots of diagrams with circles. I thought they were just doodles, but what if it wasn't that? What if it was these rings?"

They were silent for a minute, as Samantha sipped her wine. "You know, I think I do remember that they were working on some biometric thing. I overheard that word."

"Biometrics," Yolanda said, "Like on Star Trek?"

Samantha shrugged. "I told you I wasn't interested. As long as I have known Malika, she always has some hustle going. That woman believes in multiple streams of income."

"What if the rings and biometrics have something to do with each other? Yolanda, do you remember anything in Darren's files about that?" Denise made herself a note to look closer at the rings to see if there were any more clues.

"I told you, none of it made much sense to me. I was so nervous just looking at his computer, you know what I mean? I felt like an intruder in my own home," Yolanda said.

"I think I have to go." Denise gathered her things. She had to know if the rings and biometrics were related. Her gut said yes.

"But you just got here." Yolanda pouted like she was four years old. "We need this ladies night."

"We do, but do you think you can ask Darren if he was working on a biometrics project with Charles? I'm going to have someone look at the rings a little closer. I'm also going to ask Malika a few questions. I think there's more there."

Samantha pursed her lips. "More like what? You saw a few pictures on the internet. Obviously, that wasn't a secret or it wouldn't have been on the web. If nothing else, Malika can keep secrets. I've known her a long time and I can tell you that there are things that she knows that will never be told."

Denise waved to the waiter for her check. "That sounds like the most true thing I have heard all night." She paused. "You know, I still need to ask her. And there is nothing better than going straight to the source."

25
Money and Husbands

Something didn't feel right to Trent. Malika Lavigne had been kind and welcoming when they were at the Inn, but she had been a little too smug at the Beach Club for his taste. Trent thought about how almost condescending she'd been and understood why Denise didn't trust the woman.

The shadows of the trees haunted him as he headed back towards Charleston. He had to talk to her again. It was probably a bad idea not to include Denise, but she was too emotional for her own good. That woman was somehow connected to the break-in. It was too convenient that it happened while they were in town at the Planter's Inn, and he didn't believe in coincidences. There had to be a logical explanation for how they had known just how long Denise would be gone, and he would bet that Malika was part of the equation.

Kiawah wasn't the kind of place that had too many smash and grabs in broad daylight, so his bet was on some kind of inside job. It didn't add up. There were guard gates and security everywhere and no one had seen the people who'd broken in at all, coming or going. It had to be too easy to get through those sliding doors that led to the back, almost like they'd had a master key or someone had let them in.

Trent pulled into the parking lot around the Planter's Inn again. There was no cop on horseback like before, but he had no time to worry about his car as he had before. It was much earlier in the day, just past noon, and the streets were packed with people going back and forth to the markets. He took it all in as he passed.

A Gullah woman sat on the corner, her wide skirt covering all of her lower body, including her feet. She was perched on a stool, a half-finished basket between her legs and another half dozen or so smaller woven bowls, in greens and browns, surrounded her. She barely looked up as he passed, instead concentrating on completing the basket she worked on. Trent cleared his throat as he walked, without slowing down. He adjusted the strap on the satchel he was carrying, moving back around towards his front. He had no desire to engage with the woman and was not in the market for anything she was selling.

The Inn was as picturesque as it had been the first time he'd come and he still felt as if he was walking into an old-time speakeasy, but he hadn't expected to be back so soon. The large door was impenetrable to bending sunlight. Stepping through the door was akin to stepping into another universe. Blinded by the dark, Trent blinked, then rubbed his eyes, to let them adjust to his surroundings.

As before, Malika was easy to spot. She was at the back, arms folded across her chest. It appeared that she was talking with a woman, but was far enough away that Trent couldn't make out what they were saying. He stepped to the side to watch her for a bit from there. The dark-haired woman looked irritated, her head moving back and forth in a way that suggested that they might be arguing. From what he could tell, Malika was keeping her cool pretty well for someone to be yelling in her face. Every few minutes, she'd nod, either to placate or to agree, maybe both, and made movements with her hands as if to physically smooth out the tension between them.

Malika finally looked up. Trent nodded. A flicker of tension passed over Malika's face, then she recovered quickly, but not before Trent could see it. The woman she was talking to kept talking and didn't notice at first, but she finally looked away from Malika and followed her gaze, eventually focusing on Trent, too. She stopped talking, then turned on her heels and disappeared through the curtain at the back of the room.

Malika put a smile on her face as if it were a mask. "Well, hello," she said, walking towards him. "I wasn't expecting you—"

Denise burst through the door. Both Trent and Malika jumped.

Malika quickly regained her composure. "Denise. I should have known you'd be here soon. I wasn't expecting to see Trent here without you."

"What's going on?" Trent asked. "You didn't tell me you wanted to come to Charleston. We could have come together."

"Could we have?" Denise glared at him. "Did you think you would do this by yourself? Why would you think that?" She demanded.

"Uhm, what are you talking about? There are things that we talked about yesterday and I wanted to ask Malika myself."

"I see," she said. "So, you're still investigating me, then? What happened to wanting to help me find closure and all that crap you were talking yesterday?"

Trent looked from Malika to Denise. "Can we talk about this later? I was just about to talk with Malika and ask her some questions."

"Were you now?" Malika said. "How can I help you? I don't want to be in the middle of a lover's quarrel. You two should handle that."

Denise shot daggers with her eyes. "Trent, I'm sure you have a lot to discuss, but you know this isn't your investigation to conduct, right? You said you weren't investigating me anymore. That you hadn't taken that job." She paused, her eyes boring holes in Trent's face. "Are you sure that's the case, Trent? You seem to be very invested in <u>my</u> business."

Trent moved closer to Denise, putting his hands on her shoulders. "Babe, I'm as invested in it as you are."

"Please don't call me that."

"Call you what?"

"Babe. Pet names. I don't like it."

"Okay." Trent's voice was filled with hesitation. He wasn't quite sure what he'd done to make Denise so angry.

"I don't need you to save me."

"I'm sorry. I only want to find out what happened to help make things easier for you. You're so stressed."

"You know what? I'm not your woman. I'm not your girlfriend. I'm not sure that I'm even your friend."

"Okay. I get it." Trent nodded. He tried to keep a neutral face but Denise was making it hard.

She continued. "We don't have that kind of relationship. I do appreciate your help but you've overstepped this time."

"I'm sorry, then." He apologized again. The last thing he wanted was to push her away. "Please tell me what you need me to do."

"I don't have to tell you anything."

"Okay, then," Malika interrupted, "It looks like I'm in the

middle of something that I shouldn't be in the middle of here. Maybe we should go upstairs and talk about it."

Denise looked around. "I don't want to go upstairs and talk about anything. I need some answers and I need them now."

Trent touched Denise's elbow, willing her to calm down with his eyes. "Denise, please let me."

She paused for a minute, looked from Malika to Trent, then nodded.

"Okay," Malika said. "Answers to what exactly?"

Trent took a deep breath. "Malika, it looks like your husband owned a whole lot of hotels. You want to tell me what happened to them?"

Malika paused, "I don't see how that is any of your business, but if you must know, I sold them. I had no desire to be in the hotel business on that scale."

"Well that means you are a very wealthy woman then, right? They must have gotten you a good chunk of change." Denise crossed her arms over her chest.

"None of that is a secret. What is your point?" Malika struggled to maintain her composure. "I really don't have time to sit here and be grilled by you for no apparent reason. You're not even a cop, are you?"

Trent shook his head. "It's not my intention to make you feel grilled. And I assure you, I am not a cop. What I am is curious. I was paying attention at The Beach Club and it seems like when you came into the room, Darren left. I'd love to know what's going on."

"Did you think to ask him what was his issue? It seems like he was having a problem, not me. And what does my dead husband's holdings have to do with someone who apparently has a chip on their shoulder about heaven knows what?"

Malika walked towards the side of the room. "I really can't tell you anything about Darren. I can only talk about me." She paused. "And if you must know, it's public knowledge what happened to those hotels."

"We missed it," Denise said.

Trent and Denise made eye contact, and he could tell that she was not buying the story that Malika was telling, either.

"I sold those properties. Every last one, except this one. My husband was in a funny business that I did not necessarily want to be in. It didn't go with my brand."

"So, they didn't fit with new Malika?" There was a glint in Denise's eyes.

"No, they didn't."

"Was the brand more in line with <u>Mandy</u>, then?" Trent drew out the name as if he were savoring it.

"That's really not your business. I left Mandy in the dust a long time ago, and I'm not quite sure what you're implying. Malika Lavigne is a new and different kind of person."

"I see," said Trent. "So why did you keep Planter's Inn?"

Malika laughed. "Why not? I like Charleston. It's a charming place. It's beautiful here. And my husband bought it for me. He left me—"

"I thought he had a heart attack," Denise said.

"He left the Inn to me."

Trent and Denise exchanged glances.

"He left you an Inn. That's very nice." Denise rolled her eyes. "Did you know this wasn't always a beautiful place? For many years, there was a very seedy business going on upstairs.

"I didn't know anything about that. And no, that wasn't

how he operated this business. We used to come here all the time."

"Not how he operated this business, but the others..." Trent said.

A flash of frustration flickered on Malika's face. "I found out what my husband did long after he was dead. I was as surprised as anyone. I kept this one because I thought I could upgrade it into something more meaningful. Something that served the community."

"Hmph," Trent laughed. "Is that what you do? You serve the community? Tell me how exactly. What can you do for me upstairs?"

Malika looked offended. "I personally can do nothing for you. And again, I don't like what I think you're implying. I also don't think your girlfriend here would like it either. Actually, I told you I make fantasies come true. Whether you're a businessman who needs a place to take a meeting, a place to get away and bring your mistress, or you're a woman that's looking for company, it's none of my business. I just make things happen, that's all."

"Hmm. So, you're a Madam then?" Trent asked.

"I already told you, I'm not in the business my husband was in at all. He ran a line of sleazy, roach-infested motels where people could rent by the hour. This is not that kind of establishment. You've seen that yourself. I run a Country Club-Like place of business."

"Oh, that's good then," Denise said. "I'm so relieved you aren't running a brothel."

Malika laughed. "A brothel? You must be reading too many smut novels. I'm like a We Work hotel. I provide a place where people can facilitate meetings or do whatever they need to do, and beyond that, I mind my business."

She walked deeper into the Inn. Trent and Denise followed. Malika paused near the bar, motioning to the bartender. He immediately poured a glass of Prosecco and handed it to Malika.

"Would you like anything?" she asked.

Both Trent and Denise declined.

"I thought you were coming here as a reference. For Denise or something. Is your romance not going well already?" Malika asked.

"There's no romance," Denise replied.

Trent looked at the floor. He took a deep breath, then continued. "Can you elaborate on the kinds of meetings you facilitate?" He made air quotes with his fingers as he parroted Malika's words. "Come on. I see the look in your eyes. Shall we sit down?"

Malika didn't comment or wait for them to answer. Instead, she turned and walked further towards the back of the restaurant. They followed her to the curtain that the woman had ran through before. Malika held it to the side and waited for both of them to pass through.

They stepped into a small, dimly-lit room that held just one table set for two.

"Oh, this is cozy," he said.

"I thought so, too. It's my own private table. Sort of like a Chef's Table at a restaurant."

"Aren't those normally in a kitchen?"

"I said, <u>sort</u> of like." Her smile was terse. "I hold all of my meetings here."

"So, we're having a meeting now?"

"Please sit. Isn't that what you said?" She motioned towards a seat on the other side of the table. She waited while they both sat down. Trent removed his satchel and placed it on the floor near his feet, and Denise took a seat next to him.

Malika continued. "As I was saying, we do all sorts of things here. Outside of the business suites you saw upstairs—"

"Business suites?" Denise nodded. "Is that what that was?"

Malika ignored her obvious skepticism. "As I was saying, we specialize in getting things done. We find business capital, but our most valuable business service is connections.

"Tell me more." Trent leaned back in his chair. He planned to just let Malika talk until things started to make sense for him.

"I don't know that there is more to tell. We make fantasies, here, Trent. Plain and simple."

"Is it?" Trent said.

"Is it what?"

"Plain and simple? What you do is provide a place for people to come and hide, isn't that right?

"I know you know about the break-in at Denise's house on the island."

"Oh, there was a break-in?" She sat back into her chair. "How would I know anything about that? I haven't been to the island in two days."

"I'm sure that's not true." Trent said.

"Would you like a drink?" she asked.

"No, I didn't come here for pleasantries. I came here to get some answers."

Malika looked surprised. "Look, I don't know what you're looking for. Everyone knows about the break-in. Other than that, I have no answers for you."

"I think you do. I think you know more than you're saying. I think you know more about Charles and his business dealings and even his disappearance. I actually think you're wrapped up in this whole thing."

"I don't know what you're talking about. I'm just an Inn Keeper."

"A very wealthy one," Denise added.

"Last time I checked, you weren't doing so bad yourself. People aren't investigating you right now. Is that what the two of you are doing? Investigating me? Or just putting your nose where it doesn't belong?" Malika looked taken aback. "We're not here to discuss my finances. They're actually none of your business. Matter of fact, they're off limits."

Trent noticed a slight twitch in Malika's left eye. "They may be but I'm sure this is all connected." He paused. "What was Charles's fantasy, Malika? Why did he come to you? What was the magic sauce you had that everybody wanted? We saw pictures of you at a Gala. You were in everyone's picture, like you were the Belle of the ball."

Trent his hand on Denise's arm. There were goosebumps under his fingers. "You okay?"

She drew her hand back. "I'm fine."

"I misspoke," Trent said. He reached into his bag and pulled out a file folder. The thud it made as it dropped on the table echoed off the walls like a thunderclap in the small room.

Malika jumped back. "What is that? Are you threatening me with papers? It's not a very menacing weapon." Her eyes danced with fire like prey that had been cornered.

"I'm not threatening you at all. I don't threaten people. I don't have to."

"Well, what is this? Why is it relevant to me?"

"Oh, you know. This is the bank records for the Planter's Inn and your businesses for the past year. The amount of revenue that passed through here just does not line up with the amount of taxes you reported at the end of the year, the amount of taxes you paid for the alcohol that you should have sold. So, what's the deal Malika? Where does all the money come from?"

She stood up abruptly, leaning forward and balancing the tips of her fingers on the table. "Look, like I said, I don't have to tell you anything. Who are you anyway?"

Denise lowered her voice. She was in no mood for a shouting match. "Oh, you do, because you don't want to be disgraced. And I'll make sure that you are," Denise sneered. "You seem to like being the center of things, isn't that true? That's why you became Malika. She's more fabulous. More risky?"

"I think you do know something," Trent said.

Malika reached for the file, but Trent moved it back out of her reach. "There's something that you know and I want to know what it is. I can't stand to see Denise hurt another day."

Malika's sigh was heavy. She sat back down at the table, dropping her head in her hands. "I really don't know anything. And I want the best for Denise and Yolanda. I just provide a service to my community."

Trent leaned back in his chair. "That's all we get? Are you ready to tell me what that service is? Because if you don't, I'm going to let all your friends know that you have some secret that involves all of their husbands. Trust me. People get real funny when you mess with their husbands or their money."

Denise smiled. "And messing with both? They might just get crazy."

26

A Fan Favorite

"Tell me how the hell you know my husband?" Denise stood up quickly, almost knocking over the chair she'd been sitting in. Trent stopped it from falling backwards and stood too.

Malika's eyes widened, and she followed suit, backing away as Denise joined her on her side of the small table.

"Why were you at the marina with Charles all the time?" Denise said. "You said you saw him with another woman and you know damn well that wasn't me. You need to tell me something now, Malika." Denise fought to restrain herself. Her patience for the whole thing was wearing thin.

Malika backed up against the wall, her eyes wide. "Look, I really don't want any trouble here. I'm a peaceful woman."

"Peaceful, my ass," Denise said.

"I'm really tired of you marching up in my business and disturbing the peace in the middle of the day. This is a peaceful establishment," Malika seethed.

"Is it? I saw you arguing with someone when I came in. What was that about?" Trent said.

"That doesn't seem too *peaceful*." Denise said.

"What kind of business actually goes on here, Malika? Your husband owned thirty-two hotels, mostly in the red. Why did you get this one?" Trent voice was low, but firm.

"Woah...woah...woah," Malika said. "That's a lot of

questions, and I really don't have to tell you my business."

"No," Denise said. "But you will. You can tell us, or you can tell the cops. We'll take these files to them and they will be all over, up and through your records so thoroughly, you'll feel like you had an enema. Those papers that Trent has in his hands show that you have a lot more inflow and cashflow than this place makes. And you were just on the cover of that pretty little magazine out there, so I'm sure it will be all over the news. You don't want your reputation smeared across the Low Country. Your name will be so trashed, you won't ever set foot on Kiawah Island again. How do you think people will react when they know what really goes on here? Do you think they'll still come? Your husband's hotels were nothing but seedy holes in the wall that they rented by the hour. Do you want people knowing that? Do you want them to know what kind of business you run upstairs? I think not." Denise folded her hands across her chest. "Waiting."

"You don't know what you're talking about," Malika said. "No one will believe you."

"Does that even matter? Once the Feds get through with you, none of your secret clientele will want to come around. What do you think Trent?"

"I think you're right. It'll be hard to operate this place once you're relying on the <u>real</u> revenue it brings in."

Malika sunk into her chair. She put her head in her hands. "Okay," she relented. "I'll tell you what I do know. I know what it feels like to need information about your husband." She paused. "And yes, I do know something about that. I'll admit to that." She sighed, putting her head in her hands. "Charles came to me for a loan. He needed my help."

Denise pulled out a chair to sit down. "A loan? What help could he possibly need from you? He ran an accounting and consultant business out of Chicago. We ran it together."

"There is so much about your husband you don't know." She paused, "I will say this, he had a good heart." She sighed. "He wanted to pay back his firm."

Anxiety built up inside Denise. She couldn't believe what she was hearing. She felt as if her worst fears were coming true. "I know." Her voice was small.

"He got involved with things that he couldn't handle. He didn't know what to do and he came to me."

"Why you? Last I checked you don't have First National Bank stamped on your forehead," Trent said.

"You're right. I don't. I didn't give him money. I did help him, though. He knew that even if I didn't, I knew people that would."

"What are you talking about?" Denise's nostrils flared.

Malika laughed now. "You can always find what you need, if you're willing to pay. And Charles was pretty desperate. All I did was give Charles a way to help himself."

"You're going to have to do better than that, Malika," Denise said.

"Isn't that enough?" Malika pleaded.

Denise sat back in her chair. "Enough for what? To keep me from texting my friend at the Police Department the electronic copy of everything in that folder?" She shook her head. "I think not." She didn't bother to ask why Charles needed money. She knew. He had to put back the missing 401K funds, but why did he take it in the first place?

Malika's exhale was heavy. "All I did was arrange some

business meetings for him with people who could help him out of his dilemma. Angel investors." She made air quotes sort of speak.

"Angel investors?" Trent repeated. "How do we talk to these investors?"

Malika's face was suddenly filled with fear. "I don't know that you can. It's not what I do. If I tell you, my business will be ruined. People come to me because things are private. I've already told you too much."

"Can we get back to how you helped my husband?" Denise's eyes were like daggers as she stared at Malika.

Malika shook her head slowly as she wrung her hands. Her voice was small when she spoke again. "I don't want you to think any less of me."

"I don't think that's possible." Denise's mouth was drawn into a thin line. She tapped her fingertips on the manila folder. There was a deathly silence in the room.

Malika's face was pale now. She licked her lips as she contemplated her next words for what seemed like an eternity. "Like I said. I don't want you to suffer. I was just trying to help. Charles needed money."

"Tell us something new, please," Trent said.

"I have a certain clientele that invest in businesses and in whatever really. For a price." She swallowed hard. "People get lonely, you know? Sometimes after a divorce or if the person is in a sexless marriage. Women as much as men. Women get ignored all the time."

Trent and Denise exchanged glances. Tears now streamed down Malika's face. "Okay?" Denise said.

"I just help the women, that's all. They pay…"

Denise gasped and Trent put his hand on hers. She was not liking the direction this discussion was taking at all. "They pay for what!"

"Company. They pay for company. For whatever. I didn't ask questions. I just made the introductions."

Denise stood to her feet. "You're a Madam? You pimped out my husband?"

"Keep your voice down, please," Malika said. Her eyes were bloodshot. "I'm not a pimp. I'm a facilitator. I facilitate introductions between people looking for a mutually beneficial arrangement. Sometimes it's because they need money. Sometimes it's other things."

"What does that mean? Do you know what happened to him?" She screamed her words.

"How would I keep track of your husband when you couldn't even do it?" Malika said.

Before Denise knew what happened, her hand made contact with Malika's face. She slapped the other woman so hard she surprised herself, and the force of the blow threw Malika onto the floor. Trent hopped up and threw his arms around Denise, pulling her back. "She's not worth it, Denise. Now is not the time to catch a case."

Denise didn't struggle. She let Trent pull her towards the door.

Malika whimpered as she lay there on the floor, her hands covering her face. "I don't know what happened to him. I swear I had nothing to do with that." She drew her mouth into a tight line as she stood up, then smoothed her clothing. "I will say, my clients asked for him. A lot."

27

Swipe Right

After meeting with Malika, Denise was too mad to care that she was in the marina on a boat, again. "Can you believe that?" she said. She paced back and forth in the small space inside the boat.

Trent nodded. "I can. In my line of work, I've seen things too crazy not to believe. This isn't even the most unbelievable. Do you need a drink or something?"

"Can we have her arrested?"

Trent hugged Denise, rubbing her back. "For what? She hasn't been charged with any crime. Not yet."

"Someone needs to pay."

"For what? It feels wrong, but all we know really is that Malika introduces willing people to other willing people. I don't think she's a killer. She's a living dating app. I don't get the impression that she's a thief, either. I understand that you want someone to pay or at least find out where the money went, but you can't get what you're mad about mixed up in your head."

"I know what I'm mad about, Trent." He tried to rub her

back again, but she pulled away.

"Maybe, but you don't seem to know where to direct your anger."

Denise spun around. "Whose side are you on?"

Trent threw his hands up in surrender. "I wasn't aware there were sides here."

"I'm sorry. You're right." She sighed. "I need to focus." She pulled the rings out of her pocket. "We need to have someone check these out."

"I can handle that. I'll see what my contact can find. We can drop these off on the way to the police station. I'm interested to see what they have to say."

Denise shrugged. "I don't have high expectations for these people, but I'll go with you. If they could figure this out, they would have already."

"In their defense, have they had a chance yet? You told me yourself that most of the investigation was handled out of Chicago, right?"

Denise didn't answer.

"Are you good, though? It's probably not a good idea for you to slap anybody, throw things or have any kind of temper tantrum in front of the police." He grabbed his keys from the countertop. "The lonely officer might rejoice in throwing you in that jail cell they have in the back."

Denise smiled, grateful that Trent had found a way to diffuse her anger. "I promise. I'm good. Frustrated, but good. I feel like the answers I'm looking for are at our fingertips."

Trent crossed his fingers and held them up. He hoped they were close to answers, too.

The ride to the police station took less than ten minutes.

The only other cars in the parking lot were the two matching, vintage Rolls Royce's that served as the island patrol cars. They sat at the front of the building, windows rolled down. Denise looking at the poor excuse for a police vehicle and shook her head. They were not high-speed chase ready, that was for sure.

She mulled over what she'd learned so far. Although Malika had said she wasn't involved in Charles's death or disappearance, Denise didn't quite buy it. She still had a feeling that Malika knew more than she was telling. She might not have killed him, but she was not that far removed from whatever had happened to him. She was sure she'd find out soon enough.

It was much earlier in the day than when she'd been there before, but there was still no one at the front desk, just as there had been no one there the last time. The small building that served as the police station felt deserted. Denise rang the bell on the desk, half expecting to have to wait. Surprisingly, Officer Jones came out quickly. This time, he walked towards Denise with a purpose she hadn't experienced before, and it felt much better than the brush off he'd given her earlier.

"Thank you for coming down."

"I was surprised when you called. Last time we were here, I got the impression you expected someone else to take this on." Denise said.

"I can see how our last exchange would leave you with that impression. This shouldn't take too long." He shook Denise's hand first then Trent's.

"What shouldn't?" Denise asked. "You were kind of vague on the phone."

"Let's go to my office first and I'll fill you in. This way."

They followed him down a short hall to his office. Jones

walked around his desk and sat down. "We've been taking a closer look at the intrusion you had the other night. As far as you know, is there anyone that could be angry with you? They didn't take much, right?"

Denise nodded. "They didn't. No enemies as far as I know, although lately I've been finding out a lot of things I had no idea about."

"Oh?" Officer Jones said.

"Nothing major." Trent cleared his throat. "What did you find out?"

"I was perplexed about these break-ins. I mean, no one saw anyone coming or going. It occurred to me that maybe that's because whoever did it was supposed to be on the island."

"So, you're thinking workers?"

Jones rocked in his seat. "Or people dressed like them. They can come and go all day long as they please. These people don't sign in or out, other than once a day. After that first time, the guards just wave them on, no matter how many times they come and go. I got to thinking, what if a truck signed in, then changed staff later? We'd never know. I don't know why they would be interested in your house though." He paused. "Do you have anything you want to tell me? Anything at all."

"What are you implying? Mrs. Martine is as confused as the rest of us," Trent said.

"Are you her lawyer?"

"She doesn't need one."

Jones was silent as he looked from Trent to Denise. "Okay. There have been so many times when people close to home know what's going on. And small details make the case."

"Why would I have someone break into my own house?

That's ridiculous."

"Maybe it is." He opened a draw in his desk and pulled out a green and white tote bag. It was in a large, Ziploc bag. "Do you recognize this?" Jones pushed the bag across his desk.

"How'd you get this? It's my conference bag. I got it at last year's GemStones, Inc. conference."

"We figured it was yours," Officer Jones said. "There are only a few people who it could belong to. We googled it."

Denise smiled. "Yeah, I guess there would only be a handful of us that would be members in a social club for Black women. Where'd you find it?"

"In a suspect's locker."

"So you have a suspect?" Trent asked. "Why didn't you start there?"

Jones nodded. "We do. She says the bag belongs to her, though. After I looked it up, we knew that couldn't be the case. She said she found it at a Goodwill."

"Highly doubtful." Denise folded her arms across her chest. "The closest GemStones Chapter is in Charlotte, although we are trying to get one going on the island. Even if anyone did donate the bags to Goodwill, the chances of it being in one in Charleston are quite low. And this is the bag from last year. It's only a couple of months old, early for someone to be tossing it out. I used it to bring stuff down here when I came."

Jones nodded and stood up. "Do you have time to look at a lineup?" Denise's heart raced. A lineup? This was like TV. She nodded.

"We just want to know if you recognize her or not. See if it's someone you know. Victims often know the perp. Follow me."

Officer Jones led them to a room adjacent to his office. Denise looked into the dimly-lit room before she entered. It was almost empty and big enough for maybe four people. The far wall was taken up by a window that looked into another room behind it. He closed the door behind them. "You ready?"

Denise nodded and flicked the light switch. As soon as the room went dark, he pressed a button on the wall. Denise could hear the muffled sound of a buzzer in the other room. The door into the other room opened, and several women walked in. They stood against the wall with their backs to the chart that showed their heights. Denise checked them out. Three of the four women looked disheveled and disinterested, as if they'd just rolled out of bed. The fourth had been crying.

"Quarter turn to your right." All of the women turned right.

"Any look familiar?" Jones asked.

"Quarter turn again." The women turned again, now standing with their faces to the wall. They turned two more times. Denise searched their faces. One by one, they were asked to take a step forward.

Denise squinted. "Can you have number three step forward again? She looks familiar." She leaned closer to the window. She'd seen the woman before, but she just didn't know where. She was young-ish, maybe early to mid-twenties. A baby. Her dirty blonde hair looked like she'd cut it herself. Her tear-stained face was near colorless and pale, and there were dark circles under her eyes.

"What's wrong, Denise?" Trent asked.

She shook her head. "I'm not sure. She looks familiar. She's the only one though. I've never seen any of those other women in my life."

Officer Jones nodded. "Okay, that's all we need."

"That's it?" Denise said. "That's all you needed?"

"That's it," Officer Jones said. "I'll let you know when I have anything else, and you let me know when you figure out where you know her from."

28

Taxi, Anyone?

"Are you sure you don't want to stay at my place tonight?" Trent asked. He pulled his truck into Denise's driveway.

"I'm going to have to face it eventually." Denise shook her head. "As much as I am reluctant to stay in my own house, I don't believe lightning strikes three times in the same place. I'll be fine." Her face was streaked with worry, her words more of an affirmation than confirmation. "I feel like if I said it aloud, then it is so."

"I get that."

"I don't really want to stay alone in this house, but feel like it's the best thing to clear my mind."

"It probably doesn't feel like the safest thing in the world right now to stay alone in your house after strangers have been through it." His eyes filled with empathy.

"I'll be fine. I might not get any sleep, but I will reset the security alarm. That should help give me some peace of mind."

Trent didn't want to push. He could go a long while without experiencing angry Denise again. "Do you want me to at least come in and check things out?"

"Trent, I'm going to be fine." She leaned over and kissed his cheek. Sooner or later, she'd have to stand on her own two feet so she might as well start now. "I'll check in with you later tonight, and I promise I'll text if I need anything."

"That's going to have to do, I guess."

"What are you going to do now?"

"We still need to get the information back about those rings. And I have something else I want to investigate."

"Oh? Care to share?"

Trent shook his head. "Not yet. It's just something that occurred to me." He paused. "Tell me again, what was the day Charles took his boat out last?"

Denise sighed. "Why does that matter?"

"It doesn't. It's just that we've heard stories about him being on his boat, but was he alone?"

"It never occurred to me that he wouldn't be, at least not before Malika." Denise's stomach was in knots as she considered all that she had learned in just a short time.

"Exactly." Trent paused. "I'm going to take a look at the sign-in logs at the marina. There might be some information there."

"If that's what you want to do." Denise's shoulders slumped. "I would think that the police already looked at that."

"Maybe they have. Everything we've been told said that he usually took the boat out alone, but we've learned so much more. I'm guessing it won't hurt to look again through a new lens, right?"

"Okay," Denise said. He was right. The small police department on the island seemed barely invested in the investigation. "You let me know if you find anything. You are coming to the party tomorrow, right?"

Trent coughed. "I have been hearing about this infamous

party since I stepped foot on the island. I wouldn't miss it." He stayed to watch her get into her house, then waited a few extra minutes to make sure that she was okay. He held his breath, half expecting her to come running out, screaming her head off any minute. Deep down he understood Denise's reluctance. They'd had a great time together, but it was normal for her to be hesitant to be drawn into an emotional entanglement just yet, just as it was normal for her to be reluctant to stay in her house after a break-in. She was still tied up with the baggage of her marriage and the shambles her life had been left in.

The more he thought about it, the more he was positive that there actually had been someone in her house that first day, and that whomever he'd seen outside her house had not been a golfer. They probably had been waiting for them to leave, planning their entrance, or at least being a lookout for the people who did eventually break in. Part of him wanted to just stake out her living room to make sure Denise was safe, but he knew that would probably make her even more wary and he didn't want to be the one to cause any more stress.

The marina lot was fuller now. Trent pulled into a spot away from as many people as he could. Denise had made him more aware of the size of his truck and he didn't want to have another door ding encounter. He'd never thought about how that might be inconsiderate until she'd pointed it out. It was amazing how a few short days could change one's perspective on things.

He rang the bell on the window of the marina office, then pressed his nose to the glass to see if he could spot anyone. From where he stood on the pier, the place looked to be buzzing. The small room behind the window appeared to be full of people.

The sign-in log had been left outside the window, a red pen still attached to it by the piece of yarn just long enough for someone to sign the book. Trent turned the book around so he could sign it, and then paused. The book was several inches thick. *How far back did it go?* He'd meant to go inside and make a formal inquiry, but what he wanted was right in front of him, and from the looks of things, that might take longer than anticipated.

Trent glanced inside the sign-in office again. There was a small convenience store inside, and just like earlier, it seemed to be packed. The Fourth of July was the next day, and people were getting their last-minute store runs on holiday supplies. This wasn't new; boaters would be paying for gas here and grabbing beer to drink while watching the fireworks, just like everyone else on the island. Trent licked his lips. He considered taking the entire book back to his boat, but that was certainly not a good plan. As crowded as the marina was, there was bound to be a high volume of people coming and going today, and the chances were high that someone might miss the book. He glanced around again. Of course there were cameras. Removing the book would be conspicuous on the tape.

There were questions in his mind. Denise had said that Charles's boat had come in and he hadn't been on it, and based on what Malika had said, she'd seen him at the marina with people on the boat. What are the chances that he'd been alone the day he went missing?

Trent looked over his shoulder and quickly flipped back to the date Charles had taken his boat out. His heartbeat thundered in his ears as he ran his finger down the page, trying to decipher all of the various handwritings. After the first page, he found what he was looking for.

C. Martine. Going to slip number six. That would have been Charles. No guest that he could see. Someone signed in two minutes after that, but they were going to slip number five. But what if they'd lied? He used his phone to take a quick picture of the page, and the two pages that come after for that day. Trent flipped the book back to the original page, then headed towards his boat.

As soon as Trent got below-board, he turned on the computer. He waited for the machine to come to life, then air-dropped the pictures he'd taken to transfer them to his computer. The machine beeped, and he clicked on the first one to enlarge it. He was going to cross reference all of the sign-ins with all of the sign-outs for that day. He already knew that he wouldn't see Charles's name, but what about everyone else?

It took almost an hour for Trent to account for every name. He matched almost every signature, cross referencing two days past the date in question, just in case someone had slept on their boat. Forty-five minutes in, there were just two unaccounted for, Charles and one other person. He zoomed in and tried to decipher the writing. All he could make out was a first initial. The letter J. Going to Slip 5.

Trent stretched and went back up top. His boat sat at the end of the pier. The majority of the boat slips here had been designed to house boats under thirty-eight feet long. At forty-two, he was limited in which spaces he could pull into. The majority of the boat owners were also home owners, and had no intention of living on their boats long term. These were primarily weekend vessels.

He sat in his Captain seat on the bridge of his boat and

surveyed the marina. There were a few taper buoys out in the water. These white overflow moorings bobbed up and down in the water, the blue stripe on the tall end swinging back and forth. Like in the Buster's Place cove, a visitor could hook up to one of those and take a water taxi to shore. He hopped off his boat and strolled down the pier. He slowed near slip six. It was empty now, but he could tell from the detritus on the pier that it was occupied. Slip seven was also occupied, but the boat was in the space. *Planter's Party.* No mystery there. That was Malika's boat. The windows were shut and the blinds were drawn.

Slip Five was empty. There was a rope across the end so that no one could just pull up and use it, but a "for rent" sign hung on both sides so it could be visible from land and water. Trent looked around. There were signs of neglect everywhere.

"Hey, you there?" a voice called to him. "Can I help you with anything?" A man stuck his head out of a slip a few spots away.

"Not really. I'm just checking this spot out to see if I want to rent it for the rest of the season." Trent smiled.

The man stepped out on to the pier. "Is that you, down the end there?" He pointed in the direction of Trent's boat. "That ain't fitting in here, even if you're the best captain on earth and grease the sides with Crisco. You'll hit the top."

Trent laughed. "I can hope. I like that these slips are covered. I get nothing but sun all day. You know what I mean?"

"Well, the perils of owning a big ass boat! I'm sure you more than make up for that little drawback. She's a nice one. I wanted one like that but my wife—"

"Say no more. I get it. Too bad."

"Ain't no one been in this slip on a permanent basis in

almost two years."

"Really?" Trent said. "What's wrong with it?"

"As far as I know, nothing, but what do I know. Lots of people choose to keep their boats on the other side of the island I think. They just pull up to a buoy when they're here and water taxi in to the bar."

"Probably is cheaper that way," Trent said. "But seems like an easy way for all sorts of people to come and go."

"I told my wife the same thing. Those people never have to sign in since they don't really enter from the land. We can't tell who's been here and it's all fun and games until something goes missing. They just get ferried right up to the pier."

The man kept talking, but Trent could barely hear him. They shook hands and did introductions, but Trent was focused on the water taxi dingy. You would never have to sign in or out if you took a water taxi. That was all he'd heard. Whoever J was, they'd never signed out.

29
Party Central

The party might no longer be at Yolanda's house, but
the prep for it had never moved. Even before she got there,
Denise felt like she'd ended up at party central. The narrow street
leading to the entrance was littered with catering trucks and a
myriad of cars that Denise didn't recognize. She couldn't get
anywhere close to Yolanda's driveway, so she pulled over, taking
care to park mostly on the grass so that other cars could get
through. Security might not have able to keep intruders out of
her house, but there was no doubt in Denise's mind they
wouldn't hesitate to give her a ticket for poor parking.

She walked as close to the middle of the road as she
could. It was early in the day and she didn't trust that all of the
gators had gone to hide from what was promising to be a day
with record heat, and she wanted to avoid the bugs. The island
had the biggest water bugs she had ever seen, and that was saying
a lot being that she'd spent most of her life in Chicago.

There was no answer when she knocked. Denise pushed
the door open and walked into what felt like an eerily empty
house. The kitchen was a mess. She frowned. Yoli wasn't great at
cleaning, but she was certainly adept at hiring a housekeeper.
Denise could tell that Yolanda had been doing work here, but
where was she?

"Yoli!" Denise waited, expecting her friend to come running in at any minute. Yolanda had known she was coming. She looked h the house, out over the pool, half expecting to find her taking her morning laps there. The only motion in the water was that of the pool cleaner creeping along the bottom. She was probably in the bathroom, Denise thought.

Just as she was about to text Yolanda, Darren walked in. "Oh," he said and stopped in his tracks. "Is Yolanda with you?"

"I was hoping you would be able to tell me where she was. I was supposed to meet her."

He frowned. "I think she went to the store," Darren said. "Can I get you something? This place is worse than Union Station." Darren comparing the house to the main train station in Chicago painted a vivid picture for Denise.

"I can tell." She looked around the room. Normally very tidy, it looked like an explosion had happened in the kitchen. "I thought the party moved?"

"Yeah, me too." He walked towards her. "Water?"

Denise nodded. She opened her phone and quickly read the message from Trent.

Trent: *We have to talk about the water taxi.*

She frowned.

Denise: *I'm at Yoli's.*

"My wife has made every vendor check in here. Even the staff."

"Staff? We have that now?"

Trent: *Does Yoda mean anything to you?*

Denise: *You mean like Star Wars?* She waited as blue status dots flashed across her text message window.

Trent: *That was a service mark or something inside the rings, very faint. When you blow them up, it says Yoda.*

"She's hired every off-duty beach club worker. Every last one of them." Darren handed Denise a bottle of spring water.

She looked up and they locked eyes. Things slowed down around them. A memory of their garage flashed in her mind. Yoda. Both of their license plates said Yoda. Denise cleared her throat. "Darren, when will Yoli be back?"

"Should be soon, I think. Make yourself at home." He turned to walk away.

"One question before you go." Denise's hands trembled. "What are you working on nowadays? I wasn't sure how you found a way forward after Charles—"

"Yeah, it's tough," Darren cut her off. "I want to continue some of the things that we were trying to bring to market before, but the prototypes never turned up. Charles had them. It's like starting from scratch."

"I bet." She cleared her throat. "I never asked. What is Yoda?"

Darren stopped walking. "Why?"

"It's on your license plates. Yoli told me before but I don't remember."

"It's an acronym. First two letters of Yolanda's name, first two letters of mine. Not very clever, I know." His eyes narrowed. "Why are you asking so many questions?"

She sipped her water. "No reason. Curiosity. I found these rings and—"

Darren whipped around. "Rings? Where? What do they look like?"

He was suddenly too close. Denise took a step

backwards. "Just metal rings. I thought they were washers or something, but then I saw the letters YODA inside, real small."

He grabbed her arm. "Where are they? I need those." His eyes were suddenly wild looking.

She pulled back. "You're hurting me!"

Darren shook Denise. "Where are they? Do you have any idea how hard I've been looking for those? What did you do with them?"

Denise's voice became calm. "Take your hands off of me, Darren."

His eyes widened. He let her go. "I'm sorry. I just got so excited. How soon can I have those rings? It would mean a lot to get them. I'm dead in the water right now."

Denise rubbed the spot on her arm where he'd grabbed her. "I didn't say you could. I think I'm going to need to see a K-1 for this business. Seems like the two of you were into something big. I guess I own that now, too. Biometrics is it?"

Darren took a step towards Denise, his eyes wide. "Who told you that?" he demanded. "Everything is secret."

At that moment, Denise recognized a crazy in his voice that she wanted no parts of. The hairs on the back of her neck stood at attention. "You know," Denise looked around the room. How long would it take her to get to the exit anyway? "I think I'm going to go over to the venue. I can meet Yolanda there."

Darren blocked her way. "Wait, she's coming back. I can get you something stronger than water. I've been so busy, we haven't had time to catch up at all." He walked into the kitchen again. "You gals drink Prosecco all the time, right?"

She flinched. *Gals?*

"We have some here." Glasses clinked.

"I'm not sure that's a good idea. I should go. Folks will be waiting."

"Okay." Darren looked so sad that Denise felt bad. "Let me fill you in on the Yoda part before you go. You're right, you would own Darren's part of the idea." He licked his lips. "Look, I can make you an offer on what you would own right now. I'm not really interested in taking on another partner."

"You're not?"

"No, partners are too hard. They always leave and you can't replace what they brought with them. Charles left. He had all the contacts. Jamel wanted too much."

Denise's heart jumped. "Jamel? My Jamel? What does he have to do with it?"

"He was an early investor, but he and Charles had a disagreement, so we bought him out."

"He never mentioned it." She frowned.

"He was a little salty about it," Darren continued. "When Charles disappeared, we were so close." He paced the room.

"Close?"

"We had working prototypes. We were looking at selling for close to ten million. Investors were on the hook." He put his head in his hands. "Then Charles…" Darren choked up. "He never told me what he did with the prototypes. I was going to start over. Except I didn't have starting over money. That dried up when Charles disappeared. But now that you found them, I can get the investors back in line, you know what I mean?" He stepped closer. "This can be a win-win for all of us. I can get the deal closed and get you your part without you having to wait for a formal death declaration."

"I don't know." Her head was starting to hurt. "Seems

complicated. I'd need to look over the documents first to get a better understanding."

"Okay, then. Let's talk later." His face beamed. "I can't tell you how happy this makes me. I was thinking of doing some crazy things to make it work. You've saved my life."

Darren grabbed her shoulders and hugged her. He kissed her on her cheek and Denise tensed. He smiled, then rushed off to his office. "You can let yourself out, right?"

Denise didn't like the thought of being responsible for someone's life, at least not like this. Darren had gone from one end of the spectrum to the other in the space of ten minutes, and that didn't feel good to her. She made a beeline for the door. Yolanda was right, something <u>was</u> off with her husband, but she wasn't surprised. It was becoming clear that he and Charles had been off together.

30
Casing the Joint

Yolanda peered into Darren's office even though she knew he wasn't in there. "Darren?" She looked around, then stepped inside, making her way over to his desk. His screen was unlocked.

Just as she sat down, a text appeared on the screen and she jumped. It was hard to get used to the way mac computers mirrored text messages.

Darren: *Skype in two minutes. We need to discuss Yoda.*

Yolanda frowned. Yoda? "Darren?" She called out to him. He certainly had his phone with him and would have seen that message.

Blue dots appeared in the message window, indicating that Jamel, whomever he was, was typing a response. Yolanda didn't have time to read it. Charles walked through the office door, startling her.

"What are you doing at my desk?" The gruffness of his voice sent chills down Yolanda's spine.

She stammered. "I, uh, was waiting for you. Got a minute? We need to talk about—

"Actually, can it wait? I have to take an important call coming in." He waved her away from behind the desk, and slid into his chair.

Yolanda didn't have time to answer. Just as she opened her

mouse, the tell-tale two level ring tone of skype sounded on the computer.

Darren turned his chair towards the computer, waving his hand again. Yolanda pursed her lips, and instead of leaving as she knew he expected to, she took the two steps across the room and settled into the side chair in the corner. She didn't care if Darren wanted her to leave or not. The tone in his voice made her feel like she wanted to know what this call was about, too. She hadn't seen him be so animated for quite some time. He glared at her and she pulled her earbuds from her pocket, stuffing them in her ears, then pretended to look at her screen. Yolanda opened a browser on her phone, then quickly signed into Darren's iCloud. She paused a minute, then quickly brushed any feelings of guilt away. Had she done this sooner, she might not feel as if her husband was keeping her in the dark.

She watched as Darren frowned, then slammed his hands down on the desk. She jumped. Her heart pounded in her head.

"You good?"

Darren typed furiously. "Yeah, I'm good."

Yolanda thought she'd been discovered, but Darren didn't seem to be concerned with her at all. She focused on her own screen and couldn't help but feel just a little bit accomplished. More than one of them in the house had a taste for cloak and dagger. She watches as Darren's texts appeared on her screen.

Jamel: *I'm on a plane. I can't use skype.*
Darren: *I have news.*
Jamel: *Can it wait? I get into Charleston in a few. We're on approach.*

Darren's heart leapt.

Darren: *Are you coming here?*

Jamel: *Of course I am. I wouldn't miss the party of the year for anything.*

"Oh," Darren said out loud.

Yolanda smiled as their eyes met, then moved her head slightly. Darren would think she was listening to music.

He looked back to his screen.

Darren: *Who invited you?*

Jamel: *What's wrong? Did you think I didn't know the pretty people? Denise told me to come down, so you know I always do what the Boss Lady asks. Ha ha.*

Darren: *Well, Boss Lady found the prototypes. Our asses are saved.*

Jamel: *You're funny. Your ass may be saved, but you still need to get me my money. It was a loan, my man.*

Darren: *I know.*

Jamel: *Loans are meant to be paid back.*

Darren: *After I close the deal, I'll have all the money in the world.*

Jamel: *That ain't got a thing to do with me. You made that clear before. I still can't believe you had the balls to come to me in the first place. It's a good thing I don't hold grudges. Not many people would have helped you like I did after being pushed out like you guys did me. We had a deal. I need my money, Darren. And I need it fast. Now that you have the prototypes, you won't need it anymore anyway.*

Yolanda looked down and tried to act as if she were not watching her husband.

Darren exhaled heavily.

Darren: *We will discuss it while you're here and we can get things started again. She has the prototypes on the island. We can get them today.*

Yolanda's pulse quickened. This was starting to sound

dangerous. Darren finally looked up.

"Denise, did you need something?"

Yolanda removed one of her earbuds. "Did you just call me Denise?"

"What?" Darren's eyebrows shot up in surprise. "No."

"You don't know my name now? I know you ain't calling me by my bestie's name." Yolanda stood up. "I need a hand with some groceries.

Darren sighed, then ran his hand over the top of his head, from front to back. "Yeah. Be right there, babe."

"Denise was here?" Yolanda asked. "I left two bags just outside the door."

"She was. I thought you would've passed her. She was looking for you." Darren pecked his wife on the lips as she walked by him.

"Wow," she said. "What's gotten into you?"

Darren smiled. "Nothing, babe. Things are looking good again, that's all. I'm so sorry about the way I've been acting lately. Thank you for being patient." He kissed her again.

Yolanda pulled back and gave her husband the side eye. "Have you been drinking?"

"Of course not. I can't let my woman know how much I appreciate her?"

She inhaled, a smile slowly making its way across her face. He was back. "I can think of a few other ways for you to show your appreciation." Yolanda winked, laughing. She didn't know how long this version of Darren would stay, but she was going to be grateful for the visit, even if he was going to be pissed off when he discovered she'd read his texts.

By the time Denise arrived, there were people going in and out of the small pavilion like a steady stream of ants. Denise clenched her teeth. This would actually have been a very good time to stay away from the melee that this party had become, except she couldn't. Yolanda was embracing her Duchess of Delegation brand and it was not beyond her to consider her grace period over and to delegate something new to Denise. With all that was inside Denise's head, she had no desire to take on any task, no matter how meaningless, and desperately wanted to just talk to her friend, although it was doubtful she'd be able to get Yolanda alone now.

The grey-shuttered pavilion stood sentinel over the shoreline, looking over what was now barely above a trickle of water cutting a ribbon through the seagrasses between Kiawah Island and the mainland. The tide was low and the sand and grass teemed with marine wildlife. A wooden walkway came from the building, jutting out well into the marshland, ending in a picture-perfect gazebo that was a favorite of wedding parties or those in search of the refract Low Country selfie spot. Denise paused. The party might have been more personal when it was at Yolanda's place, but this view was stunning, she had to give her that.

Denise was ignored when she finally made her way inside the pavilion. There were at least ten people working. They were spreading plastic table cloths on the tables and hanging decorations with a fever frenzy. She looked around the room, recognizing a few faces from the beach club. The young man that had helped with their towels was there. He walked in front of Denise, his arms filled with table linens. "Oh, hey," he said. "Are you looking for Mrs. McAlister?"

Denise smiled. "Yeah, have you seen her?"

"I have. She was here a bit ago and went back to the house. Would you like me to track her down for you?"

She nodded.

The young man dropped his linens on a nearby table, then used one of his hands to keep the whole pile from slipping to the floor. He touched a small microphone pinned to the lapel of his black shirt. "Lady is here for Mrs. Mac. Can someone let her know?"

Denise listened as the voices on the radio talked to one another. "I didn't mean to be any trouble. I can just go find her myself."

He shook his head. "I don't mind. This Clear-Com thing is easier on all of us." He tapped his headset. "It's too hot to be running back and forth like a chicken with its head cut off. You can just sit and wait and I'll get you some sweet tea, okay?"

"I am kind of parched." She swallowed, now more aware of the dryness in her throat.

"We don't mind doing stuff for the McAllister's. They hire us for everything, and I know I need the extra money."

She thanked him, and accepted the drink he poured from a nearby pitcher. "I don't want to be in the way. Is it okay if I sit over here?" She pointed at the bench near them.

"Suit yourself. I need to finish." He grabbed his linens again, juggling them all back into his arms, then scurried away.

Denise settled in, admiring all of the work that the team Yolanda had hired was doing. She shook her head. Yolanda might think she'd handed the planning over to Samantha and her crew, but it was obvious that the event, which was a well-oiled machine from the looks of things, had Yolanda all over it.

She took a sip from the drink he'd handed her, and then sat in the chair. Her eyes narrowed. *The McAlister's hire us for everything.* She flashed back to the Beach Club. The woman at the check-in desk. She'd seen her before. She was also in the lineup at the police station. Had she been hired by someone to case her house? Darren had been so desperate. Denise touched her arm. She could still feel the squeeze of his fingers from when he'd grabbed her. Denise took a deep breath and swallowed hard. At this point, nothing would surprise her.

31

The Kindness of Man

Trent could barely find a parking spot by the time he had made it to Dabner's place. His heart beat thundered in his ears as he struggled to contain his rage. He leaned on his horn. A car drove in front of him, well below the posted speed limit. He was positive that the skiff driver, the one who operated the water taxi, had answers that would help Denise.

This time, the parking lot was packed. He drove across the gravel too fast, going straight to the parking lot and right to the water's edge. As he passed the wooden building, Dabner appeared out front, waving his fist in the air.

Trent slowed and killed his engine, hopping down from his truck.

"You know good and well that ain't no parking space." Buster glared at him.

"I won't be long. Do you know where the guy is that drives the water taxi?" He used his head to point to the cove. The water taxi skiff was anchored there, just under the ancient willow tree that shaded the area.

Dabner wiped his hands on a red towel he carried with him. "What do I look like, a damned information desk?"

Trent closed his eyes and sighed. His patience was running thin. "Look, I'm just trying to help a friend."

Dabner's face softened. "He's probably on the other side

of the building. He smokes over there while he waits."

"Thank you. I appreciate it."

"Hope it works out, son. And move that truck, okay?"

Trent nodded. "Ten minutes." He walked off in the direction that Dabner had indicated. In less than four steps, his shirt was soaked through with sweat.

Sound seemed to disappear as he stepped around the wooden building. The back end of the building was up on stilts, suspended over the water's edge. He paused. Water made a licking sound where it met the pebbly beach, and the smell of the brackish water and mildew filled Trent's nose. The peace was suddenly punctuated by the vibration of his phone. He glanced at the notification on the screen.

Denise: *You coming soon? We need to talk.*

Trent stopped walking to answer her. *I made a pitstop. I'll explain later. Be there soon, though.*

He looked up to a man looking at him. "You lost?" He held a cigarette in his hand and leaned on one of the poles that supported the building.

"Uh, no. I don't think so." He paused. "You the guy that runs the water taxi?"

The man took a puff from his cigarette. "Most days. Unless it's not. I'ma need to finish this here smoke before I take you out. I'm on break."

Trent shook his head. "Oh, you misunderstand. I don't need a ride. I have a few questions."

"You popo? I don't know nothing." He shook his head for emphasis. "You know the island cops got everything covered so you best go back down to Charleston or wherever you came from."

"I'm not the police. "I'm looking for information. To help a friend."

He took another drag on his cigarette, longer this time. "Hmph. Is that right? Your friend. Not mine."

Trent fought to maintain his composure. "Dude, I don't have time for this. I have to get to a party and—"

"Oh, so you're invited to that dance party them folks have over there every year? You one of *them?*" He chuckled. "I should have known. Your clothes told me you wasn't one of us."

"Do you remember everyone you taxi? Really I'm only interested in one day. Maybe someone you only taxied one way? From the marina."

The man seemed more still than a few moments before. He took his time answering. "You 'posed to make small talk first. Before you get in bed with a person."

"How much?" Trent thrust his hand into his pocket and took out his wallet, flipping it open.

The man held up his hand. "Not everyone can be bought. That's the problem with you people." He shook his head. "What day?"

Trent's mouth dropped open. He hadn't expected it to be this easy. For a minute, his faith in the kindness of man was restored. "It was a while ago. Do you keep a log of the trips you make?"

"Nah. Many of my clients wouldn't like that. I don't ask no questions, ya' dig?"

"Remember names?"

He nodded. "Sometimes I don't ask no questions though. It's better that way."

"Is it?" Trent said.

"Sure is. That's how I get better tips." He snuffed out his cigarette butt.

"I thought you said you couldn't be bought?"

The man nodded. "I did. But I do accept tips."

Trent smiled. "Let me tell you what I got then.

32
Party Crasher

When Denise invited Jamel, she hadn't expected that he would actually come, and now here he was, standing across the pavilion from her in the middle of the biggest party the island had ever seen. The invitation had been a cursory thing, almost an afterthought, extended because Denise felt bad and somehow responsible for all that he and the rest of the staff were going through.

There were a lot of people between them and as far as she could tell he hadn't seen her yet, but he looked to be in heavy discussion with, of all people, Darren. That part was not a surprise, especially after her encounter with Darren earlier. He shook a few hands and didn't appear to be a stranger to many. He gesticulated when he spoke and his hands gave away the passion of the discussion.

She scanned the crowd. Denise still had no idea where Yolanda was, but didn't doubt that she was somewhere close. That one wouldn't be too far from the action, in fact, Denise expected her to be the puppeteer at the center of and overseeing every detail of the production.

It was getting hard to see through the crowd, which was steadily growing. It felt as if everyone within a thirty mile radius had been invited. Denise did not recognize most of the guests, so they were no islanders. When she'd come in, she'd passed a line of cars with day passes from island security displayed in their windows. A steady stream of people emerged from a bevy of luxury cars, descending on the pavilion in all manner of white outfits. Denise sighed as she watched people walk pass her on the way to the bar. The ladies were serious about their theme of cool white. She was sure if she's looked hard enough she might find a tag or two still attached. At least the white would make everyone look cool, even if they really were standing outside in the sweltering heat.

Denise kept her eyes on Darren and Jamel as she fired off a text to Trent. Had he known about the relationship between them and Charles? Although he'd said he was off the case, there was a part of her that was still very apprehensive. Her heart wanted to trust him, but her head still wasn't too sure.

Denise: *You coming soon? We need to talk.* She wanted to believe that there were no secrets between them now, but how different could he be from everyone else? How different could he be from the Trent he had been in college? People did grow, right?

Trent: *I made a pitstop. I'll explain later. Be there soon, though.*

Her nose flared. After her encounter with Darren, she didn't feel comfortable. As much as she hated to admit it, she welcomed the feeling of being just a little bit protected when Trent was around. Darren certainly would not have put his hands on her if Trent were there.

"Hey." Yolanda tapped her on the shoulder and she almost jumped out of her skin.

Denise's eyes had been trained on Darren and Jamel, so she hadn't seen her approach. "Girl, you scared the living daylights out of me."

"You've been in the punch already? I'd be careful if I were you. The next thing you know you'll wake up naked, on someone's boat, with a wedding ring on your finger and you won't have any recollection of how you got there." Yolanda laughed. "Having good time?"

"You watch too much TV. I have too much on my mind to have a good time." She leaned in. "Listen, did you know that Darren and Charles were inventing a biometrics device together? And that Jamel had been their partner but they kicked him out of the business?"

"I tell you I know nothing, except that Darren seems to have snapped out of whatever funk he was in. We haven't had any afternoon delight in a few months, you know what I mean?" She winked, and sipped the drink she was carrying.

Denise grimaced. "That's just more than I wanted to know right now. But I'm serious. Did he give you any clue about this?"

"None. And who is Jamel?"

Denise pointed in the direction where she'd seen Darren last. "Your husband was talking to him just a minute ago. He actually works for us, I mean, me. He's the office manager at Martin's Look. I wasn't aware that he had start up investment money."

"Y'all must pay well? Have a drink and relax, okay?" She looked around, then paused. "I really didn't think I'd see her here." Yolanda clenched her fists. "Darren swore to me that nothing was going on."

"Her who? Who are you taking about?"

"That woman, talking to Malika."

"What?" Denise craned her neck. "Who is she? And I'm surprised to see Malika here at all."

"I am not sure but we're going to find out. And what did I miss? I mean you were sort of cool with Malika, but why wouldn't; she be here? She's on my committee for this thing." Yolanda continued glaring in Malika's direction. "I need to go introduce myself to her. That's the one I told you about, the one I saw with Darren at the golf course. I'm sure she's on no one's list. You know we limited the number of guests each person could invite."

"Hold on," Denise said. "You need to know something. Malika—"

"Tell me later. You coming? Or no?" She didn't wait for Denise to answer, instead making a beeline in the crowd towards Malika.

"Hi Malika." It was almost impossible to tell that Yolanda's teeth were clenched on the other side of her smile. She hid her disdain behind her moving lips better than a master ventriloquist.

Malika turned around, a look of stress flashed across her face, but she reeled it in just as quickly as it had come. She stepped towards her friend, air kissing in the direction of first one of Yolanda's cheeks and then the other. "What a marvelous turnout. You should be proud."

"Whew." Yolanda wooed her forehead with the back of her hand. "I'm exhausted. But it couldn't have been possible without my team." She paused. "Don't you want to introduce me to your guest?"

By this time, Denise had made it across the pavilion as well. "Malika, so surprised to see you."

Malika locked eyes with Denise. "What guest, Yolanda?"

Yolanda scanned the room, but the woman was gone. "The woman you were just talking with. Who was she?"

"Oh, she's a business acquaintance."

"Really?" Yolanda said. "You invited your business acquaintances here? I thought you might want to let your hair down a bit."

Malika smiled. "Well, you know me, always on."

"Which business?" Denise asked.

Malika's eyes widened.

"Which business?" She asked again. "The Inn? Or the other thing? What do you call it?"

"What other thing? I'm thinking I'm on the outside here." Yolanda said.

"Wait? Malika didn't tell you? She creates *opportunities*." She turned to Malika. "Isn't that right?"

Malika stuttered, but couldn't manage to get any words out.

"What kind?" Yolanda asked. "Why have I never heard of this?"

"You haven't but I think Darren has. Because Charles certainly had, as I discovered. Malika filled me in the other night."

"I'm not sure I like where this is going. I—"

It was Malika's turn to talk through clenched teeth. "We can discuss it later. Now is not the time—"

"Time for what?" Darren sidled up behind his wife and put his arms around her. He kissed her on the neck. Malika's face blanched. "What are you ladies talking about over here?"

"Oh hi, Darren." Denise's smile was tight. "We were just discussing how Malika helped you and Darren. Maybe you can explain it to Yolanda."

Yolanda looked at her husband expectantly. Everyone froze as his eyes bored holes through Malika. Denise folded her arms across her chest. It was Yolanda who finally broke the silence. "Darren? Helped you how?"

"She, um, helped me, I mean she helped us."

"Is it hard to understand?" Denise was beginning to put all of the details together, but she needed Darren to say it. "Did she help the two of you find money to try and invest in your company. Or to pay back what you'd stolen from Martin's Look?"

"Darren? What is she talking about? What money?" Yolanda suddenly looked drained.

"I don't know anything about any money." Malika's previously perfect diction now had a more than a hint of southern twang in it. "I introduced them both to people who'd helped them with whatever they needed in exchange—"

"Like that woman who was just here? Darren?" Yolanda said.

"For what? In exchange for what, Malika. Sexual favors?" Denise folded her arms across her chest, her eyes full of fire. As all of the details fell into place, her anger grew.

Yolanda gasped. "What?" Yolanda's stomps were not unlike a two-year old's temper tantrum. The party grew quieter around them. "What is she talking about Darren and the answer better not be that she's crazy."

"She—"

Malika cut him off. "I resent what you're implying. I am not a madam. These are consenting adults. These are women's lives you're talking about. My clients are rich women who need company and—"

Darren lunged for Denise and she side-stepped. He tripped, barely catching himself on a nearly table.

"Stop it, Darren." Yolanda's mouth was drawn into a thin line. "You will not make a scene and embarrass me here. Whatever happened, we can discuss it later, but now, we have guests."

Darren brushed himself off. "Okay. I'm sorry. Denise, do you have the prototype? I can take it from you now."

Denise looked past him towards the entrance. Trent had finally arrived. "Oh, I never agreed to that. I think I need to have a little better understanding of how things were structured." She smiled as Trent joined them. "I need to put all the details together and then see the operating agreement for the Yoda project first." She turned to Trent. "You had some information."

Trent looked at the group. "Here?"

She held up her hand. "Are your friends close?"

Trent looked from Denise to Darren. "Sure. Always."

"Darren, why don't you tell Jamel to join us, then? And Trent, call in your friends."

33

I'ma Be 'Dere

"The Investigator called you?" Trent asked.

Denise nodded. "He did."

"You worried?"

"The only thing I'm worried about is that they have no new information and all of this has been for nothing." Denise cut the engine to her car. "We aren't going to find anything out sitting out here. "I appreciate you coming with me."

"Glad to do it." Trent nodded. "Let's go see."

The new office of the federal investigator buzzed with activity. They'd made an outpost in the last few days at the police station on Kiawah. A woman led Denise and Trent to a row of identical desks. They followed her silently through the maze, arriving at one desk that was almost at the very back of the room.

Agent Jones stood as they arrived, wiping his hands on his trousers and then extended it for a handshake. "Thanks for coming in," he said. Denise and Trent both nodded, but neither took his hand. Denise stood with her arms folded across her chest. She leaned into Trent, thankful for the arm he had around her shoulder. In the past twenty-four hours, he'd waylaid most of her fears about trusting him.

"Okay, then," he started. "Can I get you something to drink?"

"Look, Agent Jones. I appreciate the offer, but we aren't interested in niceties." Denise glared.

He held up his hands. "Look, you have every right to be frustrated."

Trent touched Denise's arm, pressing gently. "You think? This went on far too long. If she hadn't kept pressing, you guys would be right where we were the day Charles disappeared."

Agent Jones nodded. "Perhaps. I don't know that."

"No disrespect intended, but I'm feeling like you didn't know much the whole time," Denise said.

"Mrs. Martine, we are very grateful for everything you did. If you hadn't put together the information about Project Yoda we would have never realized that there was a connection. You were right; Jamel was angry after being bought out of the project. He knew that Charles had diverted money to fund his research. He was friends with some notorious folks and thought he could strong arm your husband to get the prototypes for himself."

"Strong arm? Is that what you call it?" Denise's body tensed. "When he and his friends realized that Yoda could actually be a thing, he thought he could just take it from Darren and Charles, but he couldn't. Darren knew this was coming, that's why he'd hidden the prototypes at Planter's Inn."

Trent nodded. "People get crazy where money is involved. I had no idea what we were talking about. This thing really was a good idea. Can you imagine gun locks that can only be unlocked by biometrics? So many other applications for this, too."

"Jamel and his friends watched too many movies. They wouldn't have been able to do anything with the technology yet.

It was still very young," Agent Jones said.

"I didn't know what they were working on, and neither did Yolanda," Denise added. "Jamel had worked for Charles for so long. I can't believe how ruthless he actually was. He admitted to cutting off Charles's finger."

"That's right." Agent Jones nodded. "He did. It was shocking. But Charles's fingerprint was the only one programmed to make the prototype work. We never would have known that if you hadn't found the rings."

"I almost fainted when he said it. I didn't recognize him then." She shook her head. It had been almost a week since the party and it still felt like a dream. "He killed him." Her voice caught in her throat. The mystery was solved, but it still hurt, just differently now. She'd had no clue that Jamel had even been to the island.

Trent rubbed her back. "Sorry, babe, I really am."

"I know." She attempted a smile. "And thank you for being so bull-headed and following the hunch that there had to be another way into the Marina that wasn't monitored. We have kept a boat there for five years and the water taxi never even registered."

Agent Jones softened. "Of course, he was desperate when the finger went overboard. He killed Charles in anger, then pushed him overboard. Gators took care of the rest. And when the money stopped, Darren didn't know what to do."

Denise put her head in her hands. "I still can't believe Charles would take money from the company like that. He was such an upstanding citizen. Or at least he had been. The Charles I knew was good."

"Money makes people do strange things. He saw an

opportunity and from what we could tell, he thought he'd be back before anyone noticed," Trent said. "That's how I got involved. I was hired to follow the money, but it went to a dead end, or at least it did until you had suspicions about Malika. What's going to happen to her?"

"Well, we don't like prostitution around here, even high-tech prostitution. We're still looking over her records but she'll get her just due." Agent Jones shook his head. "I imagine a lot of women that are considered pillars of society will be mixed up in this one." He chuckled. "She probably thought it was a victimless crime. Neglected wives and widows paying for company—"

"And whatever else," Denise added.

"And whatever else. In exchange for connections and financial backing. Ingenious actually." He paused. "Thanks to you and your quick thinking, we have enough evidence to convict Jamel of murder, embezzlement and money laundering."

"And Darren?" Denise asked.

Agent Jones stood, then shrugged. "We'll see. He's a mad scientist if I ever saw one. I'm not sure what he'll be charged with, if anything. That's for the court to decide."

Both Trent and Denise stood. "I guess," Trent said.

"And Kiawah. The island community is small, it can be a tough place. We'll survive though." They thanked Agent Jones and walked towards the front of the building. The doors were open, and the hum of the cicadas grew louder the closer they got to the outdoors. They paused in front of the two Rolls Royce's, still flanking either side of the doors in front of the building.

The silence between them was awkward for a moment. Trent cleared his throat. "So," he said.

"So," Denise replied.

"What's next?"

"Once they get through everything, I am going to use the proceeds from Yoda to pay back everyone's 401K, then I'm going to sell all offices of Martin's Look. Probably my house, too."

Trent gasped. "But you love Kiawah."

"I do. I don't plan on leaving. With all the paper I'll have after these two sales, I plan to build me a house inside the bigger gates with all the fancy people and get back to painting."

Trent laughed. "That sounds like a damned good plan. But what about now?"

She cocked her head to the side. "I was thinking about taking a ride on a boat. Maybe sail up the coast. Take in the Intercoastal waterway."

"That sounds nice, too."

Denise stepped in close. "Do you think you can handle that? You gon' be here?"

He chuckled. "I'ma be 'dere."

The End

Author's Note and Acknowledgements

Hey readers! It's been a minute. I've been thinking about this one for awhile, and I hope it delivered what you need. The first time I visited Kiawah Island was to attend a girlfriend's weekend. I'd been invited for a few days of hanging with friends, beach days, drinks and spa treatments by a group of women I admired. It was a fast weekend since I was coming from as far away from Kiawah as possible in the continental United States. I had no idea that ten hours roundtrip flying would be forgotten so quickly; The moment I stepped off the plane I was in love.

My friends took me to the restaurant I used for inspiration for the place in the story, and my brain went into overtime as soon as we drove into the cove. The place really did look like the perfect setting for a mystery. My friends dismissed me when I told them about my imaginations, but I filed that thought away and that became the seed for this story, that, combined with the disappearance of an old work colleague.

I've been back to the island many times, but my colleague never reappeared, leaving me wondering what could have happened to him to make him vanish and leave his wife and family behind. To this day, there have been no good answers, so I just let my imagination run wild on the page. What would you do if your husband, who had otherwise been an upstanding citizen as far as you knew, suddenly disappeared without a trace, leaving you to question everything you thought you knew about him and your reality as a couple?

If you've ever been to Kiawah Island, you'll know I took a few liberties with geography. There is no marina on Kiawah where I put it. The marina is actually on neighboring (and connected) Seabrook Island. I didn't move it in the story, I just included it as if were part of Kiawah, and before you come for me, I do know where it is. Thank you for giving me grace and allowing me to do a tiny bit of world creation.

The other places mentioned in the book are real. Andell Inn is real, and has a great happy hour, as are The Sanctuary and Beach Club. Planter's Inn is also a real place in Charleston, although I must admit I have never been inside. I fabricated the inside to fit the needs of the story. The church with the parking lot and all other landmarks mentioned do exist.

Like Denise, every time I drive onto Kiawah and take that road that seems to travel through the tunnel of trees, I feel as if I am transported to some magical place somewhere else in time. Some of that feeling is due to the history of Charleston and the surrounding areas, especially Kiawah, is steeped in, but most of the feeling is due to the amazing group of women who introduced me to Kiawah and let me peek into their circle for a few summers.

No book is complete without acknowledgement of the people that helped a story crystallize. This one and the two that follow, would not have come to be without the Kiawah Queens in my life. Marcea Lloyd was kind enough to invite me into her space and friend-circle over the last decade and become not just a dear friend, a beta-reader, and a confidant, my person, but my twin separated by 20 years. (No, I will not kill off that character just because you don't like them.) She and Duchess Wooten have both enriched my life and my writing in so many ways.

Thank you to Barry Jennings, who humors me and helps me poke holes in my stories while at the same time, supporting me in every crazy endeavor I come up with, and to my children, Sydney Horton, Kai Horton, Collier, Drake and Elle Jennings who just ignore my crazy.

For much of my family, I know I am the sister that they roll their eyes at and gets put in the "she crazy" bucket, but I know they will support me until the end. So, thank you Lynda, Dina, Stephanie, Joanne and Brandie. Love you all. And thank you, Brian, well, because you're my brother.

Thank you to my team, Yolanda Gore, for keeping me straight when it comes to my literary life, to Sara Camilli, for continuing to believe in my work, and to Alma Davenport for encouraging me to push my writing limits with work for stage.

Every writer has cheerleaders who read their work countless times to try and catch every nuance that has changed since the last revision. For me, those friends are people like Jami Ervin, and Pam Walker Williams my long-time friends, and Jennifer Silberg and Jennifer Garone, my book club buddies. It also includes re-found friends Like Charlane Brown, and The Writing Sisters Summit Cohort members and Yoga Foxx Enthusiasts who show up every Sunday for my yoga class.

I would be remiss if I didn't thank my sisters of Alpha Kappa

Alpha Sorority, Inc, My Links, Inc. Sisters, My Jack and Jill mothers and my fellow members of The Girl Friends, Inc. And Of course, book club members around the country--Thank you for your support. I'ma be 'dere.

Peace,
Nina Foxx
November 2021